KEEPERS OF A
BOOK ONE

OATH
BREAKER

MARIE BILODEAU

To all my middle-aged sisters:
Claim your power.
Embrace your power.
Use your power.

ACKNOWLEDGMENTS

This series was a long time coming, and so many people helped make it happen, whether they were aware of it or not. First of all, big thanks to my "home team": Kerri Elizabeth Gerow, Jessica Torrance, Jean-François Bilodeau, Karen and Dave Henderson, Kathy and Martin Gallant, and my mother, Suzanne Desjardins.

To writing friends who inspire and support: Brandon Crilly, Jennifer Brozek, Ed Greenwood, Julie E. Czerneda, Derek Künsken, Evan May, and more than I can count.

A very special thank you to my "writing-life partner" who reminded me that stories can be effortless and to trust my voice, Linda Poitevin aka Lydia M. Hawke. And that older characters kick ass!

Thanks to my beta readers, Kerri Elizabeth Gerow, Nicole Lavigne, Gabrielle Harbowy, and Christina Yother.

My amazing cover artist, Simon Carr, and to Deranged Doctor Design for designing it.

And, most of all, thanks to all the fans of the first series, *Heirs of a Broken Land,* for still being here after all these years, cheering the characters on. It's been fifteen years. We've all aged and changed, and so have they. Here's to continuing journeys!

AUTHOR'S NOTE

More than twenty years ago (wow), I started working on *Heirs of a Broken Land*. I wrote that story for myself, craving books about strong female characters in rich epic fantasy settings. This turned into my first published series, coming out five years later and getting me my first fans and lovely reviews.

That series always held a special place in my heart, and I had no doubt that there was more to the story of Cassara, Avarielle, and Shirina, but I wasn't sure what would happen next.

When the new editions of the trilogy came out a couple of years ago, inspiration struck. It had been twenty years since I'd written their tale, after all, and I'd changed. I was now in my mid-forties, and I wanted to read more stories about kickass middle-aged women who stand their ground and claim their power. So the answer of what to do next became simple: I just had to, once again, write the story I wanted to read.

This new trilogy, *Keepers of a Broken Land*, takes place twenty years into their future, too, and they've changed... and they're still the same. Their relationships have evolved, they've struggled and thrived, and the shadows from the battlefield still loom over them.

AND, best part, if you feel like reading this trilogy more than the first one, you can totally start here. Follow your reading joy!

Thanks for being a part of my journey,

Marie

xo

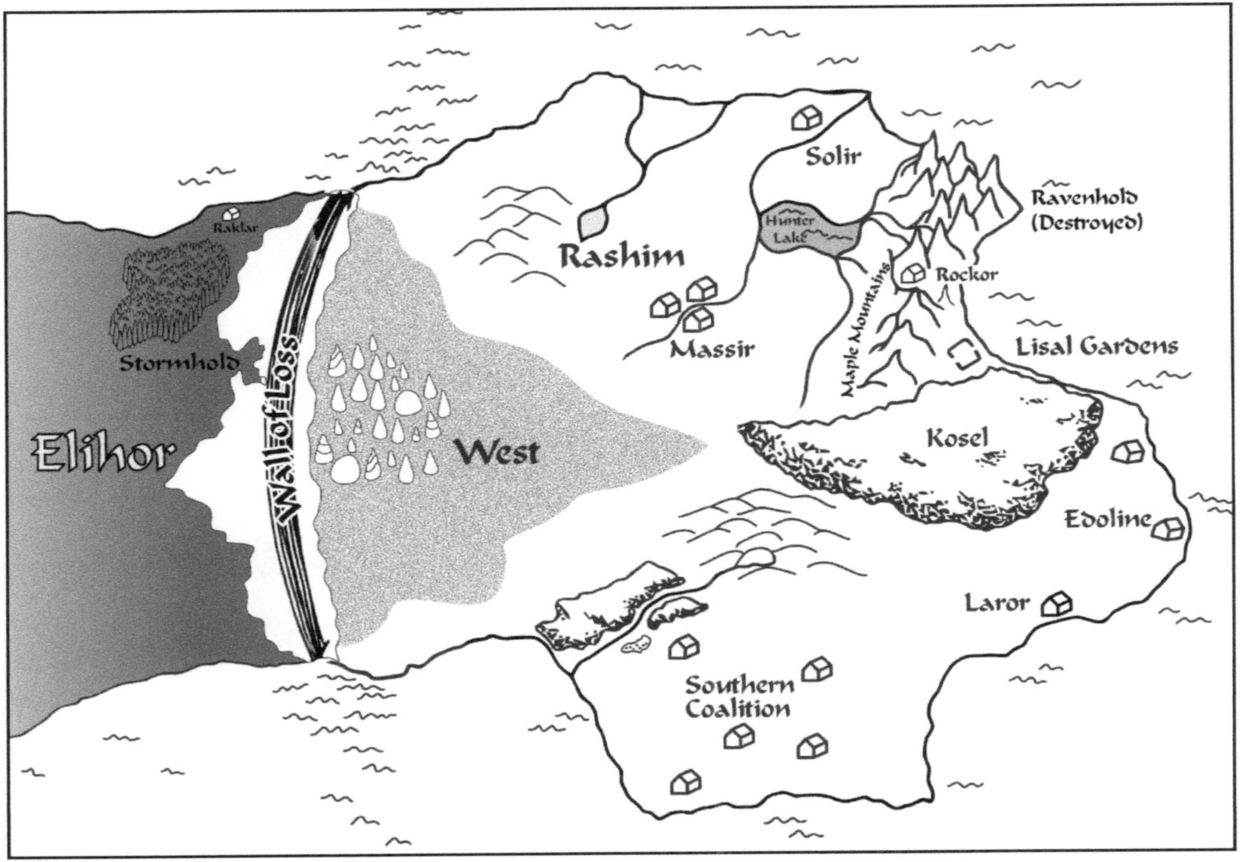

Raklar
Stormhold
Elihor
Wall of Loss
West
Rashim
Massir
Solir
Hunter Lake
Maple Mountains
Rockor
Ravenhold
(Destroyed)
Lisal Gardens
Kosel
Edoline
Laror
Southern
Coalition

———————

*A*varielle Grayloft tried hard to ignore the dockmaster beside her as she analyzed the deep claw marks in the wood. Her fingers caught in the three large scratches in what had once belonged to a ship's hull, before she turned her attention to the metal wrapped around splintered wood, the wet ripped fabric, and the other few telltale signs of what had happened to the large fishing ship.

It had been twenty years since she'd seen something like this. Twenty years hadn't been long enough.

"What do you think?" the gruff man beside her asked, arms folded. Avarielle ignored him, focusing on the wreck. The third of these in so many months.

"Same deal, isn't it?" he asked, followed by a grunt.

Avarielle turned to face Lono Haller, dockmaster of Raklar. She didn't like him and fought her instincts to scowl at him. He'd made it hard for her to get her fair share of fish, the woman from Graydon. If her son hadn't been a descendant of Elihor and his father's grandfather hadn't stood up for her, she'd have had to fight for food.

She fought the urge to just hit him and be done with it, the proximity of a monster making her alert. And itching for a fight.

He raised an eyebrow, slowly, waiting for her answer. She wanted to punch that eyebrow specifically and make sure it never rose again.

A pleasure for another day. She needed to focus on the problem at hand, the *real* problem at hand, which wasn't a blowhard of a man but rather the monster hunting these waters. He'd asked for her help, after all, and she'd made a vow to always help this village when she could, her haven for the past twenty years.

With any luck, he'd slip and fall in the water and the monster would chew on him. The thought brought a smile to her face as she focused on him. With her full attention on him, not to mention her grin, he shrank back as she towered over him. His fully black eyes still managed to meet her hazel ones, to his credit.

"It's the third one," he hissed, panic and anger bubbling out of him. Avarielle knew that anger, and how it led to rash decisions. She'd seen it happen often enough in her lifetime. She sighed and forced herself to place a hand on his shoulder, urging him to focus back on her. To stop fishing would mean less food, something they couldn't afford.

"For now, keep your boats closer to shore, Dockmaster

Haller." She invoked his title like a soothing spell, squeezing his shoulder to ground him. Predictably, he bought it, perked up, looked proud. A beat passed before he nodded.

His glance shifted sideways, toward Rojon, who had decided to stay at the edge of the docks. Her hand dropped from his shoulder, annoyed. She was proud of her son and what he'd chosen to become, but she was irritated that the dockmaster turned to him when she was the one with battle experience.

He's a descendant of Elihor. They trust him, and that's good for you, stubborn woman. Besides, there was a reason her son hadn't followed her there.

She hesitated, then pushed forward. "Survivors?"

He shook his head and his shoulders dropped.

Eli's tits. Anger bubbled inside her, and she squashed it down as far as she could, knowing there were no monsters for her to punch just yet. And she needed to tend to her son first. As she walked to join him, she was careful not to crush the moss spreading between the walkway's stones.

"It'll be fine if you step on it, Mom." Rojon waited for her at the end of the wharf, his large collection bag already filled with seeds and pods from the plants growing along the shores, hands covered in dirt, as usual. Her grandfather sat on a bench carved from stone, cane held in hand, sharp eyes studying her. In the West, he would be called Rojon's great-grandfather, but in Elihor, everything above a parent was just a grandparent. *The people of Graydon like to complicate things*, Kale had once joked to her. Well, things were complicated now, though she wished they weren't.

She forced her worries down and kissed her son on the cheek. Her son was as tall as she was, just shy of twenty. Completely dark eyes looked back at her, like his father's. The breeze ruffled his hair—red, like hers. He stood out in Elihor and would stand out in Graydon, too.

She guided him to the bench and sat him between her and the old man. Kale's hand went to Rojon's back, as though understanding some bad news would be delivered to his grandson. The weight of what she had to do pressed on her again, the anger seething just beneath it.

"Rojon." She took his hands in hers, callused from gardening tools instead of swordplay, unlike hers. Her son had grown up in a world recuperating from unimaginable loss, the path to healing riddled with plague and hardship, but he'd never known direct conflict and loss. She took a deep, shaking breath. Best he heard it from her. "I'm sorry, Rojon. Torbolem was part of the crew."

"Did he make it?" Rojon choked the words out. She cupped his cheek and he folded into her. She held him as grief poured out of him. Kale's eyes caught hers, their darkness matching her son's but their intensity matching her own.

"Why do these attacks keep happening?" Rojon asked once he'd caught his breath. The winds shifted, the scent of meats and spices calling to them. It neared suppertime, villagers gathering in the pubs to support each other and find comfort in numbers. They might not know that monsters had attacked the boats, but they certainly knew something was wrong, and they were losing friends.

The village felt as though it collectively held its breath, waiting for the next blow, its citizens keenly familiar with the dread of waiting. The helplessness of it.

"I don't know," Avarielle said, looking toward the still-growing forest to the south, where nested her home.

"Who would do this?"

Avarielle was equally unsure about that. She wanted to keep her son in the dark, for him to keep his innocence and gentle love of plants and architecture. A war waged within her—the mother, wanting to protect her son. The warrior, knowing protection came from being prepared. And the veteran of the Days of Blood, who'd always known this day would come yet had hoped it wouldn't. The past, at times, seemed impossibly far. At other times, it breathed down her neck.

"Not who but rather what," she whispered, ensuring only Rojon and Kale would hear. The old man didn't look surprised. Her son glanced at her, rallying himself from the blow of losing his friend.

"You think monsters?"

"I saw claw marks on the edge of the ship." She lowered her voice again as a few people walked by, looking equally worried. "Maybe something broke free from beneath the waters," she suggested. He nodded, pondered possibilities. His lowered head reminded her of his father. His thoughtful eyes reminded her of her older brother, after whom she'd named him. He'd died when he was just twenty. Rojon's age.

She wanted her son's face to know the wisdom of wrinkles, like Kale's. And for his hands to be free of sword calluses, his skin free of scars.

"Why don't we eat and then bring some food to Torbolem's parents and offer our aid?"

He nodded, the crush of loss slowly replacing the distraction of the mystery of what lived under the lake. Grief coiled around Avarielle's heart, for the young boy who'd played with her son, the closest thing to a brother he would ever know. She pushed it back, unwilling to fold into it, not while her son needed her, not before she could ensure everyone's safety.

～

The silent meal ended, and Kale chose to stay back, weary from a long day. The old man had been slowing down, and Avarielle's worry blossomed again. Grandfather to Kryde, who was Rojon's father, Avarielle had leaned on him to help her raise Rojon. Now he leaned on her to help him in turn. Though he'd never voiced a complaint, she could see him slowing down, his hands more inflamed and crooked during the rainy season, his steps slower and more uncertain.

She buried the worry in her heart, kissed him gently on the cheek, and squeezed his hand. As though sensing her worry, he patted her hand. "Tell Torbolem's parents that their son forever lives in my heart."

"I will." His heart. The heart of a descendant of Elihor, legendary sorceress after whom this land had been named. The same heart as Rojon. Her stomach churned, and she wished she hadn't eaten but also didn't want to be caught on an empty stomach, should her magic be needed.

Her cursed magic.

Stop it, stupid woman. She growled at herself as she led Rojon out of the pub, a few people looking at her, waiting to see if the strange hazel-eyed woman from the Land of Light would offer her protection once again. She took a deep breath and nodded to a few large sets of dark eyes. She preferred that they look to her than her son. She didn't want Rojon near any of this, nor feeling the crushing weight of their expectations. He was twenty, yes, but he was still just a boy to her. And his magic would be useless, if he even had any. Which they wouldn't know until it was too late.

They could leave him out of it.

Dusk fell like a heavy blanket on the village, rocked by another failed fishing expedition and the loss of a five-person crew. Worse than just losing their lives, their bodies had been lost too, which meant their memories and souls could not be properly cherished. A fate already laid upon so many of Elihor's people, the grief palpable.

Carefully built arches connected buildings, each alley leading to a small garden or single tree, a sign of growth and memory. Most of Raklar had survived the initial blaze, the easternmost edge of the town crushed but the rest remained standing, scorched stones never cleaned.

Never to forget.

Avarielle and her son walked in silence, steps quiet on the mostly cobblestone streets. Once, she'd been told, this place had been riddled with life. People and horses supporting the fishing trade.

Now it held its breath, waiting for the next blow.

A few streets down, away from the shore, they knocked on the familiar door. An apple tree grew in their backyard, planted by Laora's father, who had perished before the Days of Blood. It had survived, unlike so many of the orchards of Elihor.

Torbolem will never have a tree. She fought back against her grief, holding space for his parents' and her son's. While Rojon and Torbolem's father talked about memories and shared some tears, Laora took Avarielle aside to the courtyard, to stand beneath the gnarled tree.

"That was my boy," she said through clenched teeth, dark eyes deep pools of tears. "Do you know who did this?" Avarielle had met Laora shortly after moving there, quickly becoming fast friends, their sons around the same age. Both without mothers and with few resources, they'd leaned on each other to figure out how to survive with a newborn child in a burnt and scarred land. And, when Avarielle had had to step away to go fulfill her duty and maintain her oath, Laora had helped watch over Rojon, who couldn't yet follow.

That their sons had become like brothers warmed

both their hearts and united the families even further. They'd been inseparable except in one respect: Rojon didn't take to the sea but to the art of plants and buildings instead. She hated how grateful she now felt that he'd never developed sea legs. And it further twisted the grief for the young man she'd watched grow up alongside her own son.

"I don't," Avarielle said, looking deep into Laora's eyes. "But I promise I'll do everything in my power to find out."

Laora nodded, then slowly turned away from Avarielle and placed her hand on the solid trunk of the apple tree, forehead to bark as her anger quickly dissipated back into grief.

~

The Bloody Mountains formed a dark and impenetrable fortress in the distance, the sky above them shimmering slightly in the moonlight. *The Wall of Loss.* Kale had quickly fallen asleep, and Rojon had retreated to be alone. She fought against her instincts to go to him, letting him figure things out for himself.

He'd come to her if he needed her. He'd been fairly independent for the past few years, something Avarielle was both proud of and saddened by. Not that he'd had much choice—she'd been absent for half of his life, after all. She missed the little boy who held her tightly and folded into her lap when he needed to think. He might be too big to fold into her lap now, but she'd love to even just sit in the same room. To feel like he might still need her, and to know she was there if he did.

He'll be fine, she tried to convince herself, but still listened intently for signs of movement or anything that indicated he might need her.

After some time, she finally knelt by her bed and pulled out the large rectangular box she kept beneath it. A poor hiding place, but no one had ever bothered her there. And why would they? She was barely known there, a woman of Graydon with a child of Elihor, a child who couldn't survive in the Land of Light. They knew she'd helped some villagers survive, a few of them settling in the area. They trusted her because she'd put work in this place, like they all did. And the fact that Kale, a descendant of Elihor, had vouched for her certainly hadn't hurt.

Ignoring the layer of dust on the box, she opened it. An old blanket loosely covered its belongings. She smiled as she touched the blanket. Rojon's first blanket, technically a cloak, the color of deep blood. Too worn to still use, too precious to get rid of.

Carefully she moved it aside. Two items lay beneath. The first and largest was Graysword. She kept it there when not in Graydon. It looked the same as it always had —the blade as sharp, the hilt as shiny, the red jewel catching the candlelight and magnifying it. She resisted the urge to wrap her hand around its hilt, wanting to hold the metal in her hand, to feel the perfectly weighted blade that had seen her through so much. And linked her to such darkness.

With a deep breath, she looked beyond it, focusing on the second item in the box: a simple rock decorated with a swirl pattern that had been carved with magic.

"Just in case," Shirina had said, her face taut and drawn as they parted ways atop the Bloody Mountains, twenty years earlier, after a battle that almost claimed all their lives. The red cloak belonged to her. Once, Avarielle had hated the sorceress. Now a smile graced her lips at the thought of calling her. She'd love this, of course. That would have once annoyed her, but now it amused her.

Shirina was many things, irritating chief among them, but she was also trustworthy. She'd protected Cassara, rebuilt her Circle, and had always made sure Rojon had the learning he so craved. A gentle boy, son of two warriors, born during the final battle of the Days of Blood. Ripped from her by magic. Shirina always visited him when Avarielle was away, able to quickly travel thanks to her magic. Avarielle had never thanked her for that. She might, one day, if the sorceress proved especially non-annoying, knowing Shirina expected no such gesture and would probably scoff at it.

That made her smile more as she carefully lifted the stone and spoke the words Shirina had given her to activate it.

I had to choose words you'd never accidentally say, she'd informed her, face passive, drawn from overuse of magic, but an unmistakable glimmer in her eyes. Avarielle shook her head, a grin on her lips as she uttered the phrase.

"I need your help, Shirina."

~

Before dawn even pierced the sky, Avarielle stood within the nearby forest, stretching her arms and legs before starting her day's exercise. She loved this time most of all, when the world was quiet and all she had to worry about was her breath.

Her limbs remembered the moves by heart, the dances taught to her as a child by her mentor, and the sword movements taught by Trevon. The survival instincts she'd developed over the years of running, fighting, surviving. Her body effortlessly slipped into its old movements, her mind quieting even as the forest filled with life around her. She let that life embrace her, the sounds of nature coat her, remembering a time when even forests had grown quiet.

By the time she walked back to her home, the sun pierced the horizon, and she felt ready to tackle the day and whatever it might bring.

A figure sat on her porch, slowly standing as Avarielle approached.

"That was quick," Avarielle said softly, not wanting to wake up Kale or Rojon just yet. Shirina's lips quirked, the gray in her raven hair highlighted by the growing light, as were her white robes. The crimson circle embroidered above her heart matched the color of her cloak. The same outfit the sorceress had worn since Avarielle had met her. The same color as Rojon's first blanket.

"For Avarielle Grayloft to call for aid, I figured things must be pretty dire."

Avarielle couldn't help but smile. It was good to see the sorceress. Not because she was particularly fond of her, but they shared a common history that few would understand, standing against the greatest evil and surviving. Together.

"It's nice to see you haven't run out of sarcasm, Shirina. Are you up for a walk?"

Shirina nodded, and Avarielle slipped into the house to quickly change and leave a note for her still-sleeping family. She hated to admit it, but with Shirina there, she felt more confident they could handle whatever lurked in the water.

After years of rebuilding the Circle, surely Shirina had a few new tricks to share.

2

The warrior didn't initiate conversation, and so neither did Shirina, enjoying the sounds of the forest around her. Elihor's rebuilding and replanting had gone at a remarkable pace. Some didn't think so, twenty years in, but considering the landscape was mostly razed and over half of the land's people killed, Shirina found this nothing short of amazing.

She looked sideways to the warrior, curious. Avarielle and she hadn't chatted much since fighting Siabala and swearing to protect their deadly secret. The warrior kept her word, spending half the year at Cassara's side, protecting her for months at a time, her son raised by his grandfather and the villagers.

Kale. She looked forward to seeing him today. Shirina often visited when Avarielle was away. Partly to get more Circle history from him, since he was a wealth of knowledge about Elihor, and partly to assure the warrior that someone else kept an eye on her son.

She was sure that Avarielle knew, but the two had never chatted about it. Why would they? They led different lives, intersected only at Siabala's whims.

As always, the warrior seemed annoyingly the same, even the years being kind to her. She didn't strike Shirina as any less powerful physically, though it was strange to see her weaponless. At least, apparently weaponless. She doubted the warrior walked around without a dagger stuck somewhere on her. Probably several, though she'd never figured out where Avarielle kept them all. Still, something about her seemed more tempered, but Shirina doubted that impression would survive the test of fire.

"I assume you called me here for more than a morning constitutional?" Shirina asked, hating that she sounded out of breath. Her body had suffered from the fall of magic, and her continued use of it didn't help. Old instincts kicked in and she braced herself for the warrior's joke at her expense. But if Avarielle noticed, she didn't let on.

"There have been attacks on fishing ships," she said, voice low as they passed another home, the village wrapped in gloomy morning mist. Not conducive to safe sailing, or perhaps out of fear of monsters, the docks stretched quietly around them as they neared the water.

"This is the third ship," Avarielle said, pointing at a wrecked mound of wood and metal. "We lost good people to these attacks." The mists swallowed her whisper.

Shirina didn't immediately see signs of attack, but she slowly walked around the once-ship, knowing that Avarielle would not be mistaken in this, nor would have called her unless she truly needed help. On the stern she found what Avarielle had seen, etched in the wood grain and metal.

Claw marks.

"Has anyone spotted anything?"

"No," Avarielle said. "But no one's survived the attacks, either."

Shirina looked to the water, the waves lapping beneath the wooden dock, the scent of fish and algae mixing into an unpleasant odor. She missed her books and scrolls, and her gardens. A few ships floated in the harbor, and Shirina frowned as she watched them bob up and down with the waves.

Staring at the movement, a thought began to bloom in her, her breath catching on that terrible air. She glanced back at the mangled wreck, a ball that looked nothing like a ship. Then she glanced at Avarielle, the warrior looking out toward the sea, waiting her out.

"How was this found?" Shirina asked, forming her thoughts as she formed her words. "Shouldn't this have sunk?"

Avarielle held her gaze and didn't miss a beat.

"They were found on islands, sandbars, or even deposited on shore. Just waiting."

There she saw it, in the warrior's eyes, the familiar fire.

Someone, or something, had wanted the wrecks found. The water lapped on the shore, calm and serene.

"This feels like baiting," Avarielle said, with something akin to worry and, more worrisome for Shirina, excitement.

"It does," Shirina said, turning to Avarielle as she crossed her arms. "Have you seen the monster?"

"I haven't. But I do know that we need to find it and destroy it before it kills again."

"I'm surprised you didn't just try to do this yourself," Shirina said honestly, biting back the sarcasm begging to be unleashed.

"I've grown wise, Shirina."

Shirina nearly choked at the words.

"The creature isn't the only thing baiting, it seems. I could just teleport away, you know."

"I know," Avarielle said with a lazy grin. "But you won't."

"Give me one good reason?" She stood straighter, feeling energized by the exchange, which irritated her even more. If she was honest, which she certainly didn't intend to be with Avarielle, she'd missed her. Had missed *this*. The back-and-forth, always having to be on her toes, the quick wit. And always knowing where you stood. In the end, they'd both proved to each other their trustworthiness. That on the battlefield, they would keep each other safe.

In the battlefield of wits, however, only direct hits mattered.

"Because, like you said, it feels like baiting. And I'm not sure who they'd be baiting here except me or Rojon."

"Still not convinced," Shirina added, though she agreed. Avarielle held an ancient magic and had made powerful enemies with it. Her son was heir to an even more powerful power, wrought from the magic of Elihor. There was indeed quite a lot to bait there.

"Well, I'm going to find out who's doing this, with or without your help." Avarielle shrugged. "And I could use your help."

"There's that word again," Shirina said. "You haven't uttered it in twenty years, and now here we are, and you've said it twice already."

The warrior looked toward the sea, the mist starting to lift, the docks coming to life around them. Avarielle turned to face her, and she looked tired. Not like Shirina had seen her before, weary to the bone and grieving, bleeding on the battlefield. No, this was a different kind of tired. And one she understood all too well.

The fatigue of similar events rang like a battle call in her weary bones, too. The sorceress met the warrior's eyes.

"Where do you want to start?"

3

_A_varielle had thought Shirina would prove the most annoying part of her day, but she'd been wrong. The most annoying part of her day was her own flesh and blood, stubbornly standing in the entrance to her room and stopping her from leaving.

"Rojon, you'll stay here and I'll head off with Shirina." She kept her tone measured but commanding. Soldiers had jumped to follow her commands on battlefields at hearing that tone. Her son, unfortunately, seemed immune.

"I should go with you," he said, looking at her leather armor and the weapons she now had strapped on. He'd seen her wearing them before, and she'd trained him in combat, as had her own sword mentor, Trevon. But he was untested on an actual battlefield, and she hoped he would stay that way.

His eyes flickered to the pommel sticking up above her

back. She knew that look, that desire, her stomach turning. Her gentle boy, who loved gardens, had made bridges from their roots, could be made to love war. Bloodshed. The power called to him, too. The darkness of her blade, her legacy. She'd hoped that Kryde's blood would have tempered the curse of her own, but their son seemed just as powerless as she'd once been. But she'd been more desperate, too, with monsters roaming her land.

Monsters now roam his land, too.

"The answer is no." A whisper, echoing like a shout.

Torbolem was gone, grief and sorrow ignited in her son. Just like it had been in her when her brother had been killed. *Rojon is the same age as he'd been.* She pushed the thought deep, buried it, but was unable to release the fear clutching her gut. Her sensitive son sought blood. The power promised him that, in a way she couldn't.

"I have to go." She placed a hand on his shoulder. "I'll be back by nightfall."

At that he glanced away from the sword and looked at her, fear riddling his dark eyes.

"What if the monster attacks you?" His voice sounded strangled. Her brave boy, born in the heat of battle, fighting Siabala with his first few breaths, had not known combat since. And, unlike her people and her time, he hadn't really lost anyone until his friend. Maybe it wasn't the power he craved. Maybe he just wanted to do something, anything, the same Grayloft temper that ran in her blood firing his, too. Maybe she read too much in his actions and words, seeing herself reflected in them. Fearing he'd follow her path.

He was better than her. She'd done her best to raise him to follow his own path, away from hers. To have the peaceful life she never could.

"I can handle it," she said with a confident smile. "Besides, Shirina can teleport us out of there if necessary. She's faster and more powerful than she looks."

He looked at her incredulously but seemed to decide to trust her. He knew Shirina like a wise aunt who came bearing books. He'd never seen the sorceress wield her powerful fires in battle. Hopefully, he would never have to.

"Just be careful." He wrapped his arms around her. She hugged him back, then broke the embrace and kissed his forehead.

"I promise I will be," she said. "You help Torbolem's family today, and keep your grandfather out of trouble." He gave a short laugh at that.

"I'll walk you to the docks," he offered, and the two headed down the stairs to find Shirina and Kale in deep conversation. She joined them, trying to shake the feeling that her peaceful home in Elihor was being slowly unravelled and everything she'd grown to love would be swept away.

Just like it had once before.

The four companions walked in silence toward the docks as the sun steadily warmed the day, though the mists stubbornly clung on. Then she left her family and followed Shirina to Kale's small skiff.

She glanced back, to Rojon and Kale on the dock. They would keep each other safe. Then she forced herself to focus on the gloomy, mist-covered water and what she would face, her heart beginning to beat with the familiar rush of impending battle.

She loved her family. Was proud of her son, and all that they'd built there.

But, if she was honest, she'd missed this. The call to wield her sword, the battle cry of her instincts, the freedom of the battlefield, where decisions were based on immediate needs. No overthinking, worrying, hoping.

Only action, and the singing of her blade as it lit with magic.

4

*R*ocks and the nearby sandbar kept Avarielle busy navigating the skiff while Shirina focused on holding on to the sides and the looming wreck ahead. This wreck was bigger than what had washed up on shore, half the boat stranded on rocks. Deep gashes crisscrossed the wooden hull, which could have been produced by striking the rocks. But Shirina knew it wasn't. If nothing else, Avarielle believed a monster attacked. When it came to monsters, the warrior was second to none.

The parallel cuts showed that the creature had three claws, or at least three larger ones. A closer investigation would reveal more details and hopefully help them find and destroy this monster. With any luck, it would already be gone, though Shirina doubted that to be the case.

Avarielle managed to get the boat near the rocky island and secured it. Satisfied, she hopped out and offered her hand to the sorceress. Shirina accepted it, unused to travel on water.

"When did you get so proficient in boating?" she asked as she found herself swaying on firm land.

"Take a deep breath and close your eyes for a second. It'll help you find your legs again." She did as told, the warrior's hand on her back to steady her. "Kale's a fisherman, on top of being part of the Circle," she continued. "He taught me and Rojon everything he knows."

"Not technically part of the Circle," Shirina whispered as she reopened her eyes. "But it's his knowledge I've learned to lean on." Avarielle nodded knowingly, then headed toward the wreck. Rocks jutted out of the water around them, this being the biggest island, if it could be called that, barely ten meters long and wide, crafted of uneven terrain and rocks. With it being wet, Shirina had to concentrate on remaining standing, wishing she still had her staff, even if she'd not carried one for twenty years.

Absentmindedly, she touched the thick silver bracers on each wrist, making sure they were still there. If Avarielle noticed, she gave no indication of it, the warrior's narrowed eyes surveying their surroundings as they approached the wreck.

"The wreck was checked for survivors but not much else. They feared another attack."

What Shirina believed from a distance to be the whole boat turned out to be a piece of it, cracked in half. She glanced questioningly at Avarielle.

"They never found the second half."

The air smelled fresh, the breeze wafting in from the deep sea, the horizon shimmering with endless depths as it stretched past her line of sight. Shirina struggled to keep her footing on the slippery rocks. Avarielle, much to Shirina's annoyance, didn't seem plagued with such issues. Mists danced around the island just above the waters, refusing to dissipate despite the wind, blocking their view of the shore. With the Sight she peered into the mists but found nothing magical within them.

Shirina slowly studied the wreckage and could see no magic within it, either, not even a lingering trace. A finger upon it revealed that slime coated it. She had no idea what constituted normal in these conditions, and simply made note of it. An important part of being a sorceress was knowing what she didn't know. Something that she tried to impress on her Circle adepts.

The claw marks on the wood were deeper and clearer than those of the wreck on shore. On the second pass, she noticed something sticking out of the wood, near the top portion of a deep gash.

She glanced up, and Avarielle followed her eyes.

"Is that a claw?"

"It seems to be. Or at least a piece of one," Shirina said.

"Can you fly yet? Is that something you can do with your magic?"

Shirina looked at her with a raised eyebrow, and Avarielle shrugged. "Doesn't hurt to ask. But I guess it's up to me." She tied a rope to an arrow, pulling out her long bow, the rope uncoiling as the arrow went up and fell back down, planting deeply in the top of the wreck. Avarielle tested her rope, then started to climb.

With some work and the help of a dagger, she managed to get the piece of claw out.

Shirina looked around while the warrior whittled away the wood.

"How did it get so far from the water?" she asked, looking at the waves lapping below, the nearby sandbar turning the clear incoming water into rolling waves, some crashing onto rocks, others heading back toward the hidden shoreline.

Avarielle landed beside her.

"That's one of the questions worrying me," she said, handing Shirina the dark piece she'd extracted from the wood.

Gold flecks peppered the darkness of the claw. When she held it up against the mostly clear sky, she could almost see through it. Strong, sturdy, gold-lined and yet not fully opaque. This was no material that Shirina had ever encountered. The worse part was the realization that this was a smaller claw, caught in the wood and unable to break free. Yet it was bigger than her hand.

Avarielle hissed, and Shirina looked up. The waves intensified and struck the sandbar.

"What is—" Before she could finish her question, Avarielle tackled her and threw her on rocks, knocking the wind from her. The warrior scrambled up, pulling

Shirina along with her as a giant tail smashed the ground where they'd stood moments before, shattering what remained of the ship, splinters of wood storming into them.

"Shirina!" Avarielle shouted as something knocked into Shirina's midsection. Pain lanced through her body, breath stolen from her. Then she landed, hard, frigid waters enveloping her and dragging her down, merciless.

5

*W*hite robes and crimson cloak stumbled into the water before Avarielle could reach out, too busy trying to avoid incoming blows while not slipping on wet rocks. Dark legs crashed on the ground as a large creature erupted from the nearby sand bank, looking like a mix between a lizard and a centipede. Its shining dark blue exoskeleton absorbed the light instead of reflecting it, mimicking the gently rolling sea, making it difficult to spot unless it moved. Which it currently did, a ripple traveling from head to tail as it stretched.

Avarielle raced to jump into the water after Shirina, but a leg landed right in front of her, twice as wide as she was tall. She threw herself sideways, landed on her flank, and pushed herself back up in one swift, practiced motion. Three large claws surrounded by smaller claws skittered on the rock, scratching the stones. She studied it quickly as she scrambled back to find a weakness, but no matter where she looked, its shining exoskeleton greeted her like armor.

And Shirina had yet to re-emerge.

Anger bubbled into Avarielle with the familiar rush of adrenaline and excitement as her fingers wrapped around Graysword's hilt. Before she could draw on its magic, the creature shifted, and Avarielle threw herself between two large legs, then pushed off the rocks and into the lapping waters below.

She dove in, the white robes of the sorceress thankfully easy to spot, her red cloak unfurling in the water around her like a great hand holding her, red blood dribbling from her forehead where she must have struck the rocks.

Eli's blood. She'd brought the sorceress there to help her, not to get herself killed within seconds. She kicked hard toward Shirina, using her hands to pull herself as quickly as possible. The water shifted, dancing with bubbles as something large slipped into it, the wake propelling her forward but down. Or so she thought. Losing bearings underwater would prove deadly.

Avarielle found strength to swim faster as the ebbs of the water struck the sorceress, vanishing from view with sediment. She focused on where she'd last seen her as a rush of bubbles overtook her, a large leg landing inches from her nose.

Her lungs hurt and she forced her limbs to keep pushing down, ignoring her need for air, focusing on the next movement, the next action. Dirt swirled around her, caught in the creature's wake, though the calmer push of the water indicated it had withdrawn. Avarielle's knuckles scraped against stone and she changed course. The rocks jutted close to each other, and might form a natural barrier against it.

She hoped so as she looked around blindly.

Just as she thought she had to abandon the search and head up for air, loose fabric wrapped around her hand, followed by something soft and flesh-like. Praying to Graydon and Elihor, she grabbed the object and kicked up as it dragged behind her. Enough drag to be a body.

Air had never tasted fresher, and she gulped it greedily as she headed to shore. Her lungs burned, white dots exploding in her vision as she pulled herself to shore, still holding on to her find, relieved to see it was indeed Shirina and not some poor sailor's body. Grunting, she pulled the unconscious sorceress onto the rocks, away from the water. The wind picked up, chilling her to her bones.

She paused, instincts on high alert, and looked again toward the water. The creature sat on the sandbar, maybe even rested on it, part of its large head sticking up, looking almost like an island itself, save for the large, light-absorbing dark eyes. Avarielle crouched protectively over Shirina, trying to formulate a plan on how to get them both out alive. The creature stared at her. Could it be studying her? How intelligent was this thing? Moments after the two locked eyes, it slipped into the water, ripples following it away from their rocky perch.

Avarielle watched it go for a few precious seconds before focusing back on the sorceress, trying to ignore the shiver settling into her spine. Those eyes had seemed so… thoughtful. She shrugged it off. Maybe it had been too long since she'd been in battle, and much longer since she'd fought monsters.

Shirina's lips were turning blue, a dangerous pallor clinging her skin.

"This would be a stupid way for you to die," Avarielle hissed as she started pushing on the sorceress's chest, forcing the water out of her lungs. She'd been taught the technique of Elihor, used for generations to save sailors from treacherous waters.

Shirina spat up water, and Avarielle held her to her side so she wouldn't choke. The sorceress gasped, Avarielle keeping a steadying hand on her as she glanced around, trying to see where the monster had gone, but all that she could see was the quiet water, and no sign of the large creature that had just tried to kill them.

~

Shirina sat in silence as Avarielle rowed them back to shore. Coldness had settled in her core, and her head still hurt. Avarielle had wrapped her in a strange seaweed blanket and tended to her head, but there was little else she could do before they reached a healer.

31

She'd wanted to teleport them straight back to land and not risk coming under another attack, but they'd both known using so much power to teleport two people could wipe her out for hours, if not days. Especially when injured. And she needed her magic to deal with this creature. Of course, next time, she'd try not to get knocked into the water first.

She hadn't missed this. The churning of moments in battle. From victorious to crushed in an instant. She found herself again missing her books and gardens, and the warmth of Graydon's sun. Elihor shared the same sun, of course, but its quality seemed dimmed here, perhaps because it relied on evening light instead of morning rays.

The sun was just beginning to creep down in the sky by the time they spotted the shore again.

"This place is usually brimming with fishing vessels," Avarielle said, looking back to Shirina. She'd been making small talk here and there and keeping an eye on her, making sure she stayed awake. Shirina made a sound acknowledging the statement but didn't feel much like talking.

"Fishing is one of their main food sources," Avarielle continued. "When Siabala burnt Elihor, it destroyed a lot of animals, too. They hunt less to allow the herds to re-form. Some animals can be hunted now, but restabilizing the food chain in this land has been of high concern for the elders."

Shirina looked toward her, winced at the pain in her head.

"This isn't just about sailors getting killed," Avarielle continued. "It's about saving the people from famine, too. After everything they've been through, they're still rebuilding, and food supplies and storage still aren't producing enough to survive one bad season. And last summer did not have good crops."

"I heard," Shirina sighed, feeling forced to chat. "We've been working with the Circle of Elihor to reforge land magics and help fortify the crops. I'm afraid that's taking time, though," Shirina sounded apologetic. Once, she would have cared at showing the weakness. But now, she'd learned to temper her pride with humility. Her magic had been ripped from her before, and only the hard work and knowledge of others had allowed her to survive. People did better together, but getting them to work together proved difficult. And often annoying.

"Graydon had excellent crops last summer," Shirina offered. "You could reach out to Cassara. I'm sure she'd send what she can from Massir."

"I'm sure," Avarielle said. Their mutual friend was the most powerful queen in the Land of Light, and she would step up. If asked. Shirina looked at Avarielle, and the warrior sighed. "There's still so much distrust. I mean, so many of Elihor's people were killed in Graydon. And, even now, the few who dare come through Siabala's Rage act like they own the place. Like those from Graydon are better. It makes it hard to reach out for help when the help expects you to kneel." She winced. "Not that Cassara would ever expect or demand that."

She took a shuddering breath. "How is Cassara?"

"Good the last time I saw her," Shirina said, choosing her words carefully. Cassara was under protection from her closest witches, the ones she trusted most. If Cassara were to fall, the entire world would be doomed. But no one knew that except the three of them, and she intended to keep that secret. But as the queen of the biggest kingdom in Graydon, a target had been permanently etched on her back.

"Graydon has its own problems," Shirina continued. "And Cassara is not appreciated by all."

Avarielle's hands turned to fists, eyes shining as she looked to Shirina. The warrior had taken an oath to protect Cassara, and that oath ran deep in her blood. She'd been spending half her time in Graydon and half in Elihor, trying to split her heart between her duty and her family. Soon, she'd head back. With Rojon continuing his studies and talking of heading to Keshmeer, capital of Elihor, to apprentice with the Guild of Memories, she suspected Avarielle's next trip to Graydon would prove permanent.

The warrior seemed to be thinking along the same lines.

"Every time I go, tensions seem to be growing in the kingdom," Avarielle said, "And now, monsters stalk Elihor. Could any of this be Siabala's doing?"

Shirina looked out to the sea, toward the Bloody Mountains and the shimmering Wall of Loss, remembering the first time Avarielle had truly trusted her.

When there had been no choice, and everything had to be sacrificed to stop an ancient god from being reborn. They should have been able to end it then, but their magic, their armies… they'd been too weak by then and he too strong. He'd chiseled their strength away until not enough remained to defeat him, only imprison him.

"I don't know," Shirina answered truthfully, then met the warrior's steely eyes. "But we might as well proceed as though it is. We lose nothing by being overly cautious, and perhaps everything by hesitating."

The warrior nodded and turned her attention on approaching the docks. Shirina had just told her she needed to abandon her life there and go to Cassara's side. Her witches would protect Cassara to follow her orders, but no one would defend her like Avarielle. It didn't need to be Avarielle, really. Rojon was a man now, old enough to wield Graysword should Avarielle give him the ancestral blade and magic. Except she wouldn't. Not as long as she could wield it, intent on finishing what they'd failed to finish.

Shirina glanced up again toward the Wall of Loss, crackling over the Bloody Mountains, rays of sunset reflected within it and creating dark orange and yellow lines against a purple sky. She shivered, pulled her blanket closer. She'd felt the wall re-form, its energies crackling to life, threatening to absorb her.

But how long would the Wall hold, and what would it demand of them all once it fell?

~

Beneath the water, the creature watched and waited. It hated it up there, this close to the sun. The light burned its skin, turning its usually soft, radiant shell dark. It needed darkness to thrive, depths to survive. To stay away, far away, from land. It had wandered too near, drawn by schools of fish and the crackling sounds of the water. It wanted to leave now, to return to the depths of the ocean, to glow amidst its tunnels and rocks.

Yet there it stayed, compelled by a will not its own, drawn to the shore.

And the closer it came, the less it could control its desire to stay away and escape back to its home.

Silently, it glided at the bottom of the sea, fish scattering around it as it stalked the skiff.

Do not attack now. The orders were clear and firm.

Wait. Wait for now.

The creature waited but watched. And followed.

6

*A*varielle ate her fish stew in silence, Rojon and Kale also not in a talkative mood. Shirina glanced up at them from time to time but didn't seem to be feeling chatty either. Which suited and worried Avarielle at the same time. Her son had spent the day doing what he could to help Torbolem's parents in this, his real first brush with violent death. Avarielle had lost so many when she was young, including her parents and her brother. She wished her son never had to live through the same hardships she'd faced.

It'll only get worse. The visceral fears, sewn deep within the scars of his birth and his first battle, twisted her gut, and her hunger vanished. The usually lively pub stood muted, and fewer families broke bread there this night. Fear as thick as her own smothered the village. Fear of losing ships, of growing hungry. And of course, fear of dying, though less so, she guessed. These people had been intimately courted by death, until Siabala had been trapped again in the Wall of Loss.

And there was the greatest fear of all. That their climb back into normalcy, into life and light, was over, and soon they would stumble back down into wretched burnt lands and mass graves. The fear that this fragile hope had been just an illusion, and they weren't destined for anything more than just pain and grief. That the future had no use for them nor their children.

"Are you well, granddaughter?" Kale whispered. Her hand hurt where she clutched her spoon too tightly.

"Just... tired," she replied softly. "We all are." Dark caring eyes met hers. She never thought her family would look back at her with eyes so different, and she reached across the table and took his hand in hers. Gently so as not to hurt the fingers twisted by arthritis, but enough to feel his strength.

A quirk of the lips turned to a smile, though not the easy smile he'd once sported. Rojon stayed silent, though he did look up and take in the exchange.

"We have to figure out next steps," Avarielle said as she turned to Shirina, the sorceress's eyes sharp and alert. Almost drowning didn't seem to have slowed her down.

"Graydon just brings more pain and suffering." The hissed accusation cut through the din of the pub, silencing it. The dockmaster sat silently, looking on as his brother stared straight at Avarielle. He'd probably put him up to this.

"Go get some sleep, Loron." A sharp edge slipped into her voice. "You'll think clearer in the morning."

"A Circle witch from Graydon, and you." He pointed at Avarielle, unsteady on his feet. Of course he was drunk. Great. "You've been nothing but trouble since you got here."

"That's enough." Kale barely turned his head, barely raised his voice, but the man hesitated.

"Elder Kale, she's…"

"Leave my mother alone," Rojon practically growled, his anger seeping into his voice. He'd been quiet all day, seething, like water about to boil. She knew that feeling all too well.

"Come on." The dockmaster took his brother by the shoulders, conceding defeat. Avarielle stared daggers at him, annoyed he'd attacked her, after she'd lived there for twenty years, helping this village, and even more irritated that Kale and Rojon had had to step in.

And their voice was heard, while hers was ignored. Before she could make clear to them how irked she was, a crash resounded from the docks, followed by a scream, cut short too quickly.

Grabbing her sword, Avarielle turned to Rojon.

"Get away from the docks," she ordered. He hesitated. "Get Kale to safety," she added softly, pride and fear competing with his desire to fight.

"We can help," Kale said, looking up stubbornly, hand on his grandson's arm. Of course, the old man could also prove useless. "With distance weapons." A smile quirked his lips.

"He's right," Rojon said. "We can't just run away."

Knowing a losing battle when facing one, Avarielle handed her son her bow and quiver. Around them, the pub emptied as people ran toward their homes and families. The ground quaked as something crashed nearby. Time to go.

"Distance only," she said, and he nodded, looking pale but resolute. She wanted so badly to know he was safe, away from there. But she was all too familiar with the determination in his eyes. "There's too much of your father in you," she muttered.

"And his mother," Kale and Shirina both said at once. Avarielle ignored them.

"Be careful, and remember your training," she took a moment to say, making sure he nodded before she turned around and all four headed out the door.

"Battle will always follow him," Kale told her as they exited. "Let him know he can stand on his own two feet. I will let no harm come to him."

"Watch out for yourself, too, Grandfather," Avarielle said, voice softening.

Chaos swept over the village. The large centipede-like creature moved close to the ground, the dock now crushed debris. People ran in all directions, gripped by fear, the monster's uncertain, confused movements adding to the agitation. Large legs moved unpredictably, scurrying in multiple directions at once, its body undulating as though unsure where to go.

"Help get people to safety," she told Kale and Rojon. "Shirina and I will deal with this thing."

Rojon seemed about to argue, but a child stumbled nearby and he reached for her before she fell, his quick reflexes heartening Avarielle. Then he nodded to her, grabbed the child, and told a few others to follow him.

"I'll stay near him," Kale promised, squeezing her arm, walking fairly quickly toward his grandson.

Avarielle tore her eyes away from her family, took a deep breath, and focused back on the creature, which moved as though confused by its own appearance on land.

The clouded night came with a soft, misty rain, the creature glowing faintly in the dark. It screeched, turned on its side, looked back to the water, and smashed its head down, like something bothered it.

"It looks more like a wounded animal than an attacking one," Avarielle said, hands twitching at her side, eager to clutch Graysword and feel the magic coursing through her. "Which might make it even more dangerous and difficult to predict."

"We'll have to move quickly," Shirina offered, "before more people get killed."

"Let's go." Avarielle moved toward the confused creature, analyzing it as she approached from its right flank. The creature's skin sparkled in the growing darkness, as though coated with the canopy of stars the clouds hid from view. It was beautiful but deadly, and too dangerous to herd out to sea. If that could even be done.

Avarielle took a deep breath and freed Graysword from its scabbard. The blade greeted her with the familiar song in her mind, the magic eager to be unleashed after being dormant so many years. The second the magic sparked to life at her touch, before Avarielle called upon it, the creature's movements stopped being sporadic. Its head slowly turned toward them, making a weird chattering sound from the rounded orifice near its neck, surrounded by teeth.

Its entire body undulated up and down, legs clicking the ground in a consecutive row, like a dancing line, head bobbing back and forth as if focusing on them one eye at a time, the eyes too far apart to offer frontal vision.

Then it slithered up, stretched almost fifteen meters into the sky, legs held out as it screeched, mouth like a maw, skin turning a more muted yellowish glow.

"What is it doing?" Shirina asked.

Before either of them could figure it out, it collapsed back down, the ground shaking. And it charged. Not toward them but past them, straight for Rojon and Kale, who still led families to safety. Rojon's dark eyes grew wide, freezing at the sight of the creature charging for him. Without hesitation and a smoothness to his limbs that Avarielle hadn't seen in years, Kale stepped between him and the creature, bracing his feet to prepare for the attack. A glow spread around him, a dark shimmer she recognized, had seen it before when Rojon's father had saved her life but failed to save his own.

The magic of Elihor, which protected those they loved but failed to save the wielder.

There are worse things than dying for those we love, Kryde had once told her.

Something within her snapped and she screamed, throwing herself at the flank of the creature, calling forth the magic of Graysword and all that it would give her to stop the creature from finding her son and her grandfather. Her *family.* She braced herself and held Graysword's blade into its legs as it raced forward, chopping them off, her shoulders barely feeling the impact, her magic so strong.

Fires danced in her peripheral vision and she knew Shirina blasted it, but the creature still moved too quickly, the loss of dozens of legs not enough to slow it down. She grabbed hold of its armored shell, pulled herself up, holding hard so it wouldn't throw her off. Then she began to hack it, moving forward as best she could on its writhing form, slammed by the stench of burnt flesh and something sickly sweet. She didn't stop, didn't pause, barely breathed as she hacked down, possessed with her own need to save those she loved.

Until it stopped moving and collapsed beneath her.

Avarielle spat out some of its juices, which tasted like unrefined ale, and waded off of it, the sticky viscera slowing her down. She fought against it, almost slipping into it as she looked toward the front. Over its own large, still-smoking corpse, it was impossible to see how far it had gotten before finally stopping.

"Rojon!" she cried, finally freeing herself from its hacked remains, covered in gore. She didn't care as she raced to the front of the creature. Shirina knelt by someone, and Avarielle's heart dropped. The sorceress wasn't even trying to heal the fallen, meaning it was too late.

"Grandfather," she heard Rojon say, voice thick with tears. She felt immediate relief for the survival of her son, mixed with grief at the death of the man who'd taken her in, made sure she wasn't alone, helped her raise his grandson's child. Who'd stood up against a monster to see her son safe.

She slowly fell to her knees by her old friend. Shirina glanced at her, Avarielle surprised to see tears on her cheeks. It seemed Avarielle wasn't the only one who had been tempered by time.

The magic of Elihor had protected Rojon and everyone else but sacrificed its blood. Sacrificed Kale. His hands were folded on his chest, covering torn skin, blood pooling beneath him. A slight smile remained on his lips, knowing he'd managed to summon his ancestral magic. And he'd saved those he loved.

"Rest well, Kale," Avarielle said, gently closing his eyes. "May the chant of Elihor and the songs of the moon lead your soul to the Afterfate."

Rojon knelt beside her, and Avarielle placed a comforting arm around him as he wept for his grandfather. And his friend. And his world collapsing around him, for the knowledge that nothing would ever be the same.

Avarielle looked up to Shirina, the sorceress's features as grim as her own. Behind her, the creature's dark eye reflected the light, the strange glow vanishing, and Avarielle couldn't help but feel like they were being watched.

7

The stench of freshly burnt wood and overturned earth greeted twilight. Avarielle stood by Rojon, her son wrapped in sorrow, dirt spattered on his boots, hands clinging a shovel.

One by one they placed the six dead, Kale included, in their graves. Villagers gathered, some softly crying, others too numb to do much else but pull their cloaks closer against the chill of the air. Some didn't even do that, looking blankly ahead, like a piece of themselves had died with their loved ones.

Kale. Avarielle swallowed hard, remembering how he'd taken her in after the Days of Blood. She'd been more terrified than in any battle. Alone with a newborn who couldn't travel back to her ancestral land. Her allies leaving for Graydon. Kale had found her and given them a home. Taught her the ways of Elihor, even as he helped others rebuild.

Avarielle helped cover the bodies, urging her son to move and express his grief through actions. To spend it in sweat, not just tears. The grief would be his companion for a while, and he would learn to move through it. Which she hated. She'd never wanted this for him. His grandfather should have died peacefully in his bed, not run through by a monster, in front of him.

She reminded herself over and over again that Rojon was no longer a child. That she'd been his age when she'd faced Siabala, twenty years before. But it didn't help. She'd wanted different things for her son. Better things.

Avarielle finished covering the graves, then looked to the markers left behind, trees that would grow and reshape the countryside, fed by the bodies of those they loved. Fruit trees, the most sacred in Elihor, which would feed bodies and souls. They'd planted one for each sailor lost at sea, too.

Different ones, of course. A type of apple called Elihor's Fallen for those who were buried. And Elihor's Lost, which looked more like a plum to Avarielle, for those whose bodies did not feed the roots. Elihor's Lost dotted the landscape, full of rich dark plums planted as the world healed itself. Slowly, steadily, Elihor's Fallen grew as a crop as well.

Kale had taught her about the trees of Elihor and what the world had once looked like, telling her stories late into the nights. Just like Kale's grandson Kryde had done, before he was ripped away from her too. She'd been unable to help him. To help either of them.

She took a deep breath, forcing her hands not to turn to fists at her side. She was angry, darkness bubbling deep within her, her blood wanting to claim revenge, even though the creature had already been killed. Right now, she needed to focus on Rojon, who walked from tree to tree, spreading his concocted root feed.

His hands held her attention. They were rough, but not callused from clutching the pommel of a sword, unlike hers. Plants, earth, stone… those were the weapons he'd chosen to wield. Weapons of life instead of death. Each tree received special attention as he lost himself in his duty of tending the earth and crops. Others made way for him, looking silently as he gave each plant the same attention, trusting that he, a descendant of Elihor, would see their loved ones to the Afterfate.

He took a few seconds more on Kale's tree, and then continued with Elihor's Lost, giving them the same attention and care, ensuring their branches would eventually bear fruit.

In Elihor, you tasted your grief. You acknowledged it would always be a part of you. A part of every meal, every empty moment, every breeze in the leaves, every song over the sea. You embraced it, devoured it, tended to it, remembered it, and sat with it.

Running a finger on the sapling now covering Kale's grave, Avarielle whispered, "Until next time, old friend."

Someday, she would bite the apples covering his grave and find sweet memories. This day, she only tasted bitterness.

~

Shirina did not feel the need to participate in the grieving ceremonies of the people of Raklar. She respected them, but she was not one of them and would never be. Avarielle had spent almost two decades there, raising a son and leaning on the community for survival while helping them thrive. Regardless of the fact that she left for six months at a time to keep an eye on Cassara, the warrior belonged with the people of Elihor now more than she'd seen her ever belong to her own people in Graydon.

No, she would not grieve with them. But she would grieve privately for Kale. She would miss him, dearly, and his wisdom and knowledge. She would shed more tears on his behalf when time allowed her the kindness of space to grieve. That time was not now. Not while the mystery of this creature threatened them.

Shirina glanced back toward the orchard, where she couldn't currently see the villagers, nor they her. *Perfect.*

For the past twenty years, while Avarielle raised her child and Cassara ruled her kingdom, Shirina had focused on rediscovering the magic of Graydon and Elihor. Her old Circle had fallen, destroyed by its own greed and lack of understanding of the two strands of magic that danced in the air. Shirina had almost paid with her life for their ignorance, and most adepts had perished.

She'd dedicated her time to building a sturdier and more knowledgeable Circle. Kale had been instrumental in his knowledge. She'd visited him regularly, mostly when Avarielle was away, and he'd helped her find others with invaluable knowledge. And books that were thought to be lost.

She'd traveled from Graydon to Elihor, always ensuring her magic would stay safe, filtering the dark strands through her bracers, one created from metal of Elihor, the other from Graydon.

All preparing for the return of Siabala. They'd destroyed his body, his soul trapped in the Wall of Loss, thanks to Cassara's powerful magic. But that magic would fail, someday, and the Wall would fall. Siabala would be let loose, the magics would mix again, and the Circle would crumble.

Elihor's magic was powerful, and different from Graydon's. For centuries, Elihor's Circle, based out of Larkhold, had focused on magics that maintained the Wall, like the witches of Stormhold and Ravenhold. And all three Circles had fallen, unprepared for the onslaught, taken by surprise.

Shirina had changed the way the Circle of Graydon operated, having seen firsthand the consequences of its hubris. First, her coven did not just focus on the Wall. It focused on learning, mastering, and sharing. Witches could learn magic and experiment in safe spaces. When the lines of what was permitted blurred, the lines of what was possible expanded. And, thanks to Kale, Shirina had discovered the depth of Elihor's powers. A depth that Rojon himself should be able to access, some day, should he wish to pursue magic.

A familiar presence lurked nearby, studying her. Shirina spoke up.

"If you're going to lurk in the shadows, the least you can do is get me a cup of tea."

Avarielle stepped into the light. She'd cleaned the gore of the monster off, but now dirt covered her boots and pants. Graysword was still strapped to her back, and her leather armor sat snugly on her. She didn't trust that they wouldn't come under attack again, and Shirina doubted the warrior intended to sleep this night.

"Did you find anything?" Avarielle asked, voice low and controlled.

"Not yet," Shirina met her eyes. "I'm sorry about Kale."

"Me, too," she gave a wry smile. "He always spoke highly of you, you know. Even though I tried to tell him how much of a pain you were."

Shirina returned the smile. "He was kind and knowledgeable. I will truly miss him."

"He went how he'd always hoped to," Avarielle continued. "Protecting those he loved." She swallowed hard, eyes shining despite the misty night, covered torches casting a warm glow diffused by the rain. "So," she said, changing the subject, indicating the creature with a quick jerk of her chin, "do we expect another attack?"

"I'm not sure," Shirina said, looking back at the creature, black eyes open and dull, twice the height of Shirina and at least ten times that length. Barnacles clung to its side, dark algae to its fins. "It's from deep underwater, further than your ships dare to go, even."

"That's what I think, too," Avarielle said, then her voice dropped. "It went after Rojon."

Shirina nodded. It certainly had seemed that way. It might have just been a coincidence, but that wasn't a chance they could take. Not with the last remaining heir of Elihor.

"Can you find out anything about it? I mean, why would something from the deep waters suddenly charge Rojon? Nothing like this has ever happened, according to the elders of the village."

"There might be a way." Shirina spoke softly, and the warrior seemed to pick up on her hesitation, taking a step closer to her to hear her whispers. "I could use some of Elihor's magic to read its mind before it's too decayed."

Avarielle raised an eyebrow. "Won't Elihor's magic kill you? Also, you can read a dead creature's mind? That seems ill advised at best."

"Did you ever wonder where some of the rituals come from, Avarielle, like from Graydon and Elihor? Why some things are so similar, and others so different?"

"Is it lecture time? I'm not one of your witches, Shirina."

Shirina ignored her. "Some of those rituals were forged from the magic itself and how it interacts with the environments of both worlds. A thousand years apart made both strings of magic grow differently, but they were once the same, I believe."

She let the thought rest for a second, then pointed toward the orchard. "Why do they plant trees and eat the fruit, and plant different trees if there's a body or not, for example?"

"Because it's a way to remember?" Avarielle sounded more irritated than intrigued.

"Yes, there is certainly that. But it's also a way to preserve the memories, caught in the lifeforce of the tree before they fully vanish and are turned back to soil. It's a way to preserve knowledge."

Avarielle's face twisted. "Kale had alluded to it at one point, but I thought he was being poetic. You're saying they're *actually* eating dead people's memories?"

"In a way," Shirina nodded. "It brings comfort to those without magic, feeling closer to their loved ones. But, for someone with magic, it allows us to tap into those memories, with the right spells, of course."

The warrior's eyes narrowed. "You tapped into some memories before, I take it?"

A slight smile finally graced the sorceress' face. "An orchard had been left untouched in the remains of Larkhold, and thanks to Kale's knowledge, we managed to crack some of the magical ways to take hold of those memories, giving us access to some lost knowledge."

"That's... *Eli*, that's a creepy hobby. It's nice that you and Kale shared it." Her eyes wandered toward the orchard. It would be years before his fruit tree would be ripe enough to taste. Avarielle seemed to ponder those ramifications, then turned back to Shirina. "So, you're saying that you can speed up the process and basically taste that fruit before it's ripe?"

"In a way," Shirina cocked her head. "It's part of Elihor's magic. Holding memories dearly. So, I should be able to use it to delve into the creature's memories."

"I'm still not clear how you're going to wield Elihor's magic." To her credit, Avarielle sounded concerned. "It tried to kill you the last time it was anywhere near you."

Shirina's hand went to her throat, a scar visible under the skin, like a stain. "I think I figured it out and should be able to handle it in small portions," she looked the warrior in the eye. "It's not poison to me. I just need to process it differently so it doesn't hurt me." She held up her arms, showing her bracers. "I can store some of Graydon's magic in these to use in Elihor, which was not easy to figure out. And they can help me filter her magic so that it's no longer toxic to me."

The warrior studied her with tired eyes as she weighed the sorceress's words. In the end, her love for Rojon won out over her concern for Shirina, and she nodded.

"What can I do to help?"

"If I start to lose myself in the magic, pull me back."

Avarielle nodded, took a step closer. Shirina focused on the eye, the most direct route to the soul. She placed a hand on it, the surface still gelatinous hours after its death.

Slowly, carefully, she called Elihor's magic, filtering it through her fingers by tapping them on the slick surface, and unfurled it into the creature.

Pain. The intense sensation sliced through Shirina,

cutting her at the core. She hadn't expected it, wasn't ready to feel physical pain, and she gasped.

"Are you all right?" Avarielle stood beside her, ready to pull her back. Shirina gulped down the pain, forced her hand to remain on the creature's eye.

"I'm all right," she answered, then looked away from the warrior's brown eyes, back to the depthless ones of the monster. Her reflection looked back at her, then the world shifted, spun, and it felt like tumbling into the eye.

I'm still here, she reminded herself, knowing Avarielle would have grabbed her had she been plummeting. *Breathe.* The scent of burning and death grounded her back to the village. And a breeze from the sea unfurled her cloak behind her, the sensation comforting.

The sea. The scent changed from fresh and airy to heavy, and Shirina reminded herself that this was now the creature's memories. Taking a deep, slow breath, she grounded herself in the air of Elihor. And then she plunged in. Water surrounded her, at first dark and terrifying but then comforting. Deep down, pressure soothing, scales white and pure, glistening in the darkness. The sorceress floated with the creature, followed its memories as it glided on the sea floor, fish she'd never known to exist scattering as it ate some, then danced with the remaining.

Pain. Again, lancing through her, but this time, she was ready. Her head hurt. No, her *mind* hurt. *Too close.* The creature had wandered too close to the shore, too far up, looking for food when little was available.

Crushing. Something crushed her mind, as though trying to take control of it. *It's just a memory, just a memory, just a memory...* She repeated the words, a mantra against losing herself in the crushing blow. And then she saw him.

Rojon. Standing on the shore, near his mother, as she stood near the wreck.

Attack. The urge sparked her limbs to life, the command echoing in her mind, the voice too ethereal, too felt rather than heard, for her to pinpoint, but the darkness, the intent... She broke contact, gasping for breath. A hand touched her back, grounding her. Shirina could see her reflection again in the dead eye. Unexpected grief crashed into her, at the creature's once-beautiful life under the water.

I'll remember you.

She looked away, turning slowly, her body feeling foreign to her, as though water should hold her instead of her legs. Avarielle watched her closely, and Shirina met her questioning eyes.

"I'm afraid that wasn't as clarifying as I'd hoped it might be," she spoke with a thin voice. "But something forced it to attack. Or willed it to."

"Siabala?" Avarielle hissed the question.

"Perhaps. I'm not sure." She met the warrior's eyes. "But they were definitely after Rojon." She tensed. "As far as I could tell, the ship attacks were simply meant to draw him out so he could be spotted from shore."

Avarielle folded her arms. "Who else but Siabala would want him dead?"

In the distance, the Wall of Loss shimmered in the darkness, the magic crackling. Her Circle kept a close eye on it, and Shirina had trusted sorceresses and sorcerers working with the adepts of Larkhold within Stormhold. Still, she'd witnessed Siabala's cunning, and he'd taken down the three Circles before.

"I don't know," she said honestly. "A visit to Stormhold might be in order." Nested in the Bloody Mountains, Stormhold was the central keep of the Circle, and the one monitoring the Wall.

"What if..." She glanced around, lowered her voice further. "What if it's not just Cassara's magic tangled in the Wall? What if Rojon is part of that equation, and he needs to die for Siabala to be free?"

"I've looked closely, and can only see her magic, no matter how I twist the Sight." Then she relented. "But Elihor's magic is at its heart protective magic." They shifted away from the monster, Avarielle eager to have her son in sight. "Perhaps there are weaves of it in the Wall that I simply cannot see."

"That's my fear," Avarielle said, slowing when they spotted Rojon, who was speaking with an older woman. "Either way, taking Rojon away from here would be safer for him, until we figure this out."

"You'd trust Stormhold with your son's life?" Shirina raised an eyebrow.

"I trust *you*," Avarielle answered. "I've trusted you with his life since before he was even born." Rojon, given by

Avarielle to Shirina moments after his birth to help Cassara defeat Siabala. His first breath, his first battle.

"Of course," Shirina nodded. She loved Rojon like he was her own blood. She'd never let anything happen to him as long as it was within her power to stop it. The problem with studying magic, however, was being all too painfully aware of its limitations. And her own.

"Stormhold is where we fought Siabala the last time," Avarielle said. "If he's to attack again, he'd start there."

"I've made sure Stormhold would not fall so easily. Never again."

"We should leave tomorrow at first light."

"Agreed."

"And Rojon comes with us."

Shirina nodded. "I can't teleport all three of us. It's too far, even with the magic stored in my bracers."

"You take him, and I'll walk, then."

The sorceress studied her closely. "Through Siabala's Rage?"

"If need be."

"It'll take you a week to reach Stormhold," Shirina sighed. "What if we all took horses? Perhaps it's best if we stick together."

"We could ride," Avarielle consented, "and it would take a few days. But we need to get to them faster than that. Go with Rojon. I'll be fine following along."

Shirina hesitated, the warrior's jaw set stubbornly but not as it would have once been. She was worried too and didn't want to be separated from her son. And Shirina wasn't sure being separated from either of them would be a good idea.

"Warning Stormhold is important, if something is even happening, which we're not sure," Shirina said. "Elder Quilsam is there, and I could send him a message. Which might be a better plan than me using all my energies to arrive there and find it under siege." Seeing the warrior's look, she quickly added, "Not that we're thinking it is."

"We hope."

"We always hope," Shirina added softly. Not waiting for Avarielle's opinion, Shirina closed her eyes, focused inward, flicked her left hand, and whispered the incantation to reach the Elder. Much of Graydon used to rely on the Circle to share news and information, making the downfall of both lands easier once the Circle had been compromised.

Control the information, control the people.

The ability to send messages in an intelligible manner was a complicated spell, and only available to Crimson Circles and Elders. She felt her targeted destination open, like a light in the dark, or an empty bowl ready to be filled.

Strange activity in Elihor, perhaps related to Siabala. Shirina hesitated to mention her companions or that she was now headed to Stormhold, and chose not to. If Stormhold had been compromised, the less they knew, the better. And, with a bit of Graydon's luck, the safer their journey.

8

*F*or the second time today, Rojon stood in Avarielle's way. Not physically, this time, but just as annoyingly.

"We can't just leave them." Rojon looked at her with wide eyes.

"Rojon, we have to keep you safe," she said, trying to keep her cool. It would be nice if he could just take her word for it and get in line. But that would be too much to expect of her own flesh and blood.

"And who will keep the villagers safe?"

With perfect timing, the dockmaster slid in beside Rojon. "Elihor's Heir is correct. He should stay here, with us." With a pointed glare at Avarielle, he added, "With *his* people."

Her fist flew before she could think better of it, and it would have satisfyingly crunched against his nose had it not been held back by an unseen force, which could have only had one point of origin. *Shirina.* In an instant, Avarielle's hand was back at her side, Lono blinking, uncertain he'd felt the fist so near his face.

Shirina joined them, mentioning nothing of her obnoxious spell, despite the dark look Avarielle cast her.

Elihor's Heir. That was their true concern. Now, with Kale gone, Rojon was the only remaining thread to the mage who had lent her name to this land. And to its magic.

"Rojon will not be able to defeat such a creature," Shirina offered, "no more than his grandfather was able to, even with greater knowledge of his magic."

Rojon's cheeks darkened, and Lono pushed forward as Avarielle crossed her arms and tried really, really hard not to launch her fist at him again. Mostly because she'd have to hit Shirina first, and she was pretty sure the sorceress would be ready for an incoming blow, and that her resulting spell would not be gentle.

"How are we to take the word of a sorceress of Graydon?" He turned back to Avarielle, his hand on Rojon's arm. A vise to hold him there. "And how are we to trust you, a puppet in their Circle?"

Shirina's eyebrow rose slowly. The accusation of Avarielle being under the Circle's control was so ridiculous that it took her a moment to realize it was targeted at her. Enough time for Rojon to diffuse the situation.

"We can stay near and move people to safety if

necessary," he said, looking every bit like the proud man he had become. "But we're not leaving them helpless."

"Rojon..." Avarielle just wanted to grab her son and drag him out of there.

"I understand your concerns." Shirina's level voice cut off Avarielle's much less level one. "It stands to reason that the creature was after you, and so others will come, killing anyone who gets in the way." Lono shifted his feet. "And we don't want carelessness to result in the death of the Heir of Elihor. Perhaps another solution is best."

Rojon looked both proud and like he wanted to fold into himself at the title.

"Can you get extra help?" he asked the sorceress, ignoring Avarielle. He was probably mad at her, like she'd forced this on him. Well, he had every right to be angry, but that hardly meant she intended to leave him behind.

Shirina nodded, the sorceress tensing slightly, which only Avarielle noticed. She headed off to cast her spell in peace, and Lono walked off to tell a few gathered villagers of what had transpired, no doubt to weave heroics on his part. She turned to Rojon, but he cut her off before she could get a single word out.

"Graydon is your world, Mom, not mine. My place is here. Now more than ever."

"Rojon, you're of Graydon as much as of Elihor," she said, but knew it sounded weak. He'd never been to Graydon, only familiar with the stories that she, Trevon, and Shirina had told him.

"I'm not," he said, his jaw setting in that same stubborn

line it always did when he didn't intend to back down. "I'm of Elihor, and the last heir of its magic. I need to stay here and help."

"Rojon." Avarielle's voice took on that barely patient tilt, even though she tried so hard not to treat him like a child. A feat that would be easier if he stopped acting like one. "You won't be able to help anyone if you're dead."

"Well, I'm in trouble no matter where I am." A quick glance at Graysword's hilt. Avarielle turned her body so her head would hide more of it. She knew that glance, and knew to fear it.

"I'll keep you safe," she said, willing him to look at her. "But you need to trust me."

Her magic danced around her, still feeding her anger and power. And she could sense some of it covering her son, too, like mist they both breathed in, strengthening her but smothering him.

"Can you keep me safe?" he said, looking her straight in the eyes. Something in his face seemed different. Darker.

"Rojon—"

"You couldn't save Grandfather, and you couldn't save my father, either."

The words, softly spoken, hit their mark. He'd wanted to hurt her because he hurt. His eyes widened as he realized what he'd said, and for a moment, she thought he'd take them back. But then he clamped his jaw and stormed off.

Avarielle watched him go, forcing herself to stay still

and not go after him, willing the tides of his unfamiliar anger to wash away.

"Hush," she told Graysword, wishing she'd never had to call on that cursed magic again, blaming it for her son's outburst, while fearing that it wasn't the magic affecting him. And that, somewhere along the way, he'd realized what a terrible mother she was, and she had no counterargument to offer him.

All in all, she was a much better warrior than mother.

~

Shirina stood by a young fruit tree, probably about ten years old, on the outskirts of town. Dark purple apples hung plumply from the lower branches, beckoning her to taste bitter or sweet memories. She did not, though the ways of Elihor would not forbid her from eating it. She simply didn't want to potentially add bitterness to her own.

She'd contacted the Circle of Larkhold to ask for aid, as this was their land, and it grated her. She couldn't even fully pinpoint what exactly grated her, though she had a pretty good idea. The fact that her magic wasn't as powerful in Elihor was definitely part of it. The fact that a crimson circle lay etched over her heart annoyed her, too. The color of her rank never bothered her unless she dealt with the other circles, where she was all too well reminded that standing mattered more than substance.

Rojon stormed by, stopping by one of the saplings.

"She's just so infuriating!" he said. She was pretty sure he spoke to the tree and not her, but she chose to announce herself anyway. If nothing else, speaking with Rojon would remove her from her own head. Besides, the last thing they needed was for him to go off in some sort of rebellion against his mother.

Shirina understood the source of his frustration all too well.

"I assume you speak of your mother?"

He started but quickly recovered. He was tall, at least a foot taller than her, but the shy smile on his face was the same as when he was just a little boy.

"I understand that frustration," she offered.

"I just... I just need her to see me as able to make my own decisions."

Shirina had seen Avarielle leave him alone for half the year and never once question his decision to work with plants instead of the blade. As far as Shirina was concerned, Avarielle had all confidence in Rojon's judgment, present day excluded. But she didn't think saying any of those things would help.

"She can be rather stubborn," she said instead, then focused on the tree Rojon had been drawn to. An older tree, maybe twenty years old. Rojon would have been only a baby when this person passed away. "Friend of yours?"

Hand on bark, he smiled, the earlier anger dissipating at the touch. "One of my first," he said, then looked a bit guilty. "I never knew this person, or at least I don't remember them. A kid, only twelve when he died. I ate one of the first apples and saw a memory of him playing with his parents." His smile faltered. "I'd never really... I guess it just felt nice to see that memory. To make it mine, in a way."

Trevon and Kale had tried to fill the boy's void for lack of a father, but the villagers always went on about his dad, sealing the boy's missing dad into full-blown grief. It had been unfair to everyone involved, but few things were fair when you were born of legend. Or otherwise, it seemed.

"I saw your father once," Shirina said.

"I thought you'd never met him." Sharp eyes focused on her.

"I saw him only through Avarielle's mind, when she allowed me access, the only time she did, to help teleport us into Siabala's Rage."

The wind ruffled the trees, memories dancing. What happened if no one ate the apples, she suddenly wondered?

"What did you see?"

"I saw Avarielle near death, bloodied and beaten, broken bones, chained up like meat for the slaughter. Her eyes were closed tight from agony." His lips parted; his eyes closed slowly. He knew some of what they'd gone through. But Avarielle didn't speak much of her past, riddled in darkness, preferring to linger in this light. Shirina believed in sharing knowledge, so she continued.

"Then a man came." His eyes reopened, as though he could see what Shirina had seen. "He was tall, like you. More muscular, slightly older." A pause. "By maybe five to ten years, at most. Hard to tell, with the scars." Five to ten years. His father had not lived that much longer than Rojon, now twenty.

How strange to think of time in lives, but what other measure could the heart mark?

"She opened her eyes, and they were fierce. Your mother had been hurt, Rojon, but not broken. That, I've never seen." A slight smile. "They exchanged a few words. Made a deal. And they parted ways. Then she shut me out."

Rojon nodded, sea air reaching them with the wind. It smelled so fresh, not like death lurked beneath its calm surface.

"She tells me of him sometimes," he said. "But not much. Like she can't quite bring herself to talk about him."

"She's never been good at opening up, Rojon."

"Grandfather told me so much about him." His voice cracked, gaze fallen on the pink apples of the tree. "I just don't know what she wants from me," he said, speaking more to the tree than her. "She won't give me Graysword, even though I said I'd give everything else up for it. I'm of age, and I know how to wield it. She doesn't want to let me use my magic of Elihor, either, though I guess that's not the most useful. I need to make my own path, Rina."

Rina. A name Shirina used to hate being called by, which Avarielle had taught Rojon. But she didn't mind hearing it from him.

"You will. In truth, at some point, you'll be given no choice, Rojon. Life has a way of imposing itself. And it's not your bloodlines that will save you but your own wits. Your mom has lived her entire life with that philosophy, Rojon, always staying just one step ahead of death."

"I saw her hack that monster to pieces," he whispered. "I barely recognized her."

She had been covered in gore, Shirina mused, but decided to stay serious for the struggling Rojon.

"That's because you'd never seen her in battle. It gets ugly, Rojon, especially when monsters and magic are involved. It's not something she wants for you."

What does she want? That had been Rojon's question. Shirina would never pretend to truly understand the warrior, but decades had taught her a thing or two.

"You ask what your mom wants, Rojon. For you, it's simple: she wants you to be safe and happy. And that doesn't mean holding Graysword. In her experience, she's only ever used the sword to survive, and she wants more for you."

"Maybe she's scared she'll be obsolete if she gives me Graysword," he mumbled.

Shirina raised an eyebrow. "Rojon, your mother is still one of the most powerful warriors in all the lands. I doubt she's even thinking about that."

"She wants me to be safe, sure, but I want her to be safe, too. I only have one parent. One that I barely understand."

"She's hard to understand because she doesn't share, and she's never stopped to think about who she wants to be."

He looked at her in surprise, like she revealed some deep truth. She sighed. "Avarielle worried about the West and her people, then she worried about keeping Graydon safe." While Shirina hunted her, but she left that part out. "Then, and now, she protects Cassara because that's what her family's oath says to do. And then you were born, and she focused on you. So, when you say, 'What does she even want, anyway?' the truth is, I don't know. I'm not sure even *she* knows, because I'm not sure she's ever stopped to think about what she wants, simply doing what needs to be done, in the best way she knows how."

She was starting to sound like she was scolding him, and reined herself back in. The thought that Avarielle's own son thought she feared becoming obsolete had grated on her, and she suspected it had nothing to do with the warrior and everything to do with her own issues. Calmer words slipped from her mouth.

"Right now, she wants you safe. And I agree with her. This attack was against you. Remaining here puts others in danger."

"I can defend myself. I know how. If she'd let me have Graysword."

She paused, letting the sentiment pass, surprised at the fists forming at his sides. With a finger, she traced the outline of a low-hanging apple, the skin warm under the sun, the fruit ripe.

"Have you ever witnessed the boy's parents eating one of his memories?"

He didn't need to speak for her to see the answer on his face.

"Let's go find your mother and make a plan. Together."

～

"Lono is an ass and I'm telling everyone as such," Laora announced as she walked up to Avarielle.

"He's not wrong, either," Avarielle said, annoyed that Rojon had stalked off, and irritated at herself for not immediately going after him.

It wouldn't help. She knew it. Knew him as well as, if not better than, she knew herself. But it still irked her.

"I love my son, but some days..." She stopped herself, "Laora, I'm so sorry..."

Laora put up her hand, halting her words. "I loved Torbolem too," she said. "And if his fruit had been allowed to grow, I would have learned some of the secrets he never shared with me, and I'd have felt just as annoyed. Of that, I have no doubt."

The two shared a soft, gentle laugh. Avarielle followed Laora's gaze toward the new saplings. So many memories would grow, where no new memories could take root. But not for Torbolem. Despite Laora's words, Avarielle knew this hurt her friend most of all. That the loss had left her hollow, with no promise of relief from the fruits of grief.

"Laora." Avarielle whispered. "I have to take Rojon out of here. It's not safe for him."

"I understand, and I expect you to keep your boy safe.

I'd never seen you fight before. Didn't really know you had magic."

"My family's magic." She focused on the growing trees. "I used it to protect my people. And killed so many of your people." She'd never told anyone that, in Elihor. Why would she? The scent of burning flesh threatened to topple her into memories, of monsters swarming villages and cities.

"They were no longer who they'd once been," she answered. "Perhaps it's best no apple grew from them. Whether they knew what they'd become... and how they'd been made into those monsters... perhaps it's better we remember them through our biased lenses of family."

Avarielle had seen how Siabala created Elihor's monsters, known as Eloms, and she didn't disagree.

"Would you ever want your loved ones to eat your memories?" she suddenly asked. To her credit, Laora didn't scoff at her. A basic cultural touchpoint of Elihor was not something Avarielle had any right to question, especially after they'd welcomed her for twenty years.

"We are nothing but memories, in the end. Memories and earth. It's how we stay alive, Avarielle. How we remain a part of our families."

Most of Elihor's fruit trees had been destroyed by the flames of Siabala. Avarielle wondered if that had been on purpose. If he'd wanted to unbalance them, take away their roots and knowledge. It wouldn't surprise her. Someday, she'd finally end him.

"I guess I'm not sure I'd ever want Rojon to step into my memories, Laora. He's happier this way."

The leaves shivered from a breeze.

"He's happiest knowing his mother trusts him. And there is no greater trust than to leave an unedited legacy behind and have faith that your family will still love you despite truly seeing you for who you were."

Avarielle grimaced. Lovely sentiment. But she'd seen too much. Done too much. She hoped it wasn't a lack of faith in her son but rather a desire to stay in the shadows. She didn't need him to know everything she'd done. She didn't want to feel what it felt like to run her blade through his father's body.

"I wanted to give you this," Laora said, handing her a deep golden apple. "I assume you'll be gone soon, and I don't know when I'll see you again." *If.* The unspoken word lay heavy in the air. "It's my grandmother's, and we only share her fruit with family."

Avarielle accepted the fruit, voice choked up as she thanked her. She felt grounded again. Like Laora helped plant roots for her, deep into this village. Or, perhaps, to ensure Rojon would return. She'd lost her own son and would never get to taste his sweet memories.

"Rojon will be back," Avarielle said. "You helped raise him, Laora. He won't easily forget that."

"I want you to come back, too, Avarielle. You have a home here now. You return any time."

Avarielle nodded, knowing full well that wasn't true for her, though a small part of her wished it were.

Shirina and Rojon returned from deeper within the orchard, and Avarielle knew the sorceress had convinced her son to join them. Well, it was nice he listened to someone, at least, and although she wished he'd grant her words the same weight, she was glad he listened to Shirina.

Sensing the tension and jumping to correct conclusions of their departure, Laora squeezed her arm and went to hug Rojon. Avarielle watched him let himself be held by her, then lower his head so she could kiss his forehead, even though she had to stand on the tips of her toes. Kiss the forehead, kiss the memories, kiss the life that lives within.

At least her son would always have a place to come back to.

~

The air rippled outward, Shirina's cloak caught in the wake of the re-forming teleportation spell. Two Larkhold adepts stood before her. Crimson cloaks like her own wrapped around their shoulders, their robes black instead of her white. And both much younger than she, eyes of solid darkness observing her.

"Thank you for coming," she said, grateful the Larkhold Elders had seen it fit to concede to her demand. Only because she'd mentioned it was Rojon's wish, of course. She wished, as she often did, that the Circles worked together more easily, but cultural differences at their core seemed to force them to drift apart when they should be closer than ever.

One of the adepts stepped forward, hair shining violet highlights in the day.

"Crimson Circle Elite Jana," she said, the lilt in her voice stamping pride on every syllable. She must have been twenty years younger than Shirina, about the same age she made Crimson Circle Elite. She'd probably been just as insufferable, too.

"And this is Crimson Circle Orem." She pointed to the warlock, who simply nodded in acknowledgement. The Elders had sent more learned adepts, which boded well for the village.

"We understand that you managed to take down a monster?"

Managed. Shirina bit the retort that almost slipped out. She needed them, and she was in their land.

"This way," she simply said, turning to lead them toward the monster, the carcass having been moved carefully toward the water, where they would return it to the sea.

"I hope you didn't hurt yourself too much, using your magic in Elihor," the witch asked. Surely, she hadn't been *that* insufferable.

"I managed." She stretched out the last word. If the adept noticed, she gave no sign of it. Disappointing.

The creature stank, decomposition gases already bloating parts of its corpse. Its mind would be too damaged to safely read now, and she wasn't surprised that the adepts didn't attempt it. If they even knew how. Shirina wasn't certain this magic was even permitted. She'd not read any of it in Larkhold's libraries, though they didn't give her full access.

The adepts didn't attempt it. Nor did they get really close to it, choosing to stand back. Both looked a bit greener, the gases turning their stomachs.

"It went straight for Rojon," she said.

"You mean the Heir of Elihor."

"Yes." She did not use his title. Rojon himself felt uncomfortable with the title, so why would she impose it on him when she cared for him?

"So, we will protect him?" Jana asked, voice breathless.

"No, you will protect this village, in case other attacks should come. I will take Rojon to safety."

"Why would we protect this village if the Heir of Elihor is not here?"

Shirina tried, and failed, to soften her voice, every syllable crisp and sharp.

"Because these people might be in danger from another attack, and they deserve to be safe."

"Everyone is in danger, on some level." Jana shrugged.

"Monsters are climbing out of the sea for unknown reasons and have already killed several villagers." Shirina's voice was not growing any softer. "They have few defenses. You are adepts of the Circle and can protect them with your magic."

"Our job is not to protect them," she practically

sneered. "Our job is to maintain the Wall of Loss, or have you forgotten that?"

Shirina took a step forward, anger churning in her gut.

"I stood on the Bloody Mountains and fought Siabala himself, you insolent witch," she hissed. "I helped bring back the Wall of Loss and trap Siabala again. Do not assume to lecture me on the role of the Circle." With a deep breath, she leaned in closer to the Crimson Circle Elite. The younger witch stood her ground, but her eyes were wider, her stance rigid.

"Do you know why the Wall failed the first time, Crimson Circle Elite? Did they bother to teach you that where they failed to teach you basic manners?"

A blush crept on the adept's pale skin, and she tried to stutter something, but Shirina cut her off.

"Because the Circles, all of the Circles, failed. And many people died because of it. That blood is on *our* hands."

The adept looked like she'd been struck. She would have been maybe five during the Days of Blood. Old enough to remember. Old enough to have lost loved ones. Shirina's voice grew softer but not out of sympathy. She was tired. Tired of having to remind Circle adepts of the value of life. Hadn't they all lost enough?

"So, we owe it to the citizens of Elihor and Graydon to protect them, as much as possible, especially when some form of magic is involved. For us to stay strong, to stay connected with the people and each other, will be the greatest protection for the Wall of Loss. Do you understand?"

The adept's lips were thin, but she gave a quick nod.

"I don't know where this creature came from, but I fear it may be connected to Siabala. These people have only you to keep them safe, and I thank you for doing so."

The warlock, who'd taken a step back from his coven mate, looked over Shirina's shoulder, eyes slightly wide.

Shirina bit back a groan, knowing full well who stood there.

"We're ready when you are." She didn't need to see Avarielle to hear the joy in her voice and know that she'd overheard most of that. For some reason, the warrior delighted in the sorceress losing her temper. Which was probably why she tried to irritate her as often as possible.

"Heir of Elihor," the adepts said, lowering her head respectfully.

"You'll keep the village safe while we're gone?" Rojon asked, ignoring the title.

"Yes, of course," the Crimson Circle Elite said. Smooth. Shirina wondered how Rojon would feel going to Graydon, where he wasn't known like he was here. No wonder he'd chosen to work with plants, away from people.

"They're very committed to the entire process," Shirina said before she could stop herself. She'd blame Avarielle's bad influence for that.

"You would be safer at Larkhold, with us," Jana said, ignoring Shirina as she looked up at Rojon.

"I trust Shirina completely. I'll go where she tells me to."

She forced her features to remain neutral as the adept flushed again.

"Of course," Jana said unenthusiastically.

"Thank you for keeping my people safe." He lowered his head slightly, his longer red locks catching the sun. He could be a charmer when he wanted to be, and from the reaction of both adepts, he knew it.

"Let's go," Avarielle said. Shirina looked back at the creature one more time, remembering the feeling of being caged. The day suddenly feeling cooler, she followed her two companions to prepare for the dangerous journey ahead.

9

*E*ndings peppered Avarielle's life. She'd once been used to them, before settling into a home and routine for the past twenty years. But she'd never lost the ability to tell when an ending faced her.

As it did now.

The house stood empty. It wouldn't, for long. Avarielle had told Laora to make sure it would go to someone who needed it. To a young mother who needed a safe place for her children. To a widow looking for a house to live in peace. It had been her sanctuary and should become someone else's.

She wouldn't be back, and she knew it. Her son had already mostly left, following his own life as a builder, choosing to build instead of destroy.

And she couldn't be prouder of him.

She ran her hand over the wood dresser in her room.

She left behind most of what she'd accumulated, which wasn't much. Blankets. Linens. Small comforts for the long days and cold nights.

This house had survived the fire of Siabala, other structures absorbing the waves of magic, the area reduced to only a few remaining houses. Avarielle had loved how alone and strong her house stood, nested in regrowing woods.

She'd always known she would leave and had tried to resist making this a home. But she couldn't, because of Rojon. He'd needed friends, family. She'd needed help, more out of her depth than when facing Siabala. She'd trained her whole life to face monsters. She hadn't trained to be a young single mother in a land she hadn't even believed existed until a year prior to moving there.

Gently shutting the door to her room, she glanced into Rojon's small room at the end of the hall. He had been so cozy in it, needing the smaller space, like a cocoon to keep him safe. She wondered if that had been her fault. He'd needed comfort and safety because he'd been ripped out of her womb and thrown into battle.

She wasn't sure she'd wanted him, until she'd held him, his father's blood dry on her hands and fresh in her heart. But as soon as she gazed into his dark eyes, every priority had changed and shifted.

And so they'd found a home, where he could be safe and comfortable, without the magic of Graydon attacking him.

The last room had been Kale's. He would watch over

Rojon as she went to run, dance, or practice sword, her body aching for familiar movements when doing so many unfamiliar things to benefit her son. Without Kale, she'd have gone mad, the edges of her mind trapped with dark thoughts and despair.

The battle had been won, but her mind still reeled.

She left his bed surrounded by books. Shirina had taken his personal writings, with her blessings. Whatever Rojon hadn't wanted to keep for himself. Kale and Rojon were similar, both loving books and learning, both excited by the possibilities the world offered.

Avarielle had often felt left out of their discussions, but she hadn't cared. Rojon had flourished under him.

She closed his door, too, and then Rojon's.

It was all empty, save for a few trappings to help someone else, and for the memories she had of this place. The old stairs creaked as she went down, Shirina and Rojon's voices filtering through the open door downstairs. Avarielle took a moment to pause in front of the hearth. So many happy memories, talking, laughing, Rojon running around.

She'd lost her family as a child, though she still had her ancestral house. Her mentor, Trevon, had made it a home again, after her oldest brother had been killed. Murdered by their own people. She found herself missing him so badly, her steps slowed. She hoped she would see Trevon in Graydon, though she doubted her road would lead her to her people.

Trevon had known the importance of a home, and of

stability, for someone to grow up and find their path. He'd helped her make a home here, too, visiting often, staying whenever she went to keep an eye on Cassara. Just in case. Just in case someone would try to attack.

At first, when the Circle was weaker, it had been more important. Her magic might be called upon, and Shirina needed to grow Graydon's magical strength, or Siabala would destroy them all.

Shirina had done her work. The Circle was much stronger than it used to be, even if she still wore her crimson cloak instead of the black one for an Elder, which she'd more than earned, in Avarielle's mind. So, the Circle had shouldered more responsibility for Cassara's protection, and Avarielle had been less and less needed. Just as her son had been leaving home, exploring Elihor and learning and making a name for himself, above that of just the Heir of Elihor.

But Kale had needed her, toward the end. She cherished those moments with him, the trust he'd placed in her to help him navigate his twilight years. The tree that now grew where he was buried, which would one day bear fruit. The people who'd counted on her dwindled away, one by one, leaving her without purpose.

Like this empty hearth.

No. She took a deep breath, forced her thoughts in a different direction. She would not crumple into despair. This was a goodbye, not a farewell. She would find another home. And there would always be use for Graysword, which only she could wield.

She placed her hand on the pommel, the metal cool and familiar, like it was made to fight her palm. Someday, the Wall of Loss would fall, and she would be needed.

Now her son needed her protection. He needed her to show him Graydon and help him if any pain attacked him. For him, this was an adventure waiting to unfold. He was scared of the unknown but drawn by it as well. He was about to encounter an entire new world, and she'd help him there.

She felt better for the thought that he would need her. She'd put her own needs aside for so long. For her people, for Graydon, for Elihor, and for Rojon.

She'd always known eventually she'd leave this behind, but she'd never really thought about where it would lead, focused only on the next thing that needed doing. Everything else was too far, too nebulous, and she'd been trained as a warrior. The next action, the next moment, counted the most. And all those moments had been filled by other people's needs.

Like now, leaving to protect Cassara, to protect Rojon. Leaving her home for the needs of others. She wasn't sure she even knew how to forge her own path anymore.

"Stop it, stupid woman," she whispered, feeling no strength behind the words. She couldn't start to think like that. She had a lifetime of regrets and mistakes to make up for, and she would do so the best way she knew how: by pushing forward and using the magic of Graysword.

"Are you coming, or shall we leave you behind?" Shirina's crisp voice asked from outside.

Avarielle shook her head, a grin on her lips. Feeling better, she grabbed her bags and gently closed the door to the house that had been her home for half her life.

10

*A*ll of Elihor stretched below them, rivers crisscrossing in the lush and fertile land, a few swatches of ashes still defiantly holding out, marring its beauty. Villages and even the city of Keshmeer could be seen from there, all sites that had been mere rubble the first time Avarielle scaled this mountain, almost twenty years earlier.

They'd reach Stormhold by the morning, the road much safer than it used to be.

Avarielle stretched her legs, looked down to the beautiful land sprawled beneath them.

"Is this where you and Dad scaled the mountain?" Rojon asked, putting more wood on their small fire. Even the Bloody Mountains were coming back to life, parts of it filled with greenery and animals. The smell of ashes had long since dissipated, to be replaced by the scent of spring.

"It is," Avarielle whispered. Not this part, no. This part,

she'd scaled by herself, going after Kryde after he'd been taken by Siabala. When she still thought she might save him.

Hope. That was what Shirina asked her to have now, as they headed back to that place of broken hopes.

"Did he often travel these mountains?" Rojon asked, always so curious about his father. She was glad he was speaking again. He'd been quiet the first few days of travel, and she knew enough to leave him alone, though she really wanted to pry his stubborn head open and find out what dwelt there.

"He had one other time," Avarielle smiled. "He went up with his grandfather, to touch the Wall of Loss."

Kale.

"I miss him," Rojon said after some time.

"I miss him too," Avarielle said. "When I look at you, I see your father, Rojon."

Moments passed by in silence, the fire popping. When he spoke again, his voice mixed with the rustle of the leaves on trees. "What did he see when he came up here?"

He looked out, analyzing the land. He knew what he'd seen, having helped the land heal since he was a boy. But he was most like his grandfather, a scholar. His thirst for knowledge was as great as her thirst for battle.

You'd be so proud of him, Kryde.

"Ashes covered the entire land," Avarielle said, her voice just a whisper as well. The sorceress sat by the fire, focused on the flames, so quiet that Avarielle kept forgetting she was there. "There were no villages left and no trees. Certainly no leaves rustling in the wind. Monsters made of stone would fly up, terrifying and large, carrying the people of Elihor to turn them into Eloms. The world has changed so much." She turned to him. "I'm glad you get to hear the wind in the leaves."

He looked at the landscape, then at her. "Dad saw something else, too," he said. Avarielle raised an eyebrow. "He saw you, Mom. I think that's what makes all the difference. The people we love."

She wished Shirina was somewhere else, but decided to ignore the sorceress and kiss her son on the forehead.

"How someone so wise came from you is quite frankly beyond me," Shirina deadpanned.

Rojon grinned at Shirina.

"Thanks for helping us," Rojon said. "I know Mom appreciates it."

"Any time." Shirina smiled at him like a kind aunt. Then she turned to Avarielle, and there was that sarcastic look again. "It only took twenty years for her to ask for help, after all."

Before Avarielle could bite back, Rojon spoke up. "That's because she didn't need to. You already helped however you could."

The two women looked at him, then at each other. Avarielle sighed.

"We should probably turn in," she said. "Before this gets even more distressing."

"I'll take first watch," Rojon offered, pulling his bow near. Avarielle almost told him no, that she would take it, that she didn't need sleep as much as he did. But, seeing the look of pride on his face as he prepared to watch over them, she relented.

"Mom?" he asked as she lay down to sleep. Shirina seemed already asleep, or at least not bothering to participate. Which was just as well.

"Yes, Rojon?"

"When they took Dad to Stormhold, you went there to avenge him, right?"

She sat back up, the pit falling out of her stomach.

"I went there to save him, Rojon. I didn't know he needed avenging at that time."

She'd told him everything, or as much as she could. Knowledge might keep him safe, after all, and she wasn't always around to protect him. She'd never considered how it might inspire certain narratives of his own life. Ones built around revenge.

She'd hoped so much it would inspire him to be strong when needed that she'd never considered it might inspire darker things. She waited for him to finish, watching him struggle with his emotions. When he didn't speak again, she did.

"Rojon," she said, trying to keep her voice level. "I was mad with grief and did things I'm not proud of. I brought down the Wall of Loss, Rojon." She said the words that pierced her like a knife. It had been twenty years, but she remembered the hatred that flowed in her veins. And the desire for vengeance at any cost.

And how much it had cost so many people.

"I could have destroyed Graydon, had Cassara not stood against it." *And Graydon might yet fall if Cassara falls.*

"You did it out of love," Rojon said, always so quick to come to her defense, even now.

"I did it out of hatred, Rojon. I lost my head and acted solely with my heart. And my heart wanted revenge more than anything else."

She glanced to Shirina, the sorceress too still to be sleeping. *Damn it.* She'd have heard that, the sorceress always more trusting of the mind than the heart. They'd clashed over that, as had Cassara. Cassara, who wielded magic based on desires, not training or spells.

But setting her son straight was more important than worrying about feeding Shirina ammunition for later on. His hands were balled into fists as he held his knees to his chest, folding in, shielding his heart from further pain.

She'd grown up with so much loss that it had become a part of her blood, but it never got easier. Her son had grown up in a world that was healing, no matter how slowly, and he lacked an enemy to attack.

Her hands covered his fists. "Listen, Rojon. There will be enemies to fight someday. But revenge is a dangerous emotion to wield. It's not as sharp a blade as it should be. It dulls the senses and blurs instincts. It leads to destruction, Rojon. I know that better than anyone else."

"But you saved the world," he said, his voice sounding smaller. "That's not nothing, Mom."

"It's not," she relented. "But I didn't really save the world. I just unleashed magic wherever I could. It was

Cassara and you." She squeezed his hand. Elihor and Graydon's heirs had saved the world. She'd just protected them. "And Shirina, I suppose." She looked to the sorceress, who shifted and turned her back to them.

Another moment passed. "Would you ever give me Graysword?"

Circling back to power, always. He had the magic of Elihor running in his veins, though it mostly proved useless to its descendants. Just like it couldn't protect Kale, only those he loved. That magic was from his father. Avarielle's magic was created to destroy those of Elihor, and had almost killed her son in the womb. And would have, if not for Shirina's magic.

Damn it. It annoyed her no end how intertwined the sorceress was with her life.

"No," she said honestly, then added more gently, to remind him, "Its magic would only attack you, Rojon."

Something in the way he shifted, the slight turn of his head, told her he hadn't told her everything. It dawned on her. Damn it, this kid was perhaps more like her than his more even-tempered father.

"You tried to wield it, didn't you?" The redness splotching his face told her everything she needed to know. "But the magic didn't work, did it?" He nodded.

"Just as well," Avarielle said. "It would be a stupid way for you to die, Rojon."

She remembered the blade slipping into Kryde. How he hadn't fought, just... fallen. She swallowed hard.

"I just want to make a difference, like you did. Like Dad did."

This time, she did gather him in her arms.

"You will, Rojon. You just need to find your own path. Mine is too riddled with blood and darkness to follow. You deserve something filled with light."

When she finally let him go, he seemed determined to keep watch, looking over the horizon. Avarielle lay down, keeping Graysword close to her.

11

---

*T*he sturdy stonework of Stormhold, protected by mountains on all flanks, was held up by a thick stone pillar that led into the dark depths of Siabala's Rage, the prison that once trapped the demon. A stark reminder of what the Circle had allowed to happen.

Shirina had listened to Avarielle and Rojon speak quietly, unable to sleep as her mind pondered possibilities. It seemed the warrior blamed herself for bringing down the Wall of Loss. She shouldn't, however, something Shirina fiercely believed, and that Avarielle would never want to hear.

The Wall of Loss hadn't fallen because of one grief-riddled decision by a wounded and broken woman. The Wall had fallen because of years of manipulation by Siabala, because of the Circle's secrecy, because so many people who should have stepped up didn't. And those who did, like Shirina's mentor, were executed for trying to protect the lands.

Even years after losing her, the loss still stung Shirina. Despite being the highest-ranking member of Ravenhold's Circle, without her mentor, Shirina had lost the road she'd traveled most of her life, paved by the wisdom of Tanja.

Several black-and-white-robed Circle members traveled the stark halls, a few Crimson Circles like Shirina, some black for Elders, and others orange, blue, and green. Everyone knew her and lowered their chins respectfully as she walked by, her two companions garnering curious looks.

Rojon looked around in awe. He'd never seen the keep before, and Avarielle hadn't stepped foot there since their battle with Siabala. Shirina glanced her way; the warrior's jaw was set.

"Crimson Circle Elite," a familiar voice said, and Shirina found herself relieved that Shala was here. Her first pupil after the new coven was forged, Shala had become a trusted friend and confidante. Brash and impulsive, rare qualities in the Circle, Shirina had leveraged Shala's personality to learn to tap into magic in different ways. Ways that Avarielle and Cassara had both shown her to be possibilities.

If they were to win the incoming war, after all, they needed more tools than the pre-Fall Circle, as those had not been enough.

"Crimson Circle Shala." Shala should be Elite, but the Crimson Circle had chosen to hold off, saying she felt she needed more training first. Shirina hoped the once overly ambitious Shala wasn't rethinking her commitment to the Circle.

"Elder Quilsam alerted me of your arrival," Shala said. "It's an honor to meet you, Avarielle Grayloft," she said, nodding to the surprised warrior. "And you as well, Rojon Kolder."

"Shala has proved invaluable in rebuilding the Circle," Shirina said as they resumed walking. Shala looked up with pride, alleviating some of Shirina's fears of her leaving.

"You fear Siabala already breaks free of his prison?" Shala wisely lowered her voice so the other adepts wouldn't overhear.

"I fear that may be the case, though I'm uncertain how," Shirina admitted. Unlike the Elders of Graydon, the Elders of Larkhold did not believe in pretending to hold knowledge they did not have, encouraging adepts to help them fill the gaps. Of course, Larkhold also never instituted Harvests, forcing younglings with potential to swell their ranks by basically kidnapping them. Like she had been, as a child.

Those days were long gone, but Graydon's Circle had not revived with the strength of Elihor's, its people still regarding them with suspicion. If not for Cassara's help, Shirina wouldn't have as many adepts as she did. But still, she feared it wouldn't be enough.

"Shala," Shirina said, "I need you to send a message to

Trit, for the adepts keeping an eye on Queen Cassara to be on high alert. Just in case."

"Of course," Shala said, immediately veering off to reach the eastern part of the keep, where she could safely communicate with Graydon witches. Her witches believed that Cassara was of such vital importance because her magic had proven the most effective against Siabala. She had, after all, stopped his fires from destroying Graydon like they had Elihor.

Shirina cast a quick glance to Avarielle, the warrior's hand instinctively on Graysword's pommel. Only the three of them knew that Cassara was much more important than that. That it was her magic, and solely her magic, which powered the Wall of Loss. That if Cassara fell, so did the Wall.

The problem was that it wasn't just the three of them who knew it. Shirina was pretty sure that Siabala had figured it out long before.

Avarielle gave her a look that made it clear the warrior suspected the same thing.

Why he'd chosen Rojon as his target was what puzzled Shirina. Cassara was the obvious target. She hoped it meant he did not yet have power in the East, and so Rojon and Cassara would both be safer there. But even then, she doubted that safety would last.

They walked down the large hall, tall windows lining each side. This had been their last stop before facing Siabala on the roof of Stormhold. Where Cassara had forced them both to consider other alternatives than dying in this battle and sacrificing the then-unborn Rojon. And, in the end, it was Cassara they'd almost lost.

They'd all been too young to face off against such evil. Too young and inexperienced. They'd only succeeded because of sheer stubbornness. And Cassara's magic.

Instead of taking the final steps that led to the top, where they could see the Wall of Loss, Shirina veered to the left, toward the Elder Study. The coven of Stormhold had suffered most of all, Siabala claiming their lives before any other Circle. A few had survived the battle, but only some blue and green circles, too young in their training to bring much-needed knowledge to the table.

That coven had been destroyed by Siabala. With too little knowledge to rebuild it, its lore and practices were lost. Now it served as a meeting post for the two covens, each able to teleport to the edge of the keep in their land.

"What will this Elder be able to tell us that you wouldn't know?" Avarielle asked as they entered the library.

Before Shirina could scold Avarielle for her rudeness, Elder Quilsam piped up.

"We shall see." The Elder came into view, the old man's white hair in stark contrast to his dark robes.

"Elder," Shirina said, bowing her head in respect. "The coast of Elihor has received a few attacks from some type of monster." She stepped back, making sure that Rojon could be seen. "And they seem to be targeting Rojon Kolder."

The Elder focused on the young man. Shirina had

never met Kryde in person, but she'd seen him through Avarielle's memories. He'd been strong, and cut like a warrior. Someone Shirina was not surprised that Avarielle had fallen for.

He'd had a spark in his eyes, too, born from need and battle. She didn't know much about him. His grandfather, Kale, had spoken to Shirina about him. His curiosity, his desire to help, his loyalty, and his heart. When she looked at Rojon, she saw all those things in him, too.

Especially his bravery, not shrinking away from the eyes of the Elder as he peered closely at Rojon, as though weighing his worth. Shirina focused on Avarielle, to ensure the warrior wouldn't deck the Elder. She's seen it happen before.

"Rojon Kolder." The Elder placed a hand on Rojon's shoulder. The young man did not flinch nor back away, meeting the gaze full on. Avarielle crossed her arms. Shirina took a step toward the warrior.

"I knew your grandfather," he said, a short laugh bubbling deep in his chest. "Once a pariah to the Circle, he ended up saving much of our knowledge. And the Circle, in turn."

Rojon stood more proudly. Avarielle gave a low hiss, apparently annoyed at the Elder winning her son over. Shirina took another step. Soon, she'd be on top of Avarielle.

The Elder turned to Shirina, and she breathed a sigh of relief. Taking Avarielle and Rojon to the Circle had proven more distressing than she'd believed it would be.

"You believe he would target Elihor's blood?"

She nodded. "He seemed to hate her line more than Graydon's, though I've instructed my coven to keep a closer eye on Queen Cassara."

"Good thinking," he said. "And why do you suspect Siabala?"

Shirina raised an eyebrow. "Because the creature targeted Rojon," she offered.

"Siabala is well trapped in the Wall of Loss," he said. "The last time, it took him a thousand years to escape. Chances are it will take him centuries to do so again, and there will be plenty of warning signs."

Shirina forced her gaze to remain on the Elder and not turn to Avarielle, the only other person in this room who understood her concerns.

"If not the most obvious answer"—Shirina bit her words, irritated at being so questioned as the top witch of Graydon's coven—"then what do you suggest would just up and go after the descendants of Elihor, claiming one of them already in Kale?"

If he noticed her tone, he showed no indication. "Rojon and Kale are direct heirs of Elihor, the last ones that we're aware of," he said, as though lecturing her. She forced a deep breath in. "So, something else could have risen from the seas to destroy the bloodline."

"Or"—she managed to keep her dry tone low—"it could be Siabala, needing Elihor's blood to escape once again. Or for the bloodline to be completely eradicated.

Which is the most likely thing to be happening, considering recent events."

"I fear your judgement is clouded." He shook his head. She raised an eyebrow. Avarielle took a step forward. This time, Shirina did not stand in her way. "It's easy to see Siabala in all things now, considering how the lands still heal. But we must consider all options."

"I find those options to be quite finite," Shirina said. "So finite that there really is only one."

"Come off your damn high horse, you stupid Elder," Avarielle growled. Rojon's head whipped up in surprise at his mother's tone. He was accustomed to the loving mother figure, not the Avarielle that Shirina knew. Shirina found she much preferred this Avarielle. "You can talk semantics all you want, but Shirina actually helped defeat Siabala while you hid in your caves. So, you should listen to what she has to say, because she's the only one who makes sense in this whole cursed place."

The Elder's eyebrow rose, and Shirina both feared and hoped that Avarielle would deck him.

"Please keep a close eye on the Wall and report to me if anything seems amiss," Shirina asked.

"I will not report to a Crimson Circle Elite," he said, "but I will of course continue to do my duty."

Shirina was certain she flushed as red as her cloak, but he'd walked out of the room before she could tell him off. The warrior was already swearing up a storm even before the Elder exited.

"He can't talk to you like that," Avarielle spat out. She looked at Shirina. "Want me to deck him?"

"I do," Shirina offered with a slight smile. "But it would hardly help at this point. And he's not wrong," Shirina added more quietly. "I'm not an Elder, and he already offers me more courtesy than he needs to."

"Horse crap. He's intimidated by you because you actually faced Siabala and lived to tell the tale. You fought his armies, you gathered the Circle, found ways to unite them again, and have more guts than this entire place combined. Bloody Circle cowards."

Shirina raised an eyebrow. "Did you just compliment me?"

"Comparative compliment." The warrior shrugged. "So, I wouldn't read too much into it."

Rojon spoke up. "Why would Siabala come after me, though? I mean, he's right about that, right?"

The warrior and the sorceress shared a quick look. Yes, the Elder was right about that. There was no reason that Shirina could think of for him to come after Rojon. The magic of Elihor no longer flowed in the Wall, and so his blood and magic weren't needed to tear it down.

"Maybe he's not after you," Shirina mulled. "Maybe he's actually after you"—she turned to Avarielle—"and is trying to get to you by going after Rojon."

"He wouldn't dare," Avarielle said, eyes dark.

"He would," Shirina countered. "You know he would, and he hates you probably most of all."

Avarielle narrowed her eyes, but Rojon spoke up first. "Why? Why does he hate you most, Mom?"

"It doesn't matter," she said.

"It does." Rojon held his ground. Avarielle looked ready to snap, but took a deep breath.

"Because I killed his body in the original battle. It was a team effort, as far as I'm concerned, but I landed the final blow."

Shirina frowned, remembering something another Elder had said. "Elder Tally had said that Siabala wanted to test you more," she said. Avarielle didn't look at her, focusing on a point in the distance, a sure sign that she'd struck a nerve. "Do you know what she meant?" It had hardly mattered then, when they were rushing to destroy Siabala. Now it might be everything.

"Tally escaped," Avarielle said, slowly turning to focus on the sorceress again. Whatever memories haunted the warrior, she'd not bothered sharing them with Shirina. She doubted she had with anyone.

"She did," Shirina concurred.

"Who's Tally?" Rojon asked, looking from warrior to sorceress.

"An Elder of Graydon's Circle," Shirina answered. "She turned to help Siabala and tried to kill us all."

"She was annoying," Avarielle mumbled.

"She was," Shirina agreed. "Could she be behind this?"

Avarielle ran her fingers through her hair, looking annoyed and confused. "I don't know, Shirina. And we won't know until she shows her face, will we? Shouldn't she be dead of old age by now, anyway?"

"She was only sixty. She could still be alive and well."

"She just can't help but be irritating, can she?"

"So, what do we do?" Rojon asked, energized by the thought of an opponent he could see and fight.

Shirina looked to Avarielle, an unspoken question in her eyes. Did she want to head to Massir, to Cassara, with Rojon? Or should he stay here?

"Where are you headed?" Avarielle asked, and Shirina heard that unspoken question too. That she'd leave Rojon there with her if she stayed, trusting her to keep her son safe. "Stormhold doesn't seem like the wisest place to stay," she added gently. Shirina agreed. This close to the Wall of Loss could prove dangerous. Not just for Rojon. For Avarielle, too, even though the warrior would focus all her attention on keeping him safe.

"I'll be fine, Mom," he said, eyes flickering to Graysword. "It's not like he's after me, anyway."

"We don't know that," Avarielle said. "Even if it's just to get to me, he's still after you. We mustn't underestimate Siabala, or Tally, if that old witch is still around."

"It's never been about me, has it?" He ran his hand in his hair, frustrated.

"That would be a good thing, when it comes to monsters," Avarielle said. "And, again, we're not sure of anything. But I promise I'll keep you safe."

Rojon stared at Graysword again, and he scowled.

"I can handle whatever comes my way," he said, and

stormed off before Avarielle could answer. She watched him go, sighed, and gave Shirina a wry grin.

"There's more of me in him than I care to admit."

"I can see that," Shirina said, glad to have the warrior alone for a few moments. "Walk with me," she said, intent on finding a place where they could not be overheard. Avarielle fell in step without argument, as eager as she was to chat openly.

Shirina brought her to what she considered her own study. Much smaller than the Elder's, it held books and a living map of Elihor and Graydon, which adjusted to show the landscape, new builds, and population growth. It reminded her of how important her duty was, and how life persisted, regardless of difficulties. Two things she needed to be reminded of frequently, of late.

Avarielle walked up to the map, carefully looking over it, especially the West. There were quite a few outposts and villages still, and the Westlanders had worked hard to revitalize their war-torn land. The biggest population hubs on Graydon's side were Massir and the Southern Coalition, which kept growing. At its eastern edge, Edoline, Cassara's homeland, remained steady, though its village had grown and it certainly wasn't ignored anymore.

The warrior gave a low whistle. "It's impressive, isn't it? How far the lands have come?"

"It is. And it's a good reminder of how far we still have to go."

The warrior nodded, but Shirina doubted they saw the

map in the same light. For her, she wanted to see more Circle outposts. And not just places for adepts to learn and grow but for anyone to come and learn. For more schools and study halls. For poets to thrive and not just builders.

With another generation, they could be there. The world would be rebuilt, the population leveled off again, and people could turn their attention away from survival and toward growth. If they weren't busy rebuilding from a second attack.

That would be too much, too soon.

"Why aren't you an Elder?" Avarielle said, plopping down into one of the embroidered chairs before her desk.

"I didn't know you cared about my career progression, Avarielle."

"I don't." Avarielle waved at the map. "But I care about that. And seems to me that you could do more if you were an Elder. Including tell that other Elder to go jump off a cliff."

"I don't believe it's Elder protocol to tell each other to do that."

"Well, he can go rot in the Rage, then." She shrugged. "But honestly, you're way smarter and more qualified than him to make decisions here. You actually fought Siabala. I mean, how did he survive while Larkhold was destroyed? Because he certainly wasn't helping those who did."

Shirina sat down behind her sturdy oak desk and sighed. "He hid in the basement of Larkhold, with a few other Elders, and managed to save many adepts. If the

Elders of Ravenhold had had that foresight, we would be in a better position now."

She narrowed her eyes at Shirina. "You're not answering my question, though. Why aren't you an Elder? You're the top witch in your Circle. You're both powerful and annoying enough to be an Elder. So, why not swap your crimson cloak for a black one?"

Shirina paused and studied the warrior. It was weird having a chat like this with Avarielle. About life, and the Circle, and was the warrior really cheerleading her? Usually, such secrets were reserved for the Circle, but the Circle was changing, and Avarielle was a strong ally. One that she trusted more than most Circle adepts, she realized with some regret.

"Because only Elders or the keep itself can make you an Elder," Shirina said. "And neither is available to me."

"Can't stupid-face Elder help you?"

"I'm glad your ability to insult people remains as juvenile as ever. But no, an Elder from another Keep cannot share the wisdom I need to access."

Avarielle looked toward the map from where she sat, at the eastern edge of the sea where Ravenhold had once stood.

"I tried to access it, Avarielle," Shirina said, guessing the warrior's thoughts. "It's crumpled into the water, and I could find no trace of it."

"Circles like their secrets," Avarielle replied. "Are you sure there isn't another place where the knowledge would have been kept? It seems to me that such secrets would be best kept in multiple places in case the keep should fail, right?"

"I agree, and I've looked. But it seems that the coven failed to imagine its own thorough destruction and left no guidance on how to rebuild."

"I can't say as I'm surprised." Avarielle leaned forward, elbows on knees, focused on the sorceress. "So, what will you do differently this time around?"

"Share the knowledge"—she shrugged—"as best I can." She cocked her head sideways.

Avarielle gave a quick nod, as though satisfied.

"What? You're just going to trust me with this?" Shirina said, finding herself falling into old habits as well. If she was honest, she'd missed the warrior. The infighting. The sarcasm. The past two decades, they'd played a bit of a dance without ever discussing it. Avarielle would watch over Cassara for six months out of the year, and Shirina would ensure her safety the other six. While Avarielle was away, Shirina would regularly drop by to visit with Kale and Rojon, and make sure everything ran smoothly there.

Kale was gone now. A blow that Shirina had felt more than she'd anticipated.

Avarielle actually grinned at her. She'd missed this too. The two shared a quick laugh.

"Tell you what," Avarielle offered. "If we do find Tally, I'll knock her around to give you what you need to become an Elder."

"I'd like to do that myself, to be honest."

"Well, then, I'll hold her down, you punch."

That was something to imagine.

"Do we think Tally is behind this, or Siabala?" Avarielle's tone shifted back to the matter at hand.

"I think it's likely," Shirina said, "or other followers we weren't aware of. The Wall is holding steady, Avarielle." She paused, made sure her wards held in place. "And no one except the three of us knows that Cassara is the key to keeping it up."

"Not yet," Avarielle growled. "But could they figure it out? With magic eyes or some freaky Circle trick?"

Shirina had asked herself that question a thousand times. And she still had no answer.

"I'm not sure," she said honestly. "I've looked at that question from multiple points of view, but the truth is that I can only see the Wall with my magic, which are the pure strands from Graydon. But it looked like that before falling, too. I can't see what someone from Elihor can see, and I certainly have no access to what someone channeling Siabala's power would see. If that's even possible now. I think all his magic is trapped with him."

"Isn't his magic his soul?" Avarielle asked.

"Yes and no. His soul is formed from the strands of gray magic, the combined magics of Elihor and Graydon. Magic that kills adepts on both sides. But his followers seemed to possess their own magic. Some kind of red strand. I've never seen anything like it since, and the texts have proved less than enlightening. We're still translating texts from the ruins beneath the West, but it's taking time. Time we may no longer have."

Riches of books and texts had been discovered but of course all written in a different tongue. Translating them proved difficult, without any basic reference, as the language was unlike anything in their world. And Shirina had looked.

"Could Cassara see it?"

"Probably." It proved no end of frustration that Cassara had powers that Shirina didn't understand and would probably never be able to replicate. A descendant of Graydon himself, she's been gifted the power of one of Siabala's brothers. "But her magic is trapped in the Wall, and even pulling on a bit of it might be enough for it to crumple."

"It doesn't matter, anyway," Avarielle said offhandedly. "We can't exactly bring the queen of the most powerful kingdom in Graydon around and tell her to look at people."

"No. Not easily, at least."

"So, what's the plan?"

"We're stronger together," Shirina offered. "If we go to Cassara, the forces of Massir and the Circle can both help keep Rojon, and Cassara, safe."

"Are they targeting him or me?" Shirina knew exactly where the warrior was going with this.

"Once Rojon is safely in Massir"—Shirina leaned forward—"if we're sure they're after you, just promise me you'll tell me when you leave, so I can help keep you safe."

Avarielle looked surprised, then a slow smile spread across her lips. "I still think you're a pain."

"Same. Now give me your word, Grayloft."

A long pause as the warrior weighed her options. "As long as I feel Rojon is safe without you there, you have my word."

Shirina nodded. She could make sure of that.

"Let's head to Massir," Avarielle said, and both stood up, glancing at the map before exiting. They lacked so much information but knew one thing for certain: whether Tally or Siabala was the one moving the pieces on the board, the results would end up being the same.

Graydon and Elihor would burn in their wake.

12

Rojon wasn't sure what exactly had gotten into him. Maybe being so far away from home—blood and guts, being *above* his home, really, Elihor far below. Maybe it was heading into Graydon, a land he knew would hurt him, as it had his father and his grandfather before him. But he was only half from the land of darkness, so perhaps his mother's blood would protect him.

His mother. Avarielle Grayloft, champion of the West, hero of Graydon, wielder of Graysword... He sighed, stopped walking. He'd stormed off, without thought. He felt so... useless. His best friend was dead, his grandfather killed before his eyes, and he'd been swept away from his home, toward a land he didn't know.

He wasn't a kid anymore and didn't have to listen to his mother, by any means. But she'd barely ever imposed anything on him. Ashes, she used to just leave for months at a time, to pursue her duties as an heir of Grayloft.

Which he was too.

Except more so an heir of Elihor. He shook his head, feeling the heaviness that had clouded his thoughts while in his mother's presence begin to diminish. And his breath caught in his throat. He stood before a giant door marked with red runes glowing dark against the rock. He knew this place, without a doubt. He stood before the door to Siabala's Rage, reshaped from splintered stone. Rojon took a step forward, then stopped, the powers of the runes pushing against him, making him sweat.

His mother had been held captive there. His father had rescued her. He'd set her free in Elihor even when she wouldn't set him free in Graydon. His mother never shied away from the truth, though the details were sparse. He'd grown up on stories of his father, fed by his mother and his grandfather. But his mother didn't talk about herself as much, except about her time in the West, though he'd never walked her ancestral land.

He'd wanted to know more of his mother. Of the woman she had been, of who she was in Graydon. At home, she was a mother who taught him to fight, then left for months at a time to help Queen Cassara in Graydon.

He stood as close to the door as he could stand, sweat trickling down the side of his face, nausea twisting his stomach. He'd only met Cassara once, on the day he was born, when they'd fought Siabala. Above this very keep, where he'd been born. To fight Siabala.

Rojon had studied plants all his life, and he understood that roots could be moved and changed. Teased to create architecture, even. Branches could become shelters. He'd always wondered if part of him lived in the Bloody Mountains, where he'd been born. And where his father had died.

Yet he didn't feel a connection to this place, save for the pain keeping him grounded to the now. He took a step back, wondering if his mother would ever tell him what lay behind the door.

His attention was drawn toward a dark hallway, ambient light from the runes casting enough shadows that he could see the rooms for what they were. Cages. Lines and lines of cages, all broken, torn asunder by magic now gone, or at least dormant.

The cages had held the people of Elihor as they were slowly infused by dark magic and then unleashed onto Graydon as Eloms.

Fingers touching the sharp edges of the cages, Rojon let himself be swallowed up by that darkness, letting his instincts guide him. Darkness, leading to more darkness, but his feet led him forward, knowing where they needed to go.

Roots so deep, even he could barely tell how far they reached.

Up the stairs. One foot at a time he took the stairs, until he was standing in a large room, vaulted ceilings dressed in shadows, three concentric circles carved in the ground.

The three Circles that were supposed to hold Siabala prisoner. A sign of failure.

And the place where his father had died, killed by Siabala before his mother. She never spoke of it. Never gave him details. But he knew this was the place, as clearly as he knew that Elihor's blood ran through his veins.

A dark stain covered the ground. Rojon imagined it was his father's blood, his mother kneeling in it, grieving him...

"How did you find this place?" The Crimson Circle from earlier, Shala, stepped out of the shadows.

"My mom told me about it." He lied, partly. She'd never described the actual location. Only that it had been at the base of Stormhold.

The Crimson Circle nodded and looked up, awe on her face. "I never thought I'd see this place, Stormhold. While we fought the wars, with fires raining down from the mountains..." She stopped, turned to face him, as though grounding herself again.

"Your mother and Crimson Circle Elite Shirina would like to speak with you." She indicated he should follow, and so he did.

"Do you mind not telling my mother about this?" He asked. "She's still raw about my father's death."

Shala studied him for a few seconds, then she nodded and gave a slight smile. "Of course. I've heard Shirina tell enough stories about your mother's temper to know that I don't want to be on the receiving end."

"Thanks." He followed her back to the light but couldn't stop thinking of that dark patch on the ground, on the roots that connected him to this place, and the darkness that lingered within.

13

*A*varielle glanced around the Keep, the lands of light and darkness sprawling below, mountain peaks breaking some of the wind. Above, the Wall of Loss shimmered, barely visible to her eyes but a cascade of colors to witches, or so she'd been told. It used to hum, a sound that still stalked her nightmares. Now it sang gently, at the edge of her mind. *The Traveler's Song*, Graydon's song of reawakening, a magical incantation passed down through his blood.

To the east she could see the rippling sands of Graydon's West, with a great scar running down the length of it, where an ancient city had resurfaced, swallowing some of her people's villages. And forever breaking her people into two halves.

"I hate the sight of that thing," Avarielle growled, looking down at the sands below, imagining their warmth on her bare feet. Remembering her childhood spent running, laughing. Those few precious years after the Western Wars and before the invasion of Eloms.

"We found invaluable information down there," Shirina said.

The edges of the ancient city rippled with plants, some even pushing out of the city. So many waterways of Graydon had been sucked deep, now watering an ancient and dead city. Well, mostly dead. Some of her people had settled the strange city. Many others lived near it, enjoying the greenery and food it provided. Not to mention the hunt. Only the old wolves like the West's leader, Beck, still lived their traditional lifestyle. And Trevon, her mentor, wandering somewhere below.

"Do you think we'll ever know a time without war or strife?" Avarielle asked softly, looking down toward her ancestral land. She would have ruled that land, had times been different. Well, maybe not her, but her brother would have. *Rojon*. Dead at about her like-named son's age.

Fear gripped her and she forced herself to breathe and center on the feel of Graysword hanging off her waist. Rojon, *this* Rojon, would make different choices from her brother. He had more options, and he had her.

She'd taught him to fight but also to avoid combat and to make smart decisions. And he would never, ever wield Graysword. His father's blood would save him from taking the wretched oath she had.

"I don't know," Shirina answered equally softly. "But I know that we never will unless we try."

"You sound like Cassara," Avarielle wanted to scoff, but found that she couldn't. The princess, now queen, had seen them through difficult times. Her optimism and refusal to give up had saved Avarielle's life and her people. Not to mention her son.

"Thank you," Shirina said. The two shared a quick look, then laughed.

Rojon joined them, looking as stubborn as he had before leaving. But not as angry. That would have to do for now.

"Give us a moment," she told the two Circle witches, and stepped aside with Rojon.

He stood before her, defiant. She pointed down, toward the West.

"That's my homeland," she said, "and that scar is what Siabala left on it. It can never be removed and can never be changed."

He looked down, curious. She loved that he was still so curious about so much. That he wasn't afraid of shadows. She didn't want him to become afraid, to shy away from the world he should thrive in.

"It's beautiful," he said, taking her by surprise. She looked down, at the green outline of the break, at the sands rippling lazily in the sun. He was right. It was beautiful.

"That I could see the world through your eyes," she said, continuing to look down, voice gentle. "A scar like that runs through me, too. And through Shirina, though she'd never admit it. And Cassara. And everyone who fought on the front lines against Siabala. It's raw, and overgrown, and ever-present. It can't be erased or undone —we just have to learn to live with it. And you, Rojon, were born in the middle of it, right here." She waved at the top of Stormhold.

"And you have your own scars too, even if you don't realize it." She turned to face him, his eyes focused on her. "And I want you to know that I'm proud of you. You've forged your own path, away from the battlefield. That takes courage when born from scars, Rojon. The easier path is anger and revenge. But you chose life instead, and I hope you always will."

"I just..." He stopped, pondering his words as he looked to the west again. She gave him the space he needed. Though Shirina was obviously impatient to get going, she kept her peace too. "I just don't feel like I belong down there. I wish I could have just returned to my studies in Elihor."

A clamp holding Avarielle's breath loosened, and she took a deep breath. He didn't want revenge. He craved familiarity.

"I'm glad to hear that," she said, though her heart broke for him. "And I'm sorry, but it's too dangerous for you in Elihor right now."

"Siabala was after you, Shirina thinks."

"Shirina speculates, Rojon, but she doesn't know. If it's Siabala or Tally, something is happening, and we'd best be prepared. Cassara will help keep us all safe. I can't fight, knowing you're not safe, Rojon."

Anger flashed in his eyes again. "I don't see why you have to fight at all."

"Graysword will be needed, Rojon." The second she'd spoken the words, his eyes flashed with something else. Something she'd rarely seen in her generally satisfied boy. Greed. Desire? Thirst.

"No," she cut him off before he could say anything.

"You're selfish," he said, then seemed surprised at his own words. "I'm sorry," he immediately stumbled out. "I don't know what's gotten into me."

"We're all tired," she offered, though her voice didn't sound as gentle as it usually would.

"We should get going." Shirina stepped up. Annoyed and grateful, Avarielle nodded.

"Shouldn't we wait until morning?" he asked, giving her an apologetic smile. "We're all tired, after all."

"We are," Shirina said, "but we're also closer to Siabala's Rage than I care to remain. On this side of the Wall of Loss, Shala and I can fully use our magic, so we can teleport straight to Massir."

"I get to meet Cassara today?" Rojon looked surprised and thrilled. "Does she know we're coming?"

"She does not," Shirina conceded, "but she'll be happy to finally meet you in person. Now that you're no longer a baby."

"I remember her, I think," he spoke softly. "An impression. Warmth. And a song, like in the Wall of Loss." Avarielle and Shirina shared a quick look.

"We should go," Shirina said, nodding to Avarielle,

indicating that she would take Rojon. All thoughts of Graysword seemed to have vanished from Rojon's face as he smiled at the thought of finally meeting Cassara in person.

Perhaps once in Massir, in Cassara's presence, everything would turn out all right.

Avarielle doubted it, but she allowed herself a moment of hope.

14

_C_assara walked slowly down the hall, the breeze dancing in through the window ruffling her skirts and calming the growing warmth at her core. Once, that warmth would have indicated her magic. Now? Well, now, it just indicated that she ran much hotter than she used to.

Two of her guards followed her silently, and behind them, two Circle witches. Shirina had sent them a message a few days earlier demanding that security be heightened. Of course, Dayshon had found out, and that meant two guards and two witches trailed her like silent shadows wherever she went.

She'd tried to engage them in conversation but was informed that they needed to concentrate on potential threats. And when pushed to tell her why Shirina had demanded such an increase of security, they'd clammed up. This could of course mean two things, in her experience: they didn't want to tell her because she wasn't a part of the Circle, or they simply didn't know and didn't want to admit it.

She could have intimidated the answer out of them, but because she could do so, she chose not to. It would be so easy to take power and squeeze, choke the choice out of others to do her bidding. She'd vowed long past not to become that kind of ruler. To be kind and negotiate, and stand by the principles she'd forged in her idyllic youth. She'd managed to cling to those principles during the war with Siabala and had survived, despite her willingness to let go.

But so much time had passed, and a piece of her still lingered in the Wall of Loss, shimmering with her magic in the distance. A hollow carved deep within her, sighing with every breath. Family and the distractions of the throne had helped fill some of it. But it was still there, burrowing deep within her, growing day by day, and it proved a daily struggle not to simply bully her way through.

The fresh air calmed her, the scent of lilacs almost teasing a smile to her lips. Almost.

If she was honest with herself, which she had run out of energy not to be, she was tired. This wasn't the life she'd imagined, not even the life she'd wanted. Twenty years before, she'd needed an army to fight the growing armies of Eloms, and what had been a means to an end had required a lifetime commitment from her.

Looking back, she knew that she hadn't really believed she'd live long enough to rule the biggest kingdom in the land. The only reason she had was because of Shirina and Avarielle's stubbornness. Their unwillingness to leave her behind.

But part of her had stayed behind. And she missed that part more than she could say, her mother's amulet, *her* amulet, cold against her skin. But always there, reminding her of where she came from and, more importantly, where she'd been. Of what she'd been willing to sacrifice to stand there now. To live a life many would call charmed and perfect.

Many, but not her.

The orchards of Edoline grew far away, the sound of the surf crashing against the shores of her kingdom haunting her dreams. No, not *her* kingdom. Her family's kingdom. *This* was her kingdom. Edoline was wisely ruled by her younger brother, Jayden.

The corridor opened into the side of the throne room. She paused, stopped, turned right, and looked out the window. She did this regularly now, a simple practice to help ground her. There, she could see the gardens and the beautiful cherry trees lining them. Their blooms had covered the ground with white weeks before, the cherries almost ripe for the picking. If they managed to get any. Chants enlivened the entire garden as multicolored birds danced in the air and on the ground, attracted by the promise of food.

It had taken years of planting and efforts to get the

wildlife of Graydon back into the Kingdom of Rashim and even longer in its capital city of Massir, but it had been worth it. Their anti-hunting laws were unpopular in the kingdom, but the animals had needed time to replenish. Now, with strong herds of elks in the countryside, meat was easier to acquire, above what farms provided. As long as they didn't overhunt. Feeding such a large number of people with limited resources proved a continuing struggle.

Cassara watched a blue bird pluck a cherry and made a note to ask the royal gardener to discourage them so that they would have more of a crop. The birds could feed on other plants that the people couldn't eat.

Turning away from the gardens, she took a deep breath and focused on the task ahead. Dayshon had presided over a land committee meeting this morning, which she had thankfully not needed to attend. He would tell her everything later. She'd taken care of a proper farewell to dignitaries from the Southern Coalition, including the Princess Malir, once a foe, turned friend. The princess appreciated that Cassara always took time from her busy schedule to share a one-on-one tea with her to just chat about family, crops, and hopes for their people.

In turn, Malir kept the ties with the Southern Coalition strong, for the sake of all Graydon.

Now Dayshon and Cassara would welcome people from the city to hear their updates and news. She'd instituted this years before, when a young queen fresh from the war, still rattled by her lack of magic and riddled with nightmares.

The news had all been grim at first, with the city destroyed, Eloms having cut apart half its population. Pyres burned the night away. There was little food and water.

Then basic needs turned to greed and mismanagement of resources. Cassara had attempted to redirect resources by asking different representatives from various sectors to report in once a month informally. From farms to the arts, keeping a finger on the pulse of her kingdom. Or trying to.

She'd just wanted to be closer to her people, but even these meetings did nothing to bridge the gap.

"Queen Cassara," the Circle witch named Feylam stepped forward. Her dark skin contrasted with her white robes, the orange cloak falling from her shoulders indicating that she was quite powerful, even if not a Crimson Circle yet. Shirina only allowed her most trusted witches to watch over her when she or Avarielle couldn't, and so Cassara was inclined to at least listen to her opinion.

"Are you certain we can't talk you out of these proceedings? It seems… unwise, at least at this time."

Cassara fought the urge to simply keep walking, and turned to face her. It would be so easy to just do as she pleased and ignore everyone. That wouldn't help anyone except her own tired mind, and only for a very limited amount of time.

"I respect the Circle's position and appreciate your protection." She fought to keep the edge out of her voice. That grew increasingly difficult as the years passed too. "But this is the most important day of the month, connecting with the people. I will not be intimidated away from hearing my people."

The Circle witch wanted to say something else, obviously, but instead she just lowered her head respectfully. Once, Cassara would have insisted on hearing her thoughts. Now she just turned around and approached the large doors. Two guards opened them for her.

Dayshon already sat on his throne, a smile spreading across his lips at the sight of her. Her heart accelerated. If one thing had only gotten better with time, it was her relationship with Dayshon. Born out of need, it had become a cornerstone of her life, and she was grateful for him every day.

He held out his hand and she took it, leaned down to kiss him, a sign of affection that still made the court ripple, which both enjoyed. She sat in her throne beside his. Equal thrones, not one above the other.

"How was the committee?" she asked, while the first speaker was invited in. They currently had some privacy, even with the guards and witches nearby. The court used to be filled with gossip hunters, but Cassara had put an end to that. Most days, Cassara and Dayshon welcomed people to a much smaller room, with a table instead of thrones.

It made for more convivial conversation. Cassara had tried to remove the thrones completely, but some traditions held fast. And this had been the people's choice, wanting to be received formally, perhaps feeling that meant they would be more officially heard.

Townspeople and nobles filled the edges of the court. She had managed to institute a full-respect law, and anyone who spoke out of turn or made people feel uncomfortable was kindly asked to leave. At times, there were no witnesses at all. Today, when the town gathered, citizens were invited to witness and hear the updates as well. To feel united.

Then they all shared a meal together in the palace's largest dining hall, which was also enjoyed by all.

No. She would not be intimidated away from this day.

"Boring," he said, keeping a pleasant smile on his face as the court began to fill up. The guards kept everyone at least thirty feet away, a move that Cassara understood but that also used to leave her feeling lonely and out of touch. Now she appreciated the extra space. It allowed her to gather her thoughts and discuss things with Dayshon.

"How was tea with Princess Malir?" Dayshon asked in turn.

"Lovely," she said, then leaned in. "And also boring."

"Do you think we need a vacation?" he whispered,

looking reflectively at the people filling the hall. She took his hand in hers.

"We do," Cassara said, "and maybe someday we'll get one."

"My parents never needed a vacation," Dayshon said. "I wish I could ask them about that."

Cassara squeezed his hand. They'd perished in the Elom attack on Massir, together. There had been no time to ask questions, though his father had left writings with thoughts on the court.

"Your father said it himself in his manifesto, Dayshon, that he'd never ruled a land destroyed as much as now. Different rulers for a different time, he said. And different needs."

"Including no vacations," Dayshon said wistfully after a moment of silence.

Cassara's heart clutched as the first presenter walked forward, a kind old man who led the rebuilding efforts of the Tranak Quarters, the easternmost part of the city. Usually, she loved hearing about the updates and how the beautification and fortification of Massir continued.

Of late, she expected to hear issues, and found her own inability to positively effect change disheartening. She'd once looked forward to this, but not today. Sensing her hesitation, Dayshon squeezed her hand in turn, making her feel better.

No, she had to think differently. She held knowledge and experience that she would use to support her people. That was all she could do, and she would do it to its fullest. She leaned forward a bit, smiled at Gramire as he bowed deeply at the end of the purple carpet.

"Your Majesties," he said kindly, and Cassara found her smile came easily.

"Builder Gramire," she said, "it's good to see you again. Thank you for making the time to come see us today."

He smiled at that, always pleased that his queen and king respected his time, too. And Cassara did. The builder maintained the buildings past the castle gates, which had been closed during the attack, leaving the people to suffer at the hands of the Elom. Dayshon and Cassara still had many repairs to make, even if they weren't the ones who'd closed the gates.

They were a symbol now—that of the throne—and symbols came with history and preconceived notions.

"It's always a pleasure, Your Majesties." His gaze fell to where Cassara and Dayshon held hands, a gentle smile on his lips. He'd lost his husband in the war and never remarried, saying he'd give all his love to the people of Massir. But the old man had a gentle spot for the love of his king and queen. Dayshon's parents rarely showed affection in front of the court, and Dayshon and Cassara made a point of letting the people into their lives a bit more.

They were a symbol, yes. But they were just regular people, too. And more common ground could be found in the latter.

"I'm pleased to report—" Before he could finish his words, someone shouted in the back of the room. A

MARIE BILODEAU

commotion, and guards moved to stand before their king and queen, the two Circle witches appearing beside their thrones.

Another shout—no, this time a scream—and an explosion shook the hall, dust filling the air.

15

*S*trands of light encircled Shirina and Rojon as they vanished in her teleportation spell, Avarielle trusting the sorceress to get him there safely.

"Stay close to me," Shala said.

"And don't use my magic," Avarielle finished. "I've done this before."

Shala nodded.

"I also know that I hate this," Avarielle said. "Can you get us all the way to Massir? That's far for a single jump, isn't it?"

"Shirina set up teleportation hubs across Graydon, so I can tap into other adepts' powers, drawing on not just mine. Shirina once teleported from the Lisal Gardens to the edge of the West, and survived. But most of us can't teleport that far, so she made sure that in an emergency, we could move more quickly."

"Shirina is too stubborn to die," Avarielle mumbled, and Shala smiled proudly.

"She is. And she's teaching Orange Circles more than ever before so that Circle adepts are more ready for whatever may come."

Avarielle nodded, not surprised. If Shirina couldn't become an Elder, she'd make sure that each rank would get more magical learning. The more her witches were ready, the better for Graydon.

"Ready?" Shala asked, a warm summer breeze washing over them. Avarielle took one last look at her land below, imagined the sand beneath her feet as she danced. So close, she could almost smell it.

"Ready." Avarielle stepped closer to the Crimson Circle witch. Magic shimmered around them as Shala whispered the spell, her cadence steady as the world faded from around them, feet held up by magic, the hairs on Avarielle's arm standing on end as strands of light brushed up against her. Shala closed her eyes, focusing on the magic, not as experienced a teleporter as Shirina. The shimmer faded, and voices met Shala's, the cadence the same as the world became clearer again, shapes of adepts surrounding them, the scent of desert air filling Avarielle's lungs.

She knew exactly where they were. She'd helped Shirina set up an outpost just at the edge of the West and the East, near the end of the scar of her land. Shirina had hoped for a Circle outpost at the base of the Bloody Mountains, but there was still too much distrust between the witches and the Westlanders. There might always be too much distrust.

She pictured the land beyond it, took another deep breath of desert air, with a slight scent of jasmine, and they were whisked away again, to the next outpost, the magic dancing more thickly until it lessened again. The scent of roses. Then lavender. And then lilac as they arrived at Massir.

The teleportation spell faded and the Crimson Circle faltered after such a long traveling distance, but Avarielle knew better than to help steady her. If there was one thing she could understand, it was pride.

And she saw it on Shirina's features as she looked at her protégée. Rojon looked a bit green from the teleportation, but he looked around the outpost set in the back of the palace's gardens. Close enough to both the royal palace and its residence to be of use should something happen, and to the throne room. Just in case. Four witches surrounded them, having awaited their arrival.

"Thank you," Shirina told the other witches, and dismissed them with a nod.

"I've read about the interlocking stones in the throne room of the palace," Rojon said to Shirina. She nodded, encouraging him to continue. "They're unique in Graydon, maybe even all Elihor! And they haven't been replicated anywhere else, though some Southern Coalition countries have tried. To spectacular failures."

"They have detailed records in the palace libraries and

architectural notes, though some people say they're impossible to decipher," Shirina said. "Perhaps Queen Cassara will let you have a gander at them."

"That would be amazing," Rojon answered, stepping out and looking at the dark red lilacs growing on its edge. "Is the blooming season longer in Graydon? I've never seen this type of lilac."

Eli, it was good to hear her son more like himself again. Maybe being near Siabala's Rage had been a mistake. Before Shirina could answer, shouts erupted from within the palace.

A quick glance between her and Shirina, and she turned to Shala while Avarielle turned to Rojon.

"Stay here," they said in unison, and ran toward the chaos in the palace.

16

*S*hrieks erupted from the back of the room, dust
billowing toward them, blocking the view as
much as the guards forming a line before them, weapons
drawn. Cassara moved quickly, pulling Dayshon's
wheelchair from behind the throne. He would never let
himself be carried out unless necessary. He had lost his
feet in a long-ago Circle attack, not his pride.

"Help him," she instructed a guard calmly.

"We must go." A witch went to grab her arm but pulled
back at Cassara's look. She'd promised Shirina and
Avarielle she would be careful and hide if needed. But not
at the cost of her family.

The guards helped Dayshon maneuver onto the chair
as another explosion sounded at the front of the throne
room. Dayshon pulled her down and covered her head as
guards covered his. Cassara felt smothered by the pile of
people, dust sprinkling down from the ceiling. As soon as

it was clear that the ceiling wasn't about to fall on them, they started moving. Dayshon was more than capable of moving quickly in his chair, and he made sure she kept pace with him.

"Your Majesties." A guard indicated they should head to the safe room located down a corridor to the left of their thrones, past large windows. Before they reached the corridor, a mere foot from the thrones, white flames exploded before them.

The familiar gurgling of magic moved in her throat and chest, Cassara's eyes widening as she looked down at Dayshon. If she had her magic, she could save them. If she called on it, she would compromise the Wall of Loss. If she'd didn't and died, it would simply fall. She clutched her amulet, uncertainty freezing her limbs.

Before the fire struck them, the two adepts stepped forward, their shielding spell absorbing the ripples of fire. But not all of it; the two slammed back with the power, knocking down the guards beside Dayshon and Cassara.

She took a protective step before her husband, Dayshon screaming at her to get back. Smoke poured from the side of the thrones, blocking her view of the attackers. The chaos of the throne room had died, and she hoped it was because people had escaped, not because they all lay dead.

Cassara expected a witch to break the din, but instead, several gray-clad warriors wearing leather armor and cloth-covered faces stepped out of the smoke. Some held swords, others bows, all of them aimed at

Cassara. She stood her ground, refusing to be intimidated.

She stared at them, head held high. Dayshon wheeled himself beside her. Escaping was no longer an option, so they would face them together.

"King Dayshon, Queen Cassara." A woman stepped forward. From her voice and her movement, she was young. Maybe even still a teenager, though Cassara knew that hardly meant they could underestimate her.

Dayshon and Cassara both waited in silence for her to speak. The couple had harnessed many joint strategies over the years, and they'd learned that silence was one of their most powerful tools. Let them fill the silence and reveal their intentions.

"You are accused of crimes against Graydon. How do you plead?"

Dayshon scoffed. Cassara tensed. "Crimes against Graydon?" he spat. "Who are you to accuse us of such crimes?"

"We are the people of Graydon," she said, chin tilted up. "And we have come with demands."

Before Dayshon could answer, Cassara placed a hand on his shoulder, squeezing it gently. These people were scared, or extremists of some sort. Talking wouldn't get them far, but she sensed something in the woman addressing them. Something that she thought she could reach with the right words.

"We don't understand the accusations," Cassara said, her voice soft. "But we are willing to listen, if you put down your weapons. More guards are coming soon. We can end this now, or there will be more bloodshed, which I don't think is what you want."

The woman shifted. Moved her leg to the left. Hesitation. She hadn't expected things to get this far. Cassara paid close attention, seeing her glance sideways at a man who held no weapons. Cassara turned to face him.

"Putting away your weapons includes no longer using magic," she told the man. Even under his covered face, she could see his surprise.

"Just die, traitor," he spat out as he unleashed raging flames toward Cassara. Dayshon pulled her down, wheeling around quickly to cover her. But the fires never hit, a shield holding firmly in place, the heat licking over Cassara as Dayshon held her tightly.

A battle cry pierced the throne room. *Avarielle.*

She allowed herself to hope.

17

*S*hirina's fires slammed into the attacking man, the only one apparently able, or willing, to use magic as the others scrambled to safety. Two of her Orange Circle lay sprawled on the ground, possibly dead. The fatigue Shirina felt over teleporting vanished at the sight.

"Who are you?" she hissed as she sent wave after wave of fire slamming into him, grabbing hold of white streaks of magic and converting them to flames, chanting them into action. She understood so much more of magic now. So much more than she had before, when Ravenhold still stood.

Using the Sight, she focused on the magic, strand upon strand dancing in the palace, as though staying near Cassara, who had once wielded them with such ease. Shirina chanted, coaxed two to come behind the warlock and knock him down. He didn't see her attack coming and fell hard, screaming.

Avarielle moved with fluid, deadly grace from armed warrior to armed warrior, cutting them down, avoiding arrows and blades with practiced ease.

"Keep one alive," Cassara said, pointing to the young woman. "She's one of their leaders."

Avarielle nodded and was off after her as Shirina focused on the warlock. He'd done massive damage to this place and taken down two of her witches. Yet he still seemed full of energy and anger, like he drew from an endless well. He began teleporting, the familiar shimmer surrounding him.

"Feylam," Shirina called back, the Orange Circle witch struggling up. "Can you secure this place?"

"Yes," she said, and from the corner of her eye Shirina spotted four more adepts running in.

"Shirina!" Cassara cried, but Shirina ignored her. She would be safe with her witches.

Without hesitation, Shirina stepped into the teleportation circle, the warlock's eyes growing wide as she was caught in it, following him to wherever he'd planned on escaping.

*T*he attacker moved fast into the bowels of the castle, obviously familiar with the layout. Or just running in the hopes of escaping the rampaging warrior.

Good luck with that. Avarielle kept pace with her, the woman heading farther and farther down, taking stairs to the various cellars and storerooms that formed the basement of the castle. Avarielle followed her easily, familiar with the castle as though it were her own home. With Cassara's safety in her hands, she'd made sure to map out the area and be familiar with all of it.

Her prey turned left, into a cellar filled with dusty bottles of wine and ale. A clanging up ahead. Like a door.

Avarielle swore. There was no door in there, she was certain. Carefully she moved forward, the dusty tracks ending at a wall.

Eli's Blood, I am not letting you get away that easily.

Avarielle started looking around for the latch. The place was pretty dusty, with one nearby bottle having been handled recently.

Her sword in hand, Avarielle shifted the bottle.

And the wall began to open.

---

amelia, daughter of Rishel and Sarlak, had been assured that neither the Westland warrior nor the Crimson Circle Elite would be present during today's town hall. But, then again, she'd been told no deaths. Just words. And that idiot Vangle had unleashed magic everywhere, and of course neither the king nor queen felt very receptive after that.

How did it go so wrong? The question she asked herself over and over again, as she had since the Days of Blood. She had no answers, only understanding that things had to change. That a wrong had been committed and amends had to be made.

But this wasn't the way. She didn't mind taking up arms for the cause, had done so before, but not like this.

She ducked, kept running as stealthily as she could down the old escape tunnels beneath the castle, obviously forgotten by the royalty when the Eloms attacked. But her people hadn't forgotten. Those who toiled down there remembered.

She had no doubt the Westlander still followed her, pushing herself to run more quickly, lungs burning. If she reached the end of the tunnel, she could vanish in the streets and buildings, never to be found. The streets below were still choked with ruins and cracked stones, and she would use them to her advantage.

After what felt like hours of running, she finally reached a door and pushed it open, stepping into the old stone basement of the destroyed brewery, the sour scent of moldy ale making her almost gag.

Quick, quick, quick, she kept repeating, a new mantra to escape pursuit. She had just hopped onto the stairs leading up when the warrior erupted from the door. As she did so, mist and light filled the room, Vangle reappearing in his teleportation circle like the coward he was.

Ramelia jerked back at the sight of the Crimson Circle Elite with him.

2 0

*A*varielle missed the sands of the West and the scent of Elihor's seas, her lungs filled with dust as she erupted in the room after the annoyingly fast woman.

"Stop and I won't hurt you," she growled. *As much,* she added silently.

The woman glanced sideways, to the floor of wherever in Graydon's guts they were, where a shimmer indicated a teleportation spell coming to an end. Avarielle took a step back, Graysword before her, as the warlock from the throne room appeared.

As did Shirina.

Without hesitation, the witch slammed him with a fire spell, but he held his own, slamming back with force. The stairs buckled and the rebel tumbled down, screaming as broken glass sliced her leg open, streams of red on dusty stone.

"Get out of here!" Shirina ordered, holding the warlock at bay with a shield spell.

Avarielle didn't need to be told twice. She walked around the woman quickly, her prey clutching her leg. She noticed Avarielle and tried to unsheathe her sword, but the awkward angle and her pain slowed her movements.

"I'm trying to save you, you idiot," Avarielle hissed, grabbing the woman's sword and throwing it aside. There was no way she was walking with that leg, so Avarielle just picked her up. "Stop struggling or we'll both die."

"I will not be captured so easily!" she spat. Annoyed, Avarielle brought her forehead down on the woman's, knocking her out.

She didn't have time for this. Shirina was losing ground, the warlock pulling on powerful magic and the sorceress having already teleported across half of Graydon.

"Let's go, Shirina!" Avarielle shouted back. She threw the woman into the tunnel, far enough not to get crushed, and headed back to get Shirina.

Winds whirled upward, flames dancing as the top of the building was shorn off. Avarielle guessed they were somewhere populated and that lots of people were about to get killed unless this stopped. Pulling out a dagger from her belt, she flung it as the warlock's face, who flicked it off like an annoying insect.

"We have to go, Shirina!" The sorceress fought to hold

her ground, booted feet sliding back slowly as her strength diminished.

"I'm afraid I'm not quite done with you." The warlock suddenly turned to face her. "I'm glad Ramelia brought you here."

A blast of magic erupted from him, striking outward and undoing Shirina's wards. The sorceress flew back, Avarielle managing to stop her from smashing into the stone wall by grabbing her. But the momentum was set and she absorbed the blow of the wall waiting for them, getting the wind knocked out of her as they both fell hard on the ground.

A force pushed down on Avarielle, crushed her against stone, her hand flexing but not able to find purchase on Graysword as the magic tried to crush her.

The magic of Graydon didn't work against her bloodline, things like sleep spells. Crushing her, however, would probably work.

"No," she growled, muscles straining as she managed to push herself off the ground, her vision growing dark as she struggled against the influx of magic and the pain in her skull.

"No," she repeated, hissing the sound like a ward, unwilling to give in to his magic. Unwilling to give in to *anything*. She pushed herself up, to her knees, then to her feet, standing, back arched, teeth gritted. Energy pulsed from the warlock's hand toward her, trying to smother her. But she refused, bones shifting in her legs, blood rippling up her throat.

One step at a time she marched toward him, hoping she could reach him even as he plummeted more power onto her.

He tried to kill Cassara. Anger fueled her steps, and she managed another, the warlock mere feet away but excruciatingly far as the world buckled and shifted around her. And then he dropped without a word, only a look of surprise. Shirina stood behind him, a dagger planted clean in his back.

The magic stopped and Avarielle would have collapsed to her knees had Shirina not caught her.

"I think we should get back to Cassara and figure out next steps," Shirina said, helping the warrior to the tunnel. "Before either one of you gets killed."

21

With the attackers dispersed, Cassara wanted to make sure her people lived, but guards and Circle witches ushered her and Dayshon to safety.

"Was anyone injured?" she asked as they moved quickly down the back corridor. The old shrine of Massir, with no windows and only one entry point.

"A few were, Your Majesty," Captain Tralin said, having appeared shortly after Shirina and the warlock had vanished. "They'll be tended to. But first we must ensure your safety."

Another Crimson Circle witch appeared from the garden entrance, guards turning suspiciously toward her.

"Shala," Cassara called out, recognizing Shirina's protégée. Beside her stood a young man, dark eyes and red hair a strange combination. Cassara's heart skipped a few beats.

"Rojon?" she asked, and he looked up expectantly at her. The guards kept ushering her and Dayshon forward, but Cassara stopped.

"They're coming with us," she said, leaving no room for questions. The guards grudgingly let them through, and Rojon came to stand beside her, looking bewildered at the dust still rising from the room. Avarielle had spoken of her son at length. He was good with a blade but shy in person. Loved learning, especially about plants and architecture. Was growing up to be a builder of repute. Cassara slipped her arm in his, keeping him close.

"Stay close to me, Rojon," she said. "You'll be safe with me."

"It's nice to finally meet you, Cass... um, Your Highness. Majesty!" He seemed flustered as he kept pace with her.

"Just call me Cassara," she said, pulling him along, not willing to let him from her sight. Avarielle was family to her, and so was her son.

The guards led her and Dayshon to the back shrine turned into cozy library centuries before, the walls lined with old scrolls that had already been copied into other tomes for posterity. But the old scrolls had been preserved, their beauty irreplaceable.

"Shirina teleported out with a warlock," Cassara quickly told Shala, whose brown hair jumped wildly around her face as she looked at her with surprise.

"We'll stop any teleportation spells from landing here," Shala said, forming a plan. "Stay in here, Your Majesties."

She stepped out of the room as the guards closed the door and took position outside, leaving the three alone within. The quiet could be just as distressing after all the noise, and Cassara focused on Avarielle's son.

"Rojon." Cassara indicated her husband. "This is my husband, Dayshon."

Rojon looked at him with surprise but quickly caught himself. "My mother speaks highly of you, Your Majesty."

"Please, call me Dayshon." He held out his hand, which the young man shook strongly. "Any family of Avarielle is family to us, too."

"I wish they wouldn't do that," Cassara said, annoyed.

"Do what?" Dayshon asked, focusing back on her.

"Just shut us away when there's danger. We could help if people are hurt!"

"If they're coming after us, love, fewer people will get hurt if we're shut away, as you so aptly put."

"But Altessa—"

"Will be fine. They've already locked down the palace, and she was at home."

"They might be after my mother," Rojon blurted out.

"What do you mean?" Cassara asked, turning to him. He looked intimidated by her, which made her pause. She could be frightening. She knew that about herself now. She didn't want to be, especially not to a young man she'd only met once, when he was just born.

She placed a gentle hand on his arm and leveled off her voice.

"Why would they be after Avarielle?"

"We're not sure, which is why we were coming here," Rojon said. "But..." He hesitated, overcome with emotions. Cassara rubbed his arm, wishing she could take the pain away while also wishing he would hurry up and tell her everything she needed to know. She'd sent Avarielle after their leader. If she'd sent her oldest friend straight into a trap, she'd never forgive herself.

"We think Siabala attacked," he said, voice soft and fast. The world spun around Cassara. *Siabala.* The monster trapped by her magic. The one who'd tried to kill her, imprisoned her brother, murdered her family. The reason this had become her life. The reason she'd willingly stepped into this cage, to keep him in his.

"Mom and Shirina thought coming here would be wise, in case they were after a descendant of Graydon, too. Like they seem to be after Elihor."

"Did they attack you?" The familiar sensation of floating enveloped her. Even though she felt her two feet firmly on the ground and her hand on Rojon's arm, part of her floated. Directionless, undecided, afraid.

Terrified.

"I was," he said, voice so soft Cassara strained to hear. "And Grandfather, he..." Everything dropped away except the two of them, even Dayshon seeming far away as she focused on Rojon's dark eyes. He'd cried when he was born, in her arms as they faced off with Siabala, trying to destroy him. Trying to stop his soul from re-forming but only managing to destroy his body.

"I'm so sorry." Her voice already silken with grief, one

hand stayed on Rojon's arm, holding it firm. Her other hand reached toward Dayshon, and he took it. He would always take her hand, without question or fail.

Rojon lowered his head, unable to speak the words.

Cassara took a step forward and gathered him into her arms, just as she'd done two decades ago when they'd faced Siabala together, focusing on his pain to stifle her fear.

22

*S*hirina had never lost an adept before. Not to violence, anyway. She'd seen most of her coven destroyed, had lost peers and mentors alike. Watched her beloved keep, her home, crumble around her, destroyed by magic. Had even considered leaving the Circle. But never had she lost one of her own, in Graydon's new coven.

Some had left for different grounds, leaving behind the Circle and its ways. Others couldn't stand to be associated with a coven that had been so easily taken over by Siabala and his minions. All reasons she understood. In the old Circle, they wouldn't have been allowed to leave, the very thought considered heresy. But not in her coven. She needed witches who wanted to be there, who were committed to keeping Graydon safe. Not ones propelled by greed and desire for power, which had led to Graydon's downfall.

She'd worked hard to gain the trust of people and rebuild this Circle, from traveling to different villages and countries to aid with magic, to negotiating outpost space in borders and capitals, so the Circle could help move easily when needed.

Many had said no, especially at first. But after years of toil with her few remaining adepts, some had started to come learn the ways of magic. Some young, some old, some her age, caught in the middle. She took them all, no matter where they came from, as long as they were there for the right reasons.

To help Graydon survive, grow, and eventually thrive.

Those most gifted and trusted were assigned the most important duties. To keep an eye on the Wall of Loss. To work with the much stronger Circle of Larkhold. To make sure Cassara was safe. And, above all, to understand and preserve the deep lore of the Circle so that it wouldn't die with her. So that the Circle she'd once loved would continue in one form or another.

Sanakil had been one of those trusted adepts. An Orange Circle after a mere six years since walking into the Lisal Gardens, Sanakil was a mother, a widow, an avid gardener, and she'd wanted to make a difference. She'd lost her children in the war, and now she wanted to learn to help plants grow, to help feed Graydon's remaining children. When she'd learned that dark forces still threatened Graydon, she'd wanted to keep other families safe by standing up against them.

And she had. To her last breath.

"May your steps be steady," Shirina whispered gently as she closed her eyes. Feylam had been hit, too, but the older witch would live. Shala tended to her wounds, and the two cast a glance at each other, Shala's features drawn but determined. Shala had fought in that final war during the Days of Blood. She'd seen other witches die, had fought for their survival, tooth and nail.

She'd been invaluable to Shirina and still was.

Losing her would be an impossible blow. No, not impossible. Shirina wanted it to be impossible, because that meant her heart could be tangled and crushed like others. Like Avarielle's for Kryde and Rojon, and her people. Like Cassara's for her husband and children, and her beloved Edoline.

Shirina had come to understand one thing above all as they rebuilt Graydon: nothing would stop her. As tired as she could become, her entire life boiled down to leading the Circle. Into making it work. Nothing else mattered as much, and nothing would stop her, not as long as she still drew breath.

She stood, went to Shala. Feylam's drawn features relaxed as the healing spell took hold. Shala had already healed two other guards as well, but three were dead. And the other adepts had healed the injured citizens, but five of them had passed.

Eight people, in one quick blow.

"Do you need help?" Shirina asked, kneeling by Shala, placing a comforting hand on Feylam's arm. She wasn't a comforting person by nature but had seen Cassara comfort enough wounded and dying on the battlefield to replicate some of the motions.

"You're strong and brave, Feylam," Shirina said in crisp but gentle tones. "You will pull through this. Trust your magic and your coven."

A barely perceptible nod, and some tension released. Shala's spell was strong and true, the witch taking to attack and healing magics. She would be better than Shirina with enough time and practice, but still she would not accept the title of Elite.

"I can handle this," Shala said with some pride. "But the Grayloft needs healing and is too stubborn to accept it from anyone else."

"If she'll even accept it from me." Shirina shrugged, shared more comforting words, and stood up. In truth, she was tired. Exhausted. The day had her spend at least three times more magic than usual, and she still stood only because of her bracers' reserves. She would have to replenish them, fearing she would need them much sooner rather than later.

Avarielle leaned against the wall, looking to all the world like she was just relaxing. But she favored her right leg as she surveyed the room, and her tanned features were taut.

"Rojon?" she asked, not seeing him but not concerned since Avarielle wasn't.

"With Cassara. She dragged him with her, apparently, into the safe room. A memorable first meeting."

"Good. Are you too stubborn to let me heal you?" Shirina asked, facing her.

"Are you too stubborn to pretend you're not exhausted from using so much magic?"

"I have enough power to at least heal your leg," she said, placing a hand on Avarielle's arm, letting the magic flow down toward the leg. Magic trickled from her hand, finding the fractured bone of her leg, mending it.

Shirina frowned. "Did someone else cast a spell on you?"

"I'm barely willing to let you do it," she scoffed. Her voice was gentler when she spoke again. "I'm okay. You can stop and keep the rest of your energy."

Shirina held the magic a moment longer and removed her hand from the warrior. She was fine now already, which was strange. The warrior's leg had fractured under the pressure of the magic.

"It's Graysword." Avarielle shrugged away the sorceress's quizzical look. "It's always healed me to some degree."

Shirina nodded. She'd known that. The warrior had taken more blows than any human should be able to withstand, and she'd remained standing. She'd cast healing spells on her and had required less magic than usual.

"What's bothering you about it now?" Avarielle asked. "This isn't unusual for me, and you must have known it, even if we've never discussed it. You can be annoyingly perceptive."

"I did know, or at least suspect it," Shirina admitted. "And you're right; that's not what's bothering me, though it's the first time I've felt it in action. What's bothering me is the attack by the warlock."

"What kind of magic did he wield?" The soft-spoken words held layers of questions within them. No matter the answer, it couldn't be good. And Shirina knew.

"It looked like Graydon's. Like magic from my Circle." She met the warrior's eyes. "But he's no adept of mine."

The warrior's eyes flashed with anger. And understanding.

"We need to talk with Cassara. Now."

"And find out what the rebel knows."

Shirina left her adepts to tend to themselves and others, and followed the warrior to find answers before it was too late.

23

The doors to the safe room flung open and his mother walked in with Shirina. Ash and dirt clung to armor and robe, determination in both sets of eyes.

Avarielle headed straight to Rojon, looking him over.

"You're all right?"

"I'm fine."

She nodded and turned to Cassara.

The queen stood up, regal in her blue dress. Even the few strands of hair out of place, slowly turning from blond to silver, only added grace to her look as it glowed in the candlelight.

"And you? You're all right?" she repeated to Cassara.

"I am," Cassara answered.

The women all sat down on the gathered couches. Rojon did the same, wondering if they did so in order that Dayshon could be at the same height. He'd heard of the king of Massir. His mother respected him and his willingness to listen and grow while maintaining law and order in a rebuilding kingdom. He'd lost his feet in a Circle attack, and he'd borne his crown with honor during his reign.

A peaceful reign since the Days of Blood, until now.

"What do we know?" Dayshon asked, the king and queen's hands interlacing.

The three women shared a quick look, not missed by either man in the room. Dayshon shook his head. "You'll get used to these three, Rojon," he said conspiratorially. "They destroyed Siabala together, and suddenly it's like they share a secret code."

"I see that," Rojon said. "Any idea on how to decipher it?"

"Cassara is ticklish," Dayshon said, "so she might talk. I wouldn't try it on the other two."

They both laughed, the three women staring at them.

"Honestly, you can be so childish." Cassara shook her head, a soft smile on her face.

"And you can be so secretive," he said, though not unkindly. "All three of you. Considering Rojon and I were involved, perhaps you'd care to share the information as well."

Apparently, the three women decided Shirina should take the lead. Rojon sat up, feeling like he belonged, mostly thanks to Dayshon's support. If the king could feel left out of this circle, it was no surprise he did as well.

"The attacker used magic from the Circle," Shirina

said, then seemed to brace herself. "From Graydon." She turned to looked at Cassara, the queen having gone very still. "But it's no one I trained."

"What do you suspect?"

"One woman escaped us in Siabala's Rage, Cassara."

"Elder Tally," Cassara immediately filled in the gap.

"Who's Elder Tally?" Dayshon asked.

"She's an old Circle witch who took a vow to Siabala," Avarielle said, her voice distressingly soft. "She tried to kill us."

"No," Cassara said, looking to the warrior, who gave her a look in turn, which the queen ignored. Few people could stand up to his mother's glower, but the Queen of Rashim apparently was one of them. "She tried to kill me. She wanted to get Shirina on board and then wanted to kill her for refusing."

Cassara stopped. Waited for Avarielle to say the next words, but her jaw was firmly set.

"What did she want from you, Mom?" Rojon asked, feeling lost again in this world of battles and monsters.

"She wanted to make a gift of her," Shirina finally said when Avarielle refused to speak up. Shirina turned to look at Avarielle, but the warrior stared at a point faraway. Shirina turned to Dayshon and Rojon.

"To whom?" Dayshon asked, though he knew the answer as well as Rojon.

"To Siabala," Shirina says. "And it looks like she intends to carry through on her promise."

"That's horseshit," Avarielle said, standing up and

walking to the back wall, then turning and pacing to the other side of the room, smothering the small room with her anger. "Your guesswork is off, Shirina."

"Is it?" Shirina said. "For all we know, they went after Cassara to lure you out."

"No," Avarielle said, crossing her arms. "We're not going to let her push us, push *me* around any longer. Tell me where she is and I'll take care of her, once and for all."

"Mom," Rojon said, but she pushed through.

"This time, we finish her, Shirina."

"That was the plan the first time around," the sorceress said. "But we don't know where she is."

"Mom," Rojon said again, standing to face her. She focused on him, hands on hips, shaking with unspent anger. He knew his mother had a temper, mostly thanks to stories, but he'd rarely seen it. And it had never been used on him. "If she's trying to trap you, wouldn't she expect you to come now? You'd just be walking straight into a trap."

Avarielle's eyes narrowed. "That's why I'd bring Shirina to toss at her as a distraction."

Rojon kept pushing forward, ideas forming in his mind like building blocks for a house. "And why now? Why is she attacking you now? It's been twenty years. It's not like Siabala can be freed."

Avarielle took a deep breath, then offered him a rueful grin. "You take your smarts from your father." She turned to Shirina. "Why now?"

Shirina remained seated, eyes downcast. After a few moments, she spoke up.

"She was badly wounded and had to go into hiding. It might be as simple as it took her that long to rebuild her own private Circle, and now she's ready to strike."

"But your Circle can stop her?" Dayshon asked, hands relaxing on his armrests.

Shirina looked up and met his eyes, hands turning to fists on her lap. "Tally is an Elder. Not the best Graydon has ever had to offer, but an Elder nonetheless. I'm a Crimson Circle Elite and so have taught my adepts what I could, but…"

"You're missing some knowledge from the Circle," Dayshon finished.

She nodded. Nothing else needed to be said.

"If I can't go to her," Avarielle said, "then I'll get away from the rest of you, at least. It's foolish that we came here. I'm sorry, Cassara."

"Don't apologize." Cassara stood up, placed a hand on the warrior's arm. "We're family, and family supports each other. Rojon can stay with us, but I'll not let you go without knowing you have help, Avarielle."

"I don't want to stay behind," Rojon stepped up. "I want to help."

"Knowing you're safe is help enough," Avarielle said. "They'll use you to get to me, Rojon. I can't have that. I don't know what I'd do if I lost you."

"What's the plan? Run for the rest of your days?" Shirina asked from where she remained seated.

"No, we'll take the battle to her once we have a plan. Graysword can do damage to her. Cleaving her in two is effective damage."

"She'll expect you to come with Graysword, Avarielle." Shirina looked to Rojon. "What if Rojon took the blade? She wouldn't expect him, and he's an accomplished swordsman."

"Without battle experience," Avarielle immediately said, tensing.

"He'd just need the opportunity to use the blade, with a distraction we create," Shirina said. "The distraction could be you, if it makes you feel better."

Rojon looked at Graysword hanging from her mother's waist. Her hand covered the red jewel, and he looked back up at the two arguing women.

"He can't use the magic, Shirina," Avarielle's muscles grew tauter, her voice more threatening. Cassara's hand started to clutch Avarielle's arm, as though afraid the warrior would attack the sorceress.

"He could with my help," Shirina said. "I protected him once from Graysword's magic, remember?"

"In my womb."

"It worked once. It will work again."

"I can do it, Mom." Rojon stepped up. "I can be careful and take her down."

"I said *no.*" The sharply spoken word surprised them all. "And that's the last I'll hear of that."

Rojon opened his mouth to protest, but a sharp look from his mother quieted him. He was out of his element, but he knew he could help her. He wanted to help her and show her that he could be as strong as she was. As strong as his father was.

"What other path can we take?" Cassara gently filled the silence.

"We can ask the captured rebel what she knows," Shirina immediately said, like she'd had this plan all along. Then why had she been pushing his mother? Avarielle had told Rojon that Shirina could be secretive and have hidden agendas, but he'd never once witnessed it until now. Unless her visits to him and her lending him books had been part of an agenda? He couldn't think of any. She'd only ever followed his interests and encouraged him.

His mother would scoff at the idea, but Shirina really was like an aunt to him. With everything else falling apart in his life, he didn't want to think of Shirina becoming anything less than what he'd grown to think of her as.

"Let's start with that," Cassara offered. "If she can indicate a path to follow, we'll see it through"—she looked from Shirina to Avarielle—"together."

Rojon sat back down near Dayshon. The king met his eyes and nodded to him. Rojon felt seen and was glad when the king invited him to come to the royal residence with him.

His mother's world was riddled with monsters and battles, and despite his words, he wasn't yet sure he belonged. Or that he ever would.

24

The guards, including their captain, followed their queen up to the entrance to the dungeons. Once a thriving place, the dungeons were now rarely used. Cassara had only been there one other time, to offer the prisoners the chance to help rebuild Massir instead of rotting away in their dank cells.

She paused at the entrance.

"Captain, please wait here with your guards."

He stood straighter, a protest forming on his lips. Cassara held up her hand to appease him.

"I assure you I'll be well protected, Captain." She indicated Avarielle and Shirina.

The captain hated leaving her safety in anyone else's hands, no matter how they'd kept her safe over the past twenty years. Still, he relented, Avarielle giving him a quick wink as she slipped past him to clear the way for Cassara. In case any enemy should lurk nearby.

That seemed to calm him down, at least a little bit.

"We'll be out here should you have need of us, Your Majesty."

"Thank you, Captain." She stepped in after Avarielle, Shirina a silent and brooding shadow behind.

The stones of Massir buttressed the dungeons, the air dank with damp earth. Thick metal bars blocked in the captured rebel, who'd been stripped of armor and weapons and face coverings. She was just a young woman, maybe around twenty. She seemed so young to Cassara now, her motherly instincts wanting nothing more than to comfort her. The woman looked up with surprise at the sight of the queen.

She stood up slowly, every movement calculated, either because she was hurt or wary. More than likely both. She looked like a young woman, yes, but by her age, Cassara had defeated the greatest evil in the land, and so she would never underestimate the energy and belief of youth, which could be a well-honed weapon in the right hands.

"Why did you attack us?" Cassara spoke softly, her voice still loud in the small space. "Why did you betray your land?"

"You have a Circle witch and a Westlander around you, and you ask me why I would betray Massir?"

"I have two heroes who fought against Siabala firsthand and saved Graydon," Cassara replied, voice steady. "And two friends."

"You hoard all the power," the young woman spat. "The

magic that saved Graydon once could have helped so many. You had the power to change the world, but you chose not to."

Cassara's heart dropped. She should have just backed away. She knew from experience that minds and hearts were rarely changed by facts, not once they'd adopted an unshakable faith. She wanted to tell her that all her magic had burned away fighting Siabala. That she'd been willing to die but her friends had fought for her. That she had, over time, often wished she could have used her magic to help her people, but she couldn't, because it was gone. And she'd had to learn to embrace the power she now had, in her crown, though at times she despised it.

"Is that what you think?" Cassara said. The young woman glared at her. "Why did you never come to ask for help in the town halls, if help was so desperately needed? Which part of Rashim is in such dire need of magic?"

She narrowed her eyes, studied Cassara.

"I can't help you unless you tell me where I'm needed," the queen said.

The young woman sat down, crossed her legs and arms, and looked up. Cassara sighed.

"I came here to speak with you. I'm willing to listen, though everyone is advising me to let you rot in here. This is your one chance. No one else will listen to you."

"I'd take her up on that if I were you," Avarielle said. "No one listened to Westlanders in the East, even when our people were being slaughtered by Eloms. No one except Cassara."

The woman blazed at Avarielle. "She took our armies West to save your people instead of saving their own homes! To be slaughtered by monsters in the battlefield after you abandoned them without magic."

For a split second, Cassara was back in that battlefield, sharing whispers with Avarielle and Shirina, about taking the fight to Siabala, who had been whittling down their troops, one attack at a time. The stench of death and blood, infections in the healing camps, the lack of blankets and tents... They'd left without telling anyone except Trevon and her brother. So that others wouldn't lose faith, knowing they would not be there to protect them.

She hadn't even told Dayshon.

The sounds of the battlefield erupted again, the agony of knowing the only way to win was to leave... Avarielle's hand gently touched her elbow, grounding her again.

They'd done what they could. They'd saved Elihor and Graydon, but so many had perished, and yes, some had perished due to their decisions, no matter how right those decisions had seemed at the time.

It was easy to guess what had ignited the prisoner's anger. Understandable, even, regardless of the twenty years since. Some wounds took more than time to heal.

"Your father fought in the war against Siabala," Cassara said. "During the Days of Blood." A quaint name for the battle that had cost so many, near the foothills of the Bloody Mountains.

"And my mother," the prisoner said, biting the words. A child of two veterans, who'd faced the end of the world together. She was old enough that her mother might have even been pregnant. Like Avarielle had been.

"I'm sorry," Cassara said, feeling tired. So tired, and heartsick, and like she'd never really left the battlefield. And maybe never would, her magic entangled over the Bloody Mountains.

"You'll be even more sorry," the young woman spat. Whatever had happened to her parents, whatever nightmares they still harbored, must have been worse than what even Cassara still held. At least she was safe, and warm, and surrounded by a loving family.

"If you'd like to talk more later," Cassara whispered, "simply alert the guards. I'll make sure your leg is tended to."

The prisoner tried to hide the surprise in her eyes with another scowl.

"I don't need your pity." Some of the bite had left her voice.

"Good, because you don't have it," Cassara said. "You killed five innocent bystanders and three of my guards up there, and will be made to pay. But you can have my ear when you want it."

Cassara turned to go, but the rebel called after her.

"It wasn't me who killed them. I swear I didn't know he would attack with magic."

Cassara stopped, turned to face Shirina. The sorceress nodded and stepped toward the cell.

"He used Circle magic but was not an adept," Shirina said.

"Magic should be free for all to use," she said, though her voice lacked conviction.

"It should," Shirina agreed, "but it's dangerous in untrained hands or when used to attack. You saw yourself what it did today."

The anger that the young woman had felt toward Cassara did not seem to also spread to Shirina, and so Cassara remained silent, letting the sorceress take the lead.

"It was just ill luck." Her voice trailed off.

"That was powerful magic," Shirina persisted. "Teleportation spells like that are Crimson Circle and above. He could harm many people if he set his mind to it." Shirina paused. The young woman didn't answer, though Cassara could see her struggling. As could Shirina. "Are you certain he won't turn his magic on innocents again? Certain enough to risk more deaths on your conscience?"

"It was supposed to be peaceful."

Avarielle shifted, and Cassara could sense the warrior's tension. Peaceful protestors didn't bring weapons. But she kept her thoughts to herself.

"But it wasn't," Shirina said, her voice as crisp as ever. "You can protest and hate all of us. No one in this room does not understand that." The rebel looked surprised again. "But if you want to align yourself with murderers, you'll find no leniency in any of us." Her voice softened. "We've all witnessed what happens when good people fail to stand against evil. So, the question now is: what kind of a person are you?"

The prisoner looked at Shirina with such hatred that Cassara feared the woman would launch herself at her or clam up. Instead, she mulled it over, then lifted her chin and turned to look at Cassara. The queen met her gaze.

"His name is Vangle. The warlock who attacked."

"Do you know where he came from?" Avarielle stepped forward. "Or where we could find him?"

The woman turned toward her, then simply shook her head.

"You're holding back." The warrior took a step forward, growling. Cassara feared Avarielle would leap through the bars to throttle her. She was surprised when the young woman answered.

"It was safer, the less we knew about each other. We were just going to shout, scare the royalty, and vanish. That's it."

"How were you going to do that?" Shirina asked, before Avarielle could.

"Just heckle and threaten." She held her chin up. Defiantly.

Shirina's foot shifted slightly, and her eyes relaxed, and Cassara knew she was looking at her with the Sight. Cassara folded her hands before her, held them tightly, wanting so badly to see what the sorceress saw. She used to see it all, the strands of magic of Graydon and Elihor. And Siabala, even. How the magic danced in the air, caressing people and plants, feeding every living thing.

And then she could grasp it, turn it to her will. Not to destroy—she'd never been strong at attack magic. But to protect. To keep her loved ones safe, and her land. The power she'd wielded, only to now feel so powerless, despite sitting on the most powerful throne of Graydon. That was Dayshon's power and birthright. Her power had been the magic of Graydon, passed down for generations.

She noticed that Shirina looked to her, as though understanding what she was going through. Whatever the sorceress had been doing, it was done.

"This individual sounds dangerous," Shirina said to the young woman, now that Cassara had snapped back to the present. "If you encounter him again, I strongly suggest giving him a wide berth."

She answered with a sneer. "As if I'll ever get out of here."

"Thank you," Cassara said, ignoring her. "Your cooperation will be considered when it comes to your punishment."

Their eyes locked and Cassara could sense the fear and anger. Then the rebel sat back down in sullen silence.

Cassara turned, feeling the silent and comforting presences of Avarielle and Shirina trailing after her, just as they'd done twenty years earlier as they headed down the ancient city to face Siabala, abandoning their troops to certain death.

The shadows of the Bloody Mountain were long and still darkened their lives.

ojon had been effectively dumped in the royal house, a place he didn't know. Dayshon had gone to tend to royal duties, and now Rojon was alone, save for two guards, a maid, two cooks, and a butler, all too busy doing household things to be concerned with him. And, apparently, being a guest of the king meant he was above their station, so they didn't really speak with him, only tending to his needs.

But he had no need they could address. His first visit to Graydon, a moment he'd been waiting for his entire life, had failed spectacularly. A battle right away, breaking down in front of Queen Cassara, and then his mother embarrassing him in front of the others by refusing to let him wield Graysword. Even though Shirina's magic could protect him.

In a bid to distract himself, he began investigating the royal house, a part of the palace but also separate in some details and architecture. He ran his fingers on the wainscotting, made from a fine-grained wood he didn't immediately recognize.

Maybe his mother wasn't ready to let go of the sword yet. Truth was, he really didn't want it. He knew how to fight, but she was right. He had no practical experience. He was good at building, and architecture, and planting. Fighting was his mother's world, not his.

But he so wanted it to be, right now, even if he feared it. His grandfather had stood before him and died while he stood rooted in place. His mother had destroyed the creature, Shirina had used her magic, and him? He'd been unable to move even when Kale had screamed. Even when he crumpled under the claws of the creature.

He'd moved then. Just in time to hold him as he breathed his last, unable to hear those final words as he spat up blood. He'd died protecting those he loved, his mother had said. Rojon didn't want that. But now he feared his mother dying in the same way. What if he couldn't move to help her? What if he couldn't save her? Maybe with Graysword he would be braver. He could make sure she wouldn't die in his arms like his grandfather. He needed to prove to himself that he could stand up when needed, so he wouldn't be afraid his entire life.

And to know that he could protect those he loved when they needed him.

Like his mother, hunted by one of Siabala's followers, who wanted to gift her to him.

He ran his finger against the grain of the wood, feeling its texture and committing it to memory. It was a beautiful material for a beautiful home. Simple but regal. Not ostentatious but harkening back to the land.

A perfect choice.

Just like he should be for Graysword.

His mother had been his age when she'd faced off against Siabala. She'd been his age when she'd fallen in love, gotten pregnant, and had him ripped out of her in her final battle.

And there he was, unable to simply get out of the way. And now she'd made clear she didn't trust him with Graysword and probably never would. But who would wield Graysword, if not him? He was the only heir to the Graylofts. And to Elihor as well, although he couldn't access those powers, either. According to his grandfather, the power would manifest itself when those he loved were threatened.

Except they hadn't. Had he not loved his grandfather enough? Did he not love his mother enough? Or was that magic blocked to him too? Maybe he was just the child of legends, powerless to effect any change.

Even Graydon's magic, which should have by all rights proven painful to him just for stepping into the Land of Light, didn't seem to affect him. Did he possess Elihor's magic at all?

Sighing, he turned to walk back to his opulent room. And came face to face with a girl. No, woman. His age, maybe younger. Her blue-streaked blond hair was half-down, half-up, wide hazel eyes deep wells, pink lips quirked up in a smile.

"You must be Rojon." She took a step forward, took his rough hands in her soft ones. "It's so lovely to finally meet you. Your mom talks about you all the time."

"Altessa?" Rojon asked tentatively. His mother spoke of Cassara's children whenever she returned to Elihor, but she'd never really described what they looked like. Altessa was the oldest, only two years younger than himself, so it had to be her.

She nodded, another quick grin. "I've heard so much about you. You're like the golden child, aren't you?"

"I'm, um, I'm not blond?"

Her clear laughter filled the room. "I meant like perfect. From the way your mom talks about you, anyway."

It hardly felt like that, especially not when it came to Graysword. He shrugged, not sure what else to say. Then a grin twisted his lips, too. "I heard stories about you, too. Didn't my mother have to pull you out of a shady inn when you were sixteen?"

A slight shrug. "My mother always used to visit her people on her own when she was sixteen, so I really don't know what the big deal was."

"Your mother's kingdom is like one tiny village, isn't it?" *Edoline.* His mom's travels had brought her there, to the tiny kingdom by the roaring sea, to meet a flute-playing princess. "Do you play the flute too?"

"I play a bit," she said. "But I was just getting to know people. Talk to them where they live and eat."

"I'm sure your mom was thrilled." He laughed. Her quick smile and effusiveness were contagious. "And I can imagine my mother descending on you."

"It was pretty terrifying; I won't lie. But nothing like my mother's look once she brought me back here! I couldn't leave the palace for a whole month after that!"

She cocked her head. "I'm too much like my mom, or what she was like at my age. I guess she doesn't want me following in her footsteps. But you're not like your mom at all, which Avarielle seems super proud of."

"I don't think so." He shrugged, remembering her outburst at the thought of him wielding Graysword.

"Well, I know so. Would you like a snack or something to drink?" she suddenly asked, deciding the matter was concluded.

"That... that would be nice," he sputtered. He suddenly felt intimidated by the princess in front of him, and her easy manner and effortless grace. Her parents hadn't intimidated him this much, but she did. Probably because they were the same age.

His stomach rumbled at the thought of food, and he flushed with embarrassment. Altessa grinned.

"Follow me," she said, turning on her heel and heading through opulent room after opulent room, purple and silver lining the walls. She crossed a large, intimidating dining room and headed into a large kitchen in the back.

"Carla!" Altessa said, a tall woman peeking her head

from the back. She wiped her hands on her apron and nodded, her manner gruff but certain.

"Princess." She bowed. "What can I get for you?"

Rojon had never thought of bowing to the princess. His stomach gurgled again, this time with anxiety. He hadn't to the king and queen, either. But then, neither had his mother. Had she? He'd been so busy looking at everything around him that it had never occurred to him to do so.

"This is Rojon." She indicated him with a practiced wave of the hand. Everything she did seemed so effortless. Why was he so awkward? "He's Avarielle's son."

The cook's eyes widened, and another aide popped his head out from the back, smiling widely.

"It's an absolute pleasure to meet you, Sir Rojon," the cook said, bowing to him.

"Oh, no, I'm not royalty." He waved in protest.

"You're Lady Avarielle's son, and protocols must be followed," she said, then a wide smile split her face. "Your mother also hates it when we do so. You really are her son!" She looked at him more closely, focused on his dark eyes from Elihor, then looked away as though embarrassed her gaze had lingered. She settled for looking at his nose, which only made him more self-conscious.

"I bet you have a healthy appetite like your mom," she said, then turned to Altessa. "If Her Highness will wait in the family dining hall, we shall bring you food shortly."

Another bow. Another grin from Altessa. And once

again he followed her down some opulent corridors and through the doors closed at the back.

"There are the family's quarters, not where we receive dignitaries," she said.

Rojon stepped in and found himself breathing much more easily. The place was still beautifully decorated, but the ceilings were less high, immediately making it cozier. The furniture was plusher than wood, bookshelves lined walls, and a currently empty hearth focused the attention of this living space.

He followed her to the next room. A quaint, well-equipped kitchen, pots hanging from the ceiling and light filtering through a window overlooking a garden.

"If you want a snack while you're staying with us or to make a cup of tea, help yourself." She waved at the kitchen. "This is the family's kitchen. I think Mom always had plans to cook for us, but she's busy being royal and all. Besides," she added in a whisper, "she's a terrible cook."

He couldn't help but smile as they crossed the kitchen into a smaller dining area, a rectangular table with room enough for ten, max. A far cry from the large dining table on the other side of the royal manor.

"The table is made from trees of Edoline," she said softly, running a finger on the wood. "That's where my siblings are now, with Uncle Jayden. I wanted to go but had royal duties to tend to."

"You don't like your royal duties?" He asked, sitting down at the indicated chair.

"It's just annoying." She sat before him. "I'm the heir, so there are all these expectations on me, you know?"

"I don't really," he said. The cook and two aides arrived with entirely more food than necessary. Roasted meats, vegetables, skinned potatoes, things he couldn't even recognize, though they made his mouth water.

"Thank you, Carla," Altessa said with a quick grin. "You never fail to overfeed us."

The cook obviously looked at ease with the teasing, and the three exited the more intimate portion of the home.

"The architecture here is completely different from the rest of the house," Rojon said absentmindedly as he took a slice of delicious-looking bread from a basket. "More intimate, more earthy, too. Like it was built for people and not just for show."

Altessa stopped midbite, staring at him. He immediately fumbled an apology. Had he just insulted the heir of Rashim's throne?

"It's all right, Rojon. I guess I'd just never thought of it that way before. I like the way you describe it." She played with her soup, her spoon cutting the liquid and swooping back up. "I used to hate that we lived here when all those luscious rooms exist on the top floor of the royal mansion. At first it was hailed the sign of a true new king. But some people have just been cruel. Calling us the servant royals."

"I'm sorry," Rojon said, then followed up honestly. "I don't quite follow."

A studied glance. "These were the servants' quarters before the Days of Blood."

"Oh," he said, though he still didn't quite get it. Live-in servants? Didn't they have their own homes to go back to? Or were they expected to tend to the royals day in and day out?

"Father couldn't go up the stairs, having lost his feet in the final conflict," she said softly. "So, Mom made this place their home, offering better accommodations for servants and visiting dignitaries. She said she felt more at home in these quarters, that they reminded her of Edoline." She glanced at him, held his eyes prisoner. "I guess you've never been to Edoline?"

He shook his head. "I've only ever been here, in Graydon. We teleported."

"I heard about the attack," she whispered. "I wanted to help, but my parents are insistent that I stay here. Safe."

"Safe," Rojon answered around a bite of vegetable-and-barley soup, with round green veggies he wasn't familiar with but which exploded with taste when he bit into them. "My mom is pretty insistent I do the same."

"She is, is she?" That tone dripped sweetness and defiance, and when he looked up, he found the same look in her eyes.

He was in trouble, and he knew it.

26

*A*s soon as the door to the study closed, Cassara turned to Shirina.

"What did you see?" Of course the queen had noticed Shirina using the Sight. She'd once been more powerful than Shirina, though not as trained. A natural talent, borne from the blood of her legendary ancestor, Graydon.

"She has used some magic recently." At the slight pause, Avarielle's eyes focused on her, waiting. "But it wasn't Circle magic."

Deep purple couches and chairs lined the study, but the three remained standing in the center of the room. The trace of magic she'd seen clinging to the prisoner wasn't overly familiar to her, but she knew enough stories to be able to piece together its origin. Stories stemming from the Western Wars, and involving Avarielle's family.

"Obviously, it's not your Circle," Avarielle said. "Or do you mean it's completely different?"

Shirina turned to look at Avarielle. Her relationship with the warrior had started with an order to capture her, and her sword, in one piece. A bit she suspected by her mentor to keep her away from the Circle while Siabala's clutches dug deep into its flesh.

Avarielle and Shirina had gained mutual respect through battle and time. But trenches existed between them still, too many to cross over one lifetime.

"Green fires," she said softly. Avarielle's mother had been killed by green flames, in front of her young daughter. To her surprise, Avarielle did not explode nor hurl threats. She grew still.

Very still.

Shirina found herself missing the threats.

"The Circle always denied implanting that magic into the warriors who used it in the Western Wars." Avarielle remained still as Shirina spoke. Cassara stood rooted in place, too. Shirina pushed on. "But I do believe they were involved."

"Oh?" Avarielle spoke the word casually, almost nonchalantly. Shirina wasn't fooled. She forced herself to meet Avarielle's eyes.

"I believe an Elder would have the ability to plant a seed of magic in someone." Shirina kept her voice steady and braced herself for the blow. The warrior had accused the Circle time and time again of it. Shirina had denied it, time and time again. It had been easier before. Before, she hadn't cared what the warrior thought.

"Like Elder Tally," Avarielle said, nodding. "So, she's

basically built her own little Circle while you were building yours," the warrior continued, "except she's too lazy to do it right so is just messing with people."

Shirina stared at Avarielle. The warrior cocked her head, a pull on her lips. "Did you think I'd deck you, Shirina?"

"There's a healthy precedent."

"Well, this isn't on you. Not this one. So, how many people could she have implanted the magic in? And why wasn't it used?"

"That I'm not sure of." Shirina breathed a little easier. Avarielle had changed over time. They all had. Same people at the core but more refined. Or maybe wiser. Or, more likely, just tired of fighting the same battles over and over again. "Perhaps her training failed her?"

"Is there a specific training program to turn someone into a Circle murderer?" There was the Avarielle she'd grown to expect.

"All magic requires some sort of training to be accessed," Shirina said. "I'm not privy to how this magic is unleashed, but I assume through similar tenets as traditional magic." Think, plan, ponder. Through heavy thoughts and steady steps. Of course, Shirina had learned the power of emotions when crafting spells. And Avarielle's own blade relied on her emotions to cut down her enemies.

"Well, I do know one thing for sure." Avarielle shrugged. "You wouldn't have kept the fact that you knew this from her, unless you had a plan."

Shirina allowed herself a thin smile. "She'll more than likely try to use her magic to escape, if she can figure it out. Then I can follow her trail. This magic is raw. She won't be able to hide it, not without more training."

"Good plan," Avarielle muttered. "When you go, I'm coming with you."

"No," Shirina said. "You're the target, remember? They'll be ready for you."

"Well, you're not going alone," Avarielle hissed. "Besides, what makes you think you're not also a target? You're leading Ravenhold's Circle, Elder cloak or not. It would be to her benefit to take you out."

"Well, what do you propose, then?" Shirina said, hating that the warrior had a point. "We send Cassara?"

The two turned toward the queen, who stood rigid like a plank and so pale, Shirina feared she would faint.

"I was kidding," the sorceress said, feeling foolish for even saying so, knowing Cassara was no longer the gullible girl from a small kingdom.

"Are you all right?" Avarielle asked.

Cassara gave a small nod. "I think... I think I'm just tired from the day's events." She bit her lip and looked down, something that Shirina hadn't seen her do in years.

"No," the queen said, as though making up her mind. Still, her blue eyes shone with vulnerability. Something else she hadn't seen in years. "I'm afraid you'll hate me," Cassara whispered, looking to Avarielle. "I don't think I could stand that." She gave a short laugh. "Which is strange to say. So many people hate me already, but I've learned to live with it. I couldn't live with you hating me, Avarielle."

"Cassara—" Avarielle was cut off by Cassara's hand demanding silence.

Avarielle's eyebrow rose. "Do that enough times, and I'll probably at least be pissed at you."

"Sorry," Cassara said, then straightened her back, looked at Avarielle, and braced herself as though for a blow. "I know about the green flames." It was Shirina's turn to look surprised. "I've known about them since leaving Edoline."

"You knew my mother died from them," Avarielle said, filling the silence. Cassara nodded.

"That's why I never told you. Because I feared what your reaction would be, and I couldn't bear to lose anyone else I loved."

Shirina pieced it together as Avarielle did. There hadn't been many survivors of Edoline, and only two had been veterans of the Western Wars. The old guards of the princess, loyal all the way to the Days of Blood.

"Kaden and Carsyn," Avarielle said. Cassara's silence was answer enough.

"We've all kept secrets we felt were best, at the time," Shirina said. Avarielle focused on Cassara, the queen looking very much like a sixteen-year-old princess again, uncertain where to go or what to do.

Avarielle took a step toward Cassara and gripped her upper arms.

"You'd already lost so much," Avarielle said, "and I

probably would have killed them where they stood, so you were right to keep this from me."

"And now?" Cassara asked, looking the warrior in the eyes.

"Now they're so old, they can barely wield a sword. There's no sport in that, Cassara."

Cassara hesitated.

"They helped save you and the West. As you did. I guess the Western Wars seem so far away with the Days of Blood so near. And this new conflict incoming." Her hands dropped from Cassara's arms. The queen's hand gently touched Avarielle's arm.

"So, you don't hate me?"

"Of course not, you bloody idiot." Avarielle gathered Cassara in her arms, the queen seeming small in her grip, holding her back as tension left her body.

"Now that that's done, can we get on with the business of stopping this illicit Circle?" Shirina asked.

"It's nice that you're still terrible at being a regular person, Shirina," Avarielle said. Cassara seemed much more relaxed now and joined the conversation.

"Would Kaden and Carsyn be able to help?"

"I don't know that they'd know much." Shirina pondered options. If they were awake while being injected with the magic, they might be able to share some details, which could in turn help her figure out what was done. And prepare their defenses better.

"Studying them might gain us an advantage or at least allow us to be caught less unprepared."

Cassara nodded, now alert. "So, we have a plan. Or, two. We can follow her if she makes a move, and track her."

"Can't we track this Vangle guy?" Avarielle asked, crossing her arms.

Shirina shook her head. "He used traditional magic and knew how to hide his tracks. And he's at my level," Shirina added darkly. There might be more Elite Crimson Circles. Maybe even Elders. Twenty years was a lot of time to rebuild a Circle, especially if they had the knowledge and resources and no one to stand in their way. Nor any worries about building relationships or rebuilding Graydon.

All things that Shirina had been concerned about and contended with.

"All right, then," Avarielle said, "we follow her. And we ask the old guards for any insight. But the main question remains."

Shirina nodded, and all three stood closer. They knew her spell would ensure no one could listen in, but they found comfort in whispers.

"Does Tally know about Cassara?" Avarielle looked to the queen, who stared at Shirina.

"I don't know," Shirina said, "but I think that if she did, she'd have come at you more directly and ensured your downfall."

"Or she's biding her time for something," Avarielle offered.

"Why target you, then?" Shirina turned to her. "Why target you at all?"

Avarielle looked to the side, toward the stone wall of the study, her soft voice lost in the cold room. "Do you remember how that obnoxious Elder said she would gift me to Siabala?"

Shirina raised an eyebrow. She'd dismissed the statement immediately after hearing it. "A poor gift, I believe I said."

To her surprise, Avarielle didn't immediately tell her off.

Then, to her even bigger surprise, the warrior met her eyes and continued talking.

27

*A*varielle had never intended to speak the words she was about to speak. But she wasn't about to endanger her son, Cassara, and all of Graydon simply because she couldn't fathom speaking the truth.

Secrets like this killed. And Avarielle was more loyal than proud. Or so she liked to believe.

"Graysword's magic wasn't created to protect Graydon." The words slowly poured out of her, and she looked at Cassara. "I mean, it's been dedicated to that," she said, "and I'm glad. I'd have never even met you otherwise."

Cassara's eyes softened, a slight smile on her lips. Hers was a friendship Avarielle treasured. She had a hard time imagining life without her, and without the purpose her family gave her.

Except it wasn't her original purpose.

"But, originally, it was created to kill Elihor."

Shirina spoke first.

"Why would Graydon create such a sword with his magic?" As soon as she said the words, Shirina's eyes lit up with understanding. The sorceress stayed quiet, letting Avarielle fill the silence.

At times, she even treasured Shirina's friendship, too.

"It was created by Siabala," Cassara gently whispered, the queen reaching the same conclusion.

The warrior nodded, and she could see all the pieces fall into place. Siabala had needed three magic sources to bring down the Wall of Loss. Cassara's amulet, which had been activated by the descendants of Graydon and Elihor.

Kryde. He'd died protecting Avarielle, feeding his magic to the amulet. Giving Siabala what he wanted.

Until Avarielle had given him the final piece.

"Why would Siabala want you?" Cassara's voice was hesitant, thin. Not certain she wanted the answer to her question, knowing it had to be asked. A struggle between friend and queen, which Avarielle noted and appreciated. "Or is it just Graysword that he needs?"

She already suspected the answer but couldn't quite understand it. Not yet.

"I took an oath to protect you, Cassara," Avarielle said. "To protect the descendants of Graydon. Before I held Graysword, even, when I was too young to bear arms. I think, in hindsight, there was a reason for that, even if chances were our paths would never cross, as our families hadn't for generations."

"Just like there was a reason your family stayed in the West," Shirina said. "Near the Bloody Mountains."

Avarielle hadn't thought of that and hated that even her home in Elihor had been near Siabala's Rage. Like its grip on her refused to let go. Like it would always be clutched deep within her, tearing her raw. She took a deep breath, forced her hands not to turn to fists.

"To activate Graysword," Avarielle pushed on, "I had to take an oath with Siabala. A blood oath."

Shirina didn't seem surprised, but Cassara's hand came up to her mouth before quickly coming down again, like the young princess of Edoline had re-emerged from the queen for a brief moment.

"What does that mean?" Cassara's voice wavered, like she grieved for her friend.

Well, she could grieve all she wanted. What was done was done.

"I'm not actually sure," Avarielle said. "Honestly, I didn't even remember until Siabala himself told me." This time, she let her hands turn to fists. "I know he tested me, but I don't know for what. And I know that his brothers recognized his magic in me."

Cassara's face was drawn, like the ground shifted beneath her. Avarielle wanted to comfort her, but that wasn't her place. She'd trusted Avarielle, only to find out that she had taken a blood oath with the greatest villain this world had ever seen.

She didn't ask how the blood oath had been taken. Just

as well. Unable to face Cassara's pain, Avarielle turned to Shirina. The sorceress's face was as soothingly uncaring as ever.

"Tally could want you to access Siabala's magic." A simple answer. Avarielle liked that.

"This is why you wouldn't let Rojon have Graysword," Cassara said. "I just thought you were being overprotective." Her eyes widened a bit again. Avarielle waited her next realization out. At this rate, they'd never get through this awkward conversation. "You used Graysword while you were pregnant with him, but if the sword was meant to kill Elihor..."

"The child was fine." Shirina stepped in, sparing Avarielle. "I cast a protective spell over him." She didn't clarify that she'd only done so before their final confrontation, but Avarielle certainly didn't intend to correct her. At the time, she'd lived for revenge. For the battle and the chance to slice Siabala in two. She'd been willing to risk Rojon. To sacrifice him at the altar of her own thirst for revenge.

Willing to sacrifice Kryde's legacy.

Before she could stop herself, she murmured, "Rojon would hate me if he knew."

He'd hate her, and he'd have so much reason to. A blood oath with Siabala, choosing revenge over him, keeping him in the shadows of Bloody Mountains because part of her was compelled to stay near Siabala, and, even now, keeping the truth of his heritage from him in the only way she truly knew how. By making sure he could never take the blood oath with Siabala.

The fact that her magic targeted descendants of Elihor had proven to be a blessing. He couldn't just grab Graysword and activate the magic. It might not work for him at all.

"He could never hate you," Cassara said, suddenly beside her, placing a hand on her arm, grounding her. "And neither could I."

Ashes, she hated talking about this, but it did feel good not feeling so alone. But she wasn't ready to be forgiven just yet.

"So, now that we've all revealed a dire secret," Shirina deadpanned, "shall we all hug it out?"

"Do you want to?" Avarielle raised an eyebrow.

"Spare me," Shirina said. "Now that all our secrets and worries are out in the open, what's our plan?" She turned to Cassara, as did Avarielle.

"We'll need help, but I think we can agree that no one else needs to know what was said in this room," Cassara whispered. "And that we can't keep secrets from each other. We're keeping enough from the world and our families. We can't afford to be caught unawares." A thin smile played on her lips. "We've all seen each other at our best and at our worse. It's nice to know that someone witnessed all our struggles, even if I never imagined it would be you two."

Avarielle grinned; Shirina nodded. The three of them had walked into Siabala's Rage with barely a plan almost two decades past to put an end to him. They'd faced enemies and heartache, and had pulled through against all odds.

All in all, Avarielle was glad she wasn't alone to face her demons.

28

*D*ayshon had visited all the wounded and spoken to the families of the fallen. His legs hurt where the prosthetics hugged him, wood against scarred skin. He'd wanted to look the families in the eye. He hadn't wanted them to kneel, and so he stood.

Pain on scars. The tang of magic in his palace. Screams echoing in his mind. He wanted to move his ankle so badly. To lessen the tension that had lived there since the Days of Blood, gripping muscle and marrow. But he couldn't. He'd lost his feet, burned by magic, and to save his life, the healers had sacrificed everything below the knees.

He'd been lucky to survive. Had the Circle been able to use its magic, they might have saved more of his leg. But by then, the corrupted magic had killed most of their rank.

He stood straight, nodded as the remaining visitors

left, his loyal captain by his side, staying close in case he should need help walking. He didn't want to need help now. He'd accepted that he did often, of course, and Cassara had been his rock.

At first, he'd thought a broken king was wrong for a broken kingdom. That someone whole should lead them. Cassara had had to step into many duties while he healed, the queen taking care of everything from adapting their home to building new ones for their people. Shoring up defenses while shoring up hearts. Inspiring others to live while she gave life herself.

"Shall we head back, Your Majesty?" Captain Tralin asked softly at his side.

Cassara was now planning with Avarielle and Shirina, and whatever secret connected the three. She'd come back from the Bloody Mountains a different person, if he was honest. Still the same, but different. With a longing deep within her that he couldn't alleviate, no matter how he tried. Like a part of her had been left behind.

He'd asked the warrior once. Avarielle had darkly said that they'd all left a piece of themselves back there. That the battle wasn't over, and someday Siabala would rise again.

He'd thought it was failure that drove them. It drove the sorceress, building her new Circle, their children among their students, though not adepts. That had been Cassara's wish, to support Shirina and ensure none of her descendants would be caught so unawares in future generations.

"Let's walk the perimeter," Dayshon said, his captain nodding stiffly. Walking the perimeter meant he would be vulnerable to attack. Two Circle witches, a Crimson Cloak and an Orange Cloak, kept pace close by, as did four other guards. He was well protected, and his people might need to see their king.

He might need to see his people, too.

Dayshon's first step was clunky, the prosthetic's ankle stiff and awkward. He had to focus on his first few steps before his mind remembered how to walk with it on. He leaned his weight on his cane, using it to balance, his other hand behind his back as a counterweight.

The cane was made of the same wood as the prosthetics. From the charred remains of Massir. The tang of magic dissipated in the fresh air of Graydon. The palace hovered over the city's large expense spreading below.

Buildings and streets intertwined, built of stone and wood, though mostly stone for fear of fire. Old fountains stood silent and empty, the city now relying on water from its Circle created wells to survive. Walls encircled his people, each more damaged than the last, great gates opened but ready to close if needed. The city had recovered, gardens growing atop rooftops, laundry drying in the breeze, laughter drifting through the streets. But still, beneath the life, he could see the war-torn home he'd returned to after the final battle. Delirious from pain, he'd sworn it was a Circle trick, that his city could not have fallen so quickly. That pyres of bodies did not feed the smoke in the air.

Cassara had made enemies while he recovered. He smiled at the memories. They'd expected a shy, inexperienced girl from a small, inconsequential kingdom. What they'd gotten was a queen, fresh from battle, willing to do what it took to rebuild the kingdom and all of Graydon.

She didn't only focus on Massir but created allegiances across Graydon to share resources and food. The kingdom could have fared quite well, had it hoarded everything. But they hadn't. With his blessing, Cassara and he always forming a united front, they'd sent resources to the harder-hit regions, welcomed refugees from inhabitable areas, and reset trade routes now that half their shipping routes and water systems had collapsed.

The nobility of Massir had been up in arms, until the veterans of the Days of Blood showed their queen support. But not all of them, apparently. Some remembered that final battle, where Cassara and the others had vanished silently in the night.

She'd left him a note. A simple letter.

He'd forgiven her. He'd forgiven a lot, knowing war took its tole, refusing to give it more than it had already claimed. He had told her he trusted and cherished her, and when she'd had to test his resolve, he'd been true to his word.

But not everyone felt that way, a rebellion brewing under his very feet, such as they were.

Dayshon took the Path of Roses, a walking memorial for the veterans of the Days of Blood, red roses and thorns a symbol of what had been lost. And what had been won, the flowers blooming each year, like Massir surviving.

He often took this path, reminding himself of the friends and allies he'd lost, including Captain Jiles, sacrificing himself to stop the flames from reaching his future king. Dayshon had lost his feet but not his life.

His people easily forgave his absence, his injuries so visible, like so many veterans. But Cassara did not sport injuries so easily spotted. She'd been injured, badly. But her body bore no scars. They were all in her spirit, try as she might to hide them. Like a piece of her was still missing, even after years.

He'd never filled those places, though he'd tried. He simply had to trust that she would find her way and lean on him when needed. Or on others, if they could help more. He wasn't so proud that he would put his desire to help her over her agency to help herself.

But he feared losing her, still, a fear born years past, before battle had darkened his doorstep, when he'd ridden out to find her after she'd vanished on her way to accept his proposal. She would pull away from him again. He knew it, could sense it already. Avarielle and Shirina were closing ranks on her, protective of her in ways he respected but never quite understood.

It was them that she'd trusted in and leaned on years before.

Dayshon had no intention of letting her slip away so easily this time. But he had every intention of letting her go, if that was what she truly wanted.

He'd ruled his people through drought, post-war, near-famine, and a reconstruction unlike any other. They would weather this, too.

As would his marriage.

He'd always believed that Cassara was the right queen for the right time, and even in the wake of a rebellion targeting her, his belief did not waver.

Nor did his love.

A guard whispered something in the captain's ear. Captain Tralin nodded briskly, and the guard bowed to Dayshon and stepped back.

"Was there another attack?" Dayshon asked, fear gripping him for his family.

"No, Your Majesty. But Princess Altessa, I fear, and Lady Avarielle's son seem to have left the castle without permission."

He loved his wife but wished his oldest daughter had taken a little bit less after her.

"Do you know where she's gone?"

"To the lower levels of the city. She is being watched."

"I appreciate your foresight, Captain."

"Princess Altessa had precedents, Your Majesty."

"Please bring my daughter back, Captain. Quickly."

"Your Majesty." The captain bowed and headed off.

Dayshon watched him go, wishing he could go get his daughter himself, knowing it would be foolish to even try.

He cast a glance toward the city, his breath coming in too quickly. She'd done this before. But this time, she'd dragged Rojon along with her. He was certain the youth was smart enough to stay out of trouble, but doubted he stood a chance against his headstrong daughter.

Dayshon misstepped and caught himself thanks to his cane. He needed to get these prosthetics off and check on Cassara. And figure out how to stymie the growing flames of rebellion before they grew into a blaze and consumed all of Massir.

29

"What were you thinking?" Cassara's voice was clipped, worry bubbling out of her as anger. "We'd just been attacked in our home, and you decide you're going to go traipsing about? And drag poor Rojon into all of this?"

"I followed; I wasn't dragged," he muttered. "I'm older than she is, you know."

"I know." Cassara tried very hard to keep her anger in check. He was Avarielle's son, not hers, and just because she wanted to scold them both right now hardly meant she should. "But you're new to Graydon."

"And you should know better than to just wander off, Rojon," Avarielle snapped. "The enemies who attacked you in Elihor might very well be here, too!"

"They were after you," he snapped back, "not me. Remember, I'm not anyone's concern. And I can defend myself, with or without Graysword."

Avarielle looked like she wanted to both snap at him and console him all at once, and settled on staring daggers at him.

This was going great.

"All we're saying"—Cassara was proud of how calm her voice sounded—"is that caution is of importance at this time."

"And when isn't it the time to be cautious?" Altessa shot back. "Our families"— she locked arms with Rojon. A united front. Wonderful—"both our families are under attack. We need to stand up and show them we're not afraid and we're strong."

With fading reserves of calm, Cassara pushed on. "And we will, together. But not at the cost of your lives."

"You went off to battle when you were younger than me, Mom." Had Altessa just rolled her eyes at her? Where had she learned such manners? "And you were his age." She nodded to Avarielle and then Rojon.

Avarielle was doing no better than she was at being calm, though to her credit, the warrior managed not to snap.

"We had no choice," Avarielle said, "and that's hardly the point."

"Isn't it?" Rojon said, looking at his mother. "Had you been given the choice, would you have done anything differently?" Before she could reply, Altessa stepped in. They really were doing a great job at standing their ground. She had to give them that.

"You both accomplished so much at our age, and we're

from the same blood. We can make a difference," she said, annoyingly convincingly. "What powers you had at our age, we now have, so you can let us handle some of the harder lifting."

"She'd been doing so well," Cassara muttered.

"The power we had at your age?" Avarielle repeated. "I certainly hope you're not proposing we're ready to fade into the background while you run off with whatever magic your families offer?"

Cassara stepped in. "Honestly, Altessa, you're distressingly like I was at your age." Her daughter looked surprised at that. Cassara wasn't smiling. "And I admire your tenacity and perseverance. Both of you. But there's no torch to hand off, and no, you're not going to go riding off to war like we did simply because there's trouble brewing." She tried her best to not look as annoyed as she felt. "With any luck, this will be over soon anyway."

"Magic can be passed down," Rojon said, looking at Graysword. "If the wielder is willing."

Lips in a straight line, Avarielle didn't bother answering.

"Your mother is one of the finest warriors in all of the lands," Cassara said. "And, as you're so intent on pointing out, if someone is after her, then it's best if she's fully able to confront it, wouldn't you agree?"

He reddened, obviously uncertainty how to answer. Her daughter, however, seemed to suffer no such hesitation.

"It's the job of parents to assure their children are

ready to take the torch when the time comes. You're not doing that by stopping us from accessing our full heritage."

She looked pointedly at the amulet around Cassara's neck. It was always there, and had been since her mother's death when but a child. Magic used to flow from it, until she realized she could access Graydon's power without it, though it helped her focus.

"It has no more power," Cassara said honestly. At least, as far as she knew. "Its magic was spent in the battle against Siabala."

"And why won't you tell me why, or how, that happened?" Altessa sounded frustrated, like a child wanting so badly to understand herself. "Why won't you tell me why I'm not powerful like you were?"

Altessa's eyes shone with unspent rage and frustration. Her daughter, gifted in understanding magic, according to Shirina, had so far been unable to tap into the powers of Graydon as she had been. Possibly because of the lack of the amulet. Possibly because it was all locked away in the Wall of Loss.

Was that why she kept the amulet from her? Or was it as a shield, protection for herself? Perhaps a link back to her beloved Edoline?

"Altessa, I—"

Her daughter cut her off with a splash of golden hair as she turned around, grabbing Rojon.

"Let's go," she said. The young man didn't argue,

following behind her, slamming the door behind them. Her eldest daughter had her temper and restlessness.

Wonderful.

"I love being a mom," Cassara muttered.

"Me, too," Avarielle answered.

"Wine?"

"Wine."

"Seriously," Avarielle said as she headed to the kitchen and grabbed a bottle and glasses, as familiar with this place as Cassara. "What are we going to do about them? I doubt they'll just decide to let this go."

"I'm sorry." She winced. "My daughter can be a handful."

"She can," Avarielle took a sip of wine. "She reminds me of you."

Cassara smiled, then grew serious. "Would it be such a bad thing? Telling our children our secrets?"

"I've considered it," Avarielle admitted. "But the wider we grow the circle of knowledge, the more people might know."

"But if we don't tell them, they'll relentlessly pursue this."

"Are you sure they won't if we tell them?" Avarielle said. "You remember what we were like, thinking we could change the world?"

"And we did."

Another sip of wine.

"We did. But the world doesn't need changing right now, does it? Just some realigning?"

"We changed the world, Avarielle. Did we save it, though? Or did we just delay the inevitable? Would it be wiser to get extra help?"

"Which help? Rojon can't wield Graysword, and Elihor's magic would see him dead, like it did his father and his grandfather. And Altessa might pull magic from the Wall of Loss if her magic comes from the same well as yours, which Shirina isn't certain it doesn't."

Cassara hesitated, swirled the wine in her glass, the dark color reminding her of the amber of Siabala's Rage. She put the glass down, no longer interested.

"Look." Avarielle sat back. "We taught our children how to protect themselves. Rojon can fight, though I much prefer he stick with his studies. Altessa can shoot a bow like you, and that'll do for now. And they're smart, and apparently, they'll look out for each other." She paused. "Or drag each other into trouble, I suppose." She leaned forward. "We did our part back then, and we left some things unfinished. Now it's up to us to finish them so that our children can know the peaceful life we never could."

Her words made sense, and Cassara had played the same argument in her mind over and over again. But still, it bothered her. Her parents had kept secrets from her, which had almost seen her killed. And she kept secrets from her children, in the hopes of protecting them and all of Graydon.

"I guess I just hoped it would all be easier, somehow."

Avarielle sighed. "I know. But it's not like we have a

clear line of sight to what will happen from here, either. We don't know how we'll take the battle to Siabala, when we'll need to, and how we'll win... The road before us is foggy and there are no answers."

"This isn't a winning inspirational speech, Avarielle."

"Well, how about this." The warrior grinned and downed the rest of her drink. "We headed off in the middle of the night, without much of a plan, to take the battle to Siabala himself. And we figured it out, and we're still standing, twenty years later. So, we'll figure this out, too. As long as we do it together."

Cassara couldn't help but push back, wishing she'd just accept the words but finding herself unable to. When she'd been younger, she would have easily found inspiration. Believed in her ability to overcome anything. But now she'd known enough losses to fear them.

"I don't have my magic, Avarielle. And now rebellions brews in Massir because of what I did, leaving the battle in the middle of the night, when I *did* have magic and could have helped..."

"Stop," Avarielle said. "Look, we did the best we could with what we knew. It was war, we were losing, and we turned the tide. And no, you don't have your magic. But that's not your greatest strength, and you do yourself a disservice by deciding it was. You're robbing yourself of your own power, which is stupid because everyone else will try to rob you of power, and here you are, just doing it to yourself."

She filled her glass, sighed.

"Look, remember what I told you when you killed that Circle witch in the cave?"

"Jesimae," she whispered the name. A name she would never forget. She'd killed, to save Shirina. Taken a life instead of saving one.

"Right," Avarielle's voice softened. "I told you you'd have to find a way to live with it. And I meant it. And you'll have to find a way to live with this, too, Cassara, because it happened, and there's no going back."

"I just—"

"I'm not finished. I should have said that differently. You won't have to learn to live with it. You'll have to learn to keep moving forward despite it. To not let it be an anchor. Otherwise, you'll question everything you're doing, and you can't afford that in your role."

"I get that, but—"

"Still not finished." Cassara narrowed her eyes at the warrior but waited. "And you'll start to hesitate, and that'll stop you from using your greatest strength to solve this problem."

Cassara waited, but Avarielle looked back at her. She raised an eyebrow slowly.

"What, am I allowed to speak now?"

The warrior laughed.

"Sarcasm is one of your strengths, but also people, Cassara. You're good at people, which is why you're a good queen. So, be yourself and just talk to these rebels."

"You saw how well that went earlier," she mumbled.

"Well, yes, but she was a frontline attacker. And it did

go well. She gave us information we needed. Not everyone will be as dedicated to their cause, and maybe they just need someone to talk them off the ledge and make them feel seen and heard."

Cassara looked down at her glass. The walls of the Rage had pulsated with life around them. The color of blood, like she'd seen so much of on the battlefield.

"I have to go find Dayshon," she offered, then gave Avarielle a slight smile. "It's nice that you're proposing a solution that isn't simply hitting them."

"Blame Rojon for that."

"I'm glad you're here, Avarielle."

The warrior gave her a crooked smile. "I am too. I just wish *here* would be a little more peaceful right now."

"I'll see if I can do something about that."

Avarielle grinned, and Cassara felt more like herself again. At least for a moment.

30

From atop the Unity Tower of the palace, Shirina gazed at the city down below. It stretched far and wide, covering hills and once-lush land, generations of families having lived and died within its walls. At its borders, the city spilled beyond those walls, farther than her eyes could see.

The castle was the highest point in all of Massir, the capital of the kingdom of Rashim. There was no better vantage point than there to see the magic that danced across the city.

And yet, no matter how she tried to coax the Sight, she could see nothing. Not even the gentle movement of Graydon's magic.

"You wanted to see me, Crimson Circle Elite?" Shala stepped beside her, still calling her by her title. Of all her adepts, Shala clung most to the way things had been, but also was the most flexible to adapt for the good of the

Circle. Mental gymnastics that made her a powerful witch, and one more than worthy of the Elite title.

"Look at the city with your Sight," Shirina asked Shala, "and tell me what you see."

Without questioning her, Shala stepped up to the barrier of stone standing between them and certain death, and peered below. Shirina observed her from the corner of her eye, breathing deeply. She could see magic dancing around her pupil, strong and steady, a beacon of Circle confidence. Shala took a deep breath, hands gripping the edge of the half-wall, eyes crinkling at their edges, where age had just started to leave its trusted mark.

After a few more moments, Shala blinked, shook her head.

"I don't understand," Shala offered. "I can't see any magic below."

"I can't either," Shirina said, "which means they've found a way to block the Sight. We won't be able to track the traitor this way."

"Is it a shield or some kind of mist?" Shala asked. Very perceptive. Shirina had pondered the same thing and was pleased that Shala had easily done so as well.

"I tried the Sight below, and it still worked," Shirina said. "Which means we'll have to track her from the streets, making this endeavor entirely more dangerous."

Shala nodded. The city beneath them was beautiful, if large for Shirina's taste. She preferred the quiet Circle outposts, where she could have space to think and work with magic. Here, everyone was too close. Stone and wood buildings lined the streets, rubble still at the edges of every neighborhood, guild halls solemn and tall, promising safety should another attack befall them. Walls closed it in, several cutting through the city, signs of dangerous times.

No, Shirina much preferred being away from the streets of the city, where her white robes seemed to glow against the starker contrast of Massir. Her favorite parts were the parks, restored into communal gardens and orchards, fed by wells beneath the city. Cassara had always maintained their necessity to the harsh stone landscape of the place she now called home, though Shirina suspected Cassara simply needed a piece of Edoline to remain with her.

And Edoline was renowned for its beautiful gardens and orchards.

Massir, on the other hand, would never be like the small kingdom. Closed where Edoline was open. Stone where Edoline was soft greenery. The voices of people instead of the murmurs of the surf.

Shirina pulled herself away from her own mind and focused back on Shala, turning to face her. The woman wore her hair tied in a bun now, though Shirina missed her wilder hair. She did not presume to tell her witches what was appropriate in terms of hair, only that their attire would be that of the Circle.

"I have a special and important mission for you, Shala," Shirina said, making up her mind. "Avarielle needs to go speak with some old friends who might know something about the green flames." Shala seemed surprised, but Shirina had to take her into her confidence. Both she and Avarielle couldn't leave Cassara, and with Avarielle being the obvious target, it was wiser to remove her from the city. Even a few hours could buy them the time they needed.

The warrior could be mad at her later, but she certainly couldn't argue the truth of it. Especially once she shared her observations on Rojon.

"Others know of this?" Shala said, voice soft, understanding the heaviness of secrets.

"It was done once before by the Circle. During the Western Wars."

Shala stiffened, knowing the truth of the wars but not all the tactics. The real truth, not the one Shirina had learned from the Elders when younger. No, she'd learned the Westlanders' perspective as well, a rounded-out piece of history and not just a two-dimensional script of manipulation.

"That's... unexpected," Shala said, though Shirina could imagine the words the adept truly wanted to use.

"Is it?" Shirina asked.

"Sometimes," Shala said even more softly, "I think the destruction of Ravenhold was the best thing that could have happened to the Circle."

Shirina didn't share her thoughts on that, though she knew Shala could glean them. The Circle had been different. Some people thought better. Others, worse.

Shirina thought it was simply different, and that would have to do.

"If another Circle does exist," Shirina said, voicing her fears, trusting Shala to understand, "it may be our greatest challenge yet, and it will test our resolve."

"My resolve has already been tested during the Days of Blood." Shala stood straighter. "I decided I would fight for Graydon. What they're doing, attacking innocents and implanting dangerous magics into people... that's not supporting Graydon. I believe in your vision for the Circle, Shirina."

Shirina nodded, a slight smile playing at her lips.

"You didn't always."

"No, but now I do."

"Certainty is not something we can ever afford, Shala," Shirina gently told her pupil. "To be too certain means our minds close, and we can easily turn into something we do not want to be. That's what happened to the old Circle, after all."

Shala's eyebrow shot up. "Are you suggesting I review this other Circle's membership materials?"

Shirina laughed. It felt good. "Perhaps not. But please keep in mind what happened to the old Circle, always. And remember that this other Circle has an Elder."

"You should be Elder." Shala crossed her arms, that stubborn streak still strongly a part of her.

"It doesn't matter what should be," Shirina said, her crimson cloak billowing in the wind, as though embracing her. Or mocking her. "I am what I can be. We all must be the best we can be."

Shala looked stubbornly at her, and Shirina realized why she wouldn't take the Elite title offered so deservingly to her. Because Shirina couldn't become Elder.

"I would be proud to have you stand by my side as an Elite, Shala. You are deserving of the honor."

A deep breath, Shala's dark eyes looking toward the city below.

"I know," she said, "and someday I will accept it. I'm ambitious, and you know that." A quick grin. "But you taught me some things are worth waiting for, and fighting for."

"I never meant to make you feel like your ambition wasn't warranted. It just needed tempering."

"I understand that." She focused back on Shirina. "And I know that the Circle looks to you as their leader. As the witch who faced Siabala and survived. As the woman willing to turn from the stones of Ravenhold to the earth of Graydon, trading in staff for trowel, power for peace"—her eyes looked to Shirina's bracers—"and back again when needed. I want to learn that ability to adapt, Shirina, and I need you to trust me when I tell you I need more time."

"I trust you" was all that Shirina said, though a thousand arguments swarmed her mind. The Circle would seem more powerful with two Elites. Some training would not be available to Shala until she took the bonds of Elite. But she had told herself she would trust her adepts. That this new Circle would be different. And she had to hold herself to this, even if it was near impossible. Not to mention vexing.

"You trust me, but you're trying to get me killed," Shala said lightly.

Shirina simply raised an eyebrow.

"You just asked me to take Avarielle away from her son and the battle brewing here to face off with illegal magic-users from the Western Wars. That sounds like a suicide mission."

Shirina gave a thin smile. "It does, doesn't it? If necessary, just leave her behind and teleport back."

Shala smiled, and the two looked down upon the city, both trying to see the magical currents that would lead them to the enemy.

And both seeing nothing except the lives of thousands moving forward, blissfully unaware that the ground beneath them teemed with snakes.

31

"*No*," Avarielle said, crossing her arms.

"Avarielle—" Cassara started.

"I said no."

Cassara sighed, sat back against the small wooden chair at her dining table. Avarielle had to hand it to her that she'd raised her family in what felt like a home, not a castle. Unlike the rest of the royal mansion.

"I'm not leaving my son behind without defense. We came here for protection and to make sure you were safe, Cassara. I'm not leaving."

"Carsyn and Kaden know you and would speak with you," Cassara said. "We can't just send a Circle witch to chat with them."

"They know Shirina." Avarielle shrugged.

"They know she's from the Circle, the same one they distrust, Avarielle." Cassara shifted in her seat. "It'll be easier if you just go."

Avarielle narrowed her eyes. Cassara had gotten better at hiding her true intentions, which she supposed years on the throne would do. But she couldn't hide them from Avarielle. Not really.

"You're trying to get me out of here." She looked from queen to sorceress. Shirina met her gaze full on, but Cassara had to look away. That was all the answer she needed. "Why?"

"Because you're the target," Shirina plainly. "The further away you are from Cassara, quite frankly, the better."

"Shirina!" Cassara gasped. "That's not what I was thinking."

Avarielle raised an eyebrow. "Well, Shirina's explanation actually makes sense, and I'm willing to go with that, but now I'm curious to know what, exactly, you *were* thinking."

The queen hesitated, then relented.

"I can't stop thinking about the blood oath." The gently spoken words were still like daggers embedding in Avarielle's heart. Cassara's hand shot out, took Avarielle's, and squeezed it. "Not because I think less of you"— Cassara looked her in the eye so that Avarielle could see she spoke truth—"but because I fear for Rojon."

"I agree with her," Shirina said. "He's been different and, quite frankly, grows fixated on your blade. I'm not sure if it's because when you used Graysword for the first time in Elihor, perhaps it sparked something in him, but—"

"You're afraid he'll try to take Graysword from me?" Avarielle said, voicing her own fears. Her son had changed since coming to Graydon. It could be the adventure or the different magic, or perhaps Altessa's influence, but he seemed to be growing bolder and desired to hold the sword. It terrified her.

"I'm not sure," Cassara said, "but every fiber of my being is telling me not to risk it."

"What do you mean by that?" Even Shirina's whispers grated on Avarielle's nerves.

Cassara looked at her in surprise. "Just... just a feeling, I suppose."

"Do you have these feelings often?" Shirina peered at Cassara, studying her so harshly that Avarielle found herself fighting against her instincts to defend the queen.

"Sometimes." Cassara's eyes lit up. "Could it be my magic?" She spoke with such hope, such longing, that it tore at Avarielle's heart. Day in, day out, the peoples of Graydon and Elihor looked to the Wall of Loss. Sometimes, sunlight or moonlight caught in its shimmering wake created a cascade of light or rainbows. They stood in awe, staring at the miracle that allowed the magics to remain separate and for the people to survive.

When Avarielle saw it, she saw Cassara's sacrifice. The defensive magic that flowed through her now protected the lands, but at the cost of her magic. And the hole it had left behind.

"Some Elders could read the future," Shirina whispered. "I don't know much about the art form, or really how it works, but it's something I know has been possible in the past. That's how the Elders of Larkhold knew that something was happening with the Wall of Loss. Perhaps an Elder from their coven could enlighten us."

"They didn't seem exactly helpful in Stormhold," Avarielle said, with none of her fire. Their words on Rojon haunted her, ringing true in her heart.

"How was it, Stormhold?" Cassara asked, voice wistful. A darker shade of blue colored her eyes now, the blond of her hair mixed with some gray. The warrior could still see the girl who'd given up everything to save her small kingdom, even after letting it go. Cassara had lost herself in the magic, over and over again.

In quiet moments, when Avarielle had seen her looking toward the gardens, she saw that part of her was still lost, leaning always toward the West where the Wall was, looking absentmindedly toward it at times, humming the old music under her breath to fill the silence of her soul.

Avarielle never asked nor pressed. Perhaps it was how Rojon felt, drawn to a magic he couldn't reach. That she wouldn't allow him to reach.

"The same." Avarielle shrugged. "Well, a bit cleaner, and more live adepts in it." She hesitated, then decided to tell her. "I heard the Wall." Cassara slowly turned to face her. "I heard your song in its magic."

"In *your* magic," Shirina said, her voice like a cold glass of water splashing Cassara back to reality. She blinked, looked to the sorceress. "Your magic is all trapped in there," Shirina said, as kindly as Shirina ever said anything. "So, it's unlikely your magic is manifesting now, and you're probably just working on finely honed instincts. Your instincts saved our lives quite a few times during the Days of Blood."

The sorceress glanced at Avarielle, and she understood what the sorceress was doing. Shirina didn't want Cassara to try to grab for any of her magic, and hope could lead down dangerous roads. "Could be more akin to warrior's instincts. Don't go into the haunted swamp or you'll get eaten by monsters. Or something like that."

"I guess," Cassara said, then said with more strength, "You're right. It's silly to waste time on daydreams. Now we must act before the rebels do."

"As soon as the rebel escapes, we'll be able to follow her on the ground," Shirina said. "She's watched by trusted witches."

Avarielle sighed. "And I'll go to speak to Kaden and Carsyn, to find out if they know anything about the green flames that might help us," she growled, "but I don't like it."

"Neither do I," Cassara assured her, pushing her chair back and standing. The others followed suit. "But this is the best way to proceed."

"I'll have Shala bring you to Kosel, where they're staying," Shirina said. "She'll get you there in one jump and back after some rest. So, you won't be gone too long."

Avarielle nodded, appreciating the gesture. She hated

the thought of leaving, but Shirina was right. If Avarielle was the target, she needlessly put Cassara at risk by staying. Plus, if Rojon somehow reacted to her magic…

"Keep Shala here," she said, "in case of attack. Send someone you rely on less with me."

"You'd trust another witch?" Shirina couldn't keep the surprise from her voice.

"I'd do a lot to make sure Cassara and Rojon are safe while I'm away."

"It's settled, then," Cassara said, heading to the door to resume her royal duties. Avarielle sought Shirina's eyes out. The sorceress stared back, a hint of worry clinging to the corners of her eyes.

Great.

"I promise it'll be fast," Shirina said, "and I will watch over Cassara."

"I know you will," Avarielle said. Right now, it wasn't that which worried her.

What worried her were the enemy they couldn't see and the haunted look on Cassara's pale features as she looked west, ever west, toward the Wall of Loss and her trapped magic.

*D*ayshon sat on the edge of the bed, legs dangling over the edge of it, head lowered. Cassara shut the bedroom door and slipped in beside him, kneeling at his feet to help him remove the prosthetics. He'd worn them too long today, and the pain became much more unbearable the longer he did.

Stubborn to the last, he mostly refused anything to help with the pain. Sometimes, Cassara saw Shirina cast a gentle healing spell, which Dayshon allowed. But she was the only one he allowed to do so.

His prosthetics mixed wood and metal to allow strength and articulation, leather and fabric for as comfortable and reliable a fastener as possible. It had taken almost two years before his wounds had healed enough to even try the prosthetics, and then a long time before he could walk with them mostly normally. He'd

MARIE BILODEAU

been dedicated to the task, though at times she could feel him collapsing under his own weight.

Cassara looked up at Dayshon, who looked down at her. She pushed herself up, slipped onto the bed beside him, the knit blanket warm and solid beneath her. Her fingers found Dayshon's, and she took his hand in hers. She leaned her head against his strong shoulder, closed her eyes, basked in the scent of him, wishing they could stay there forever.

In this moment. In the light.

She meant to tell him about their findings, and the plan, in as many details as she could without betraying the others. But different, surprising words slipped out of her mouth before she could stop them.

"I'm sorry," she whispered, unable to stop the words from tumbling out, or the tears from springing forth, like a long-closed book had been opened, its spine cracked, and pages tumbled out. "I'm sorry I left you in that final battle. I'm sorry I couldn't stop Siabala. I'm sorry I couldn't keep the Wall of Loss down. I'm sorry I haven't been a better queen to your people."

Dayshon's hand unfurled from hers and he turned her gently to see him, wiping away a tear. He looked mortified.

"There's nothing to apologize for," Dayshon said, his voice both certain and gentle. "You're a fabulous queen, a wonderful wife and mother. You faced Siabala when you were sixteen and did the best you could, Cassara. More than anyone else. And," he said, raising an eyebrow, "you married me to get to my army. I mean, that's more commitment to saving Graydon than anyone else had."

She tried to smile at his attempt at humor but felt worse instead.

"But so many died because of me. So many were killed or maimed because I dragged the armies to war. And then Massir couldn't defend itself against the Eloms…"

"Cassara," Dayshon said, his strong voice snapping her to attention, "stop. You always do this, you know?"

"Do what?"

"Decide it all comes down to you." He turned her to face him. "You've been doing it since I met you. First, save Edoline. Then the West. Then all of Graydon. And I get it," he said, placing his hands on her upper arm, solidifying her. "You are important. Descendant of Graydon, wielder of great magic." She flushed at that one. She hadn't had her magic for a long time. "Avarielle Grayloft, great warrior of the West and wielder of her own magical blade, comes to protect you for months at a time, from shadows that I can't see. The Circle sticks close to you, too."

He paused, looked deeply in her eyes.

"Like you still need protection for some reason. Not just because you're queen of Massir. That in itself being impressive enough." Another pause, a crinkling of his eyes. "Cassara, you'd tell me if something else was going on, wouldn't you?"

She'd left in the night without telling him she intended

to go face Siabala. She'd never told him that her magic held up the Wall of Loss. That the moment she died or drew on it, the Wall would fall and Siabala's soul would be unleashed.

What good would it do to tell him now? He bore enough worries for a kingdom.

"The people rebelled because of me," she said softly, deflecting the question. "Because I abandoned everyone in the final battle. I'm the problem here, Dayshon, and I just... I just don't know how to make it right."

She'd face demons again before this. She'd given her life to this kingdom, for better or worse. But she'd never once considered she'd become hated enough for attacks in her palace. She should have, in hindsight.

"The people didn't rebel because of you," Dayshon said, snapping her back. "It's a reason, of course, but rebellions happen because of an abundance of reasons, piling together until the people can't handle it anymore. The war was a start. Then drought, famine, reconstruction, poverty... Massir is a big city, and Rashim a large kingdom, Cassara. When we're flush with resources, it's easier to keep everyone happy. But now? We're making decisions for everyone, whether we want to or not."

His words rang true to her mind but hollow in her heart.

"We've gone through war, famine, and strife," Dayshon added. "We'll get through this, too. Together."

She looked into his eyes, trying to believe him. But he couldn't hear what she heard. The drums of war, ringing in the West, where the Wall of Loss called to her, beckoned her come.

Together.

"Together," she repeated, clinging to the word like a talisman.

33

*R*ojon stared at the words before him without reading them, thinking back to everything he'd seen and heard since arriving in Graydon. This was hardly what he'd imagined his first visit here would be like.

Altessa sat across from him, staring out the window, not even pretending to be reading. He stole a glance at her. Straight nose, those strange hazel eyes surrounded by white, blond hair streaked with blue.

She seemed gifted with a clarity of vision Rojon envied. And, of all the people she'd ever met, she had the most in common with him, too. Well, her past, anyway.

Both children of legendary heroes with strong magic, from the bloodlines that the very lands of light and darkness were named after. Graydon. Elihor.

And both just as unable to tap in to magic or be of use,

their parents obsessed with keeping the power away from them. Rojon knew that wasn't true. He knew his mother only tried to protect him as best she could, to keep him from the same pain she'd endured. But she'd had good moments, too. She'd met his father and still loved him, even after all this time. Or the idea of him anyway, Rojon supposed. But he liked to think they were still tied together, which he supposed they were, in him.

She'd met Cassara and Shirina, the three sharing a friendship closer than anything he'd ever known. Not that his mother would call Shirina a friend, but if you could relay messages in a simple glance and sought each other out in times of trouble... well, it seemed like friendship to Rojon.

"What are you doing?" Altessa's voice cut through his musings. He was still staring at her, though his mind had wandered far away. He flushed, cleared his throat.

"Ah, um, just lost in thought."

Altessa cocked her head, then seemed to decide he wasn't being weird, and she simply nodded.

"I'm bored, too," she simply said. "What do you do in Elihor to pass the time?"

"My mom taught me a few Westland games," he said, "and we often have village meals and stuff like that."

"Mmm, sounds about as much fun as Graydon," Altessa mumbled. "What do *you* do for fun?"

He winced. He doubted he was everyone's definition of fun, especially not for someone like Altessa.

"Come on, tell me!" she insisted, leaning forward.

"You're going to think it's boring." Worse, that *he* was boring.

"You've seen my parents," Altessa said. "I doubt you're more boring than they are."

He looked at her with surprise.

"The king and queen of Rashim are boring?"

"Sure, when all you do is royal stuff, it's pretty boring."

"Oh. Well, okay, I don't really know much about royalty."

"And I don't know much about you except what your mom's told us."

"What… what did she tell you, exactly?"

Altessa shrugged. "She's super proud of you. Gushes about how you like books and learning. That you're quite an architect and builder. Tried to describe something you were doing in the capital, but it didn't really make sense. Something with water."

"The aqueducts," he said. He'd built his reputation on that project, the first one he'd left home for a couple of years back, after testing a smaller version in his village. "We needed to get water to flow better into the city and clean it, too. Underground rivers snaked under the city but too deep to be efficient. But I created a root system with Silkar trees; they're like big purple trees, kind of like your weeping willows, and basically worked the roots to draw the water up toward them instead of them going down toward it. It's a property of the Silkars, which is why all the canals in Elihor were lined with them. Dig, then let the water come to you. You have to be careful, of course, not to collapse anything by drawing water sources—"

He stopped, realizing he'd let his enthusiasm run free. "Sorry," he mumbled.

"For what?" Altessa said. "Never be sorry for who you are, Rojon. I've never found architecture fascinating until right now. So, that's impressive!"

"I guess you know my hobbies now," he winced. "Building, and reading books."

She stood up, grabbed his hand, and pulled him up to the window. Massir spread out below them.

"Tell me what you see when you look at Massir." Her voice was low, wistful even.

Rojon took a deep breath. "It's beautiful," he said, looking down the castle walls. "An integration of old styles with newer ones, defenses with day-to-day-living, stone and plants."

His eyes slowly followed the lines of the large city, which sprawled to the edge of his sight. By far the biggest city he'd ever seen.

"Gardens were built where buildings were destroyed, during the Days of Blood, I assume. The closer you get to the edge of the city, the poorer the people, with fewer gardens and more destruction. Rebuilding efforts are obvious, but there's still a lot to be done, and twenty years is a long time to wait."

He had been born on the day the war ended. His whole life and some of this city still stood in rubble.

"To the east"—he pointed, leaning into the window—"the city is more secure, because it wasn't badly hit. To the west"—Altessa leaned with him—"you can see still where the path of the invaders took them; the buildings look poorer, like no one dares repair them. But walls were added in several sections, adding a visible striation of class and economics, of dispensable and less so. It's like the city is still holding its breath for an attack, and it's never released it. This city can't, because it's built to hold its breath, and people, in."

He finished, looked back to Altessa, her hazel eyes staring at him.

"I'm sorry," he said, suddenly embarrassed. "I didn't mean to assume anything..."

"No," she said, looking down to her city, "you've just seen more of this city than I have my entire life. I always knew something felt off, but you just voiced all of it."

"It's fear," Rojon said softly. "Fear-based architecture. It's meant to protect but not strive."

"Is Elihor like that?" The two stared down at the life below them.

"Elihor was destroyed by a flash fire," Rojon said, "and there's little except building a stronger, safer Circle to protect against that. We lost forests, crops, animals, entire villages... We're building to celebrate what remains. So, no, Elihor is different. But," he added, "we also have underground safe places now, and entire underground networks where survivors hid. Some people stay there still, because it feels safer."

"But safe isn't necessarily better," Altessa said.

"I don't think so, either." He shrugged. "But we didn't see the armies of Eloms walking on this city, killing all in their path. We didn't fight Siabala and his armies. So, I guess we don't really get the fear behind it all."

"No, we didn't." Altessa crossed her arms. "But we're living now. This is our land, too, and the fear that feeds into it feeds into our lives. They at least had an enemy to fight, Rojon. How do we fight an enemy that no longer exists? How do we fight this fear?"

"Do we have to?" he asked honestly.

"Of course we do!" she exclaimed, making him jump. "This is at the heart of all of this. The attack on the palace which could have killed both my parents was based on fear, wasn't it? Fear of not being heard unless screaming loudly?"

He didn't point out that her own words were spoken out of fear that her parents could have been killed, though he enjoyed the irony that he didn't tell her because he feared her reaction.

"Are you sure they never tried to be heard before?" Rojon asked. Her eyes grew wide, her arms uncrossed and hung limply at her side.

"My mother and father would have listened," she said, resolute.

"I'm sure they would," he said. "Had they heard."

"You think they didn't know?"

"Well, your mom hosts town hall meetings, right?" Altessa nodded. "But certain people report for groups, right? What if those people aren't sharing everything?"

Altessa's mouth turned to a line.

Before she could answer, his mom stepped into the room.

"Altessa," she asked, "could Rojon and I talk alone, please?"

Altessa squeezed Rojon's arm and walked off without another word.

"She's a spitfire, that one," Avarielle said. "Can we talk?"

"I'm sorry I screwed up," he said right away, his guilt bubbling to the surface. He wanted his mom to be proud of him, but he kept getting everything wrong. No wonder she wouldn't give him Graysword, even if Shirina could keep him safe with her spells.

"You didn't screw up," Avarielle said, a hand through her hair, a sure sign of discomfort and annoyance at herself. "I did. And I'm really sorry about that."

She stood before him, just a bit taller than him. She placed her hands on his shoulders.

"You were born in the middle of battle, Rojon, and I didn't think I'd ever come back," she said, her voice soft and hypnotic. Rojon held his breath. She'd never shared much at all about how she'd felt, as though unable, or unwilling, to confront her feelings. "Then, the very first thing I did after holding you was hand you to Shirina to go fight Siabala alongside Cassara."

He didn't remember any of it, but sometimes, he could hear gentle music in his dreams from a flute and feel the tingling of magic on his skin. It might be a memory borne of retellings, or it might be real. He would never know.

"I was... Eli, I never know how to say this stuff." She took a deep breath, visibly tried to center herself. Rojon waited. He knew his mom would rather fight a thousand demons then talk about her feelings, though he'd seen her conquer that over and over again. It was part of what made him respect—and love—her so much.

"I was fighting, and bleeding, and so tired. I could hear the battle waging up above in the sky but couldn't fight that one. I was stuck on the top of Stormhold, trying not to slip in my own blood, while cutting down enemies. Then they were gone, and I was alone, staring up, hearing your cries..." Her voice broke, eyes shining. She didn't look down. Didn't back away.

"You'd just been born, Rojon, and I couldn't help you or save you. I sent you to fight Siabala, and I was powerless to save you. Just like I'd been powerless to save your father. I guess... I guess I can be overprotective of you."

"It's okay—"

"No, it's not. It's not fair to you, and I'm sorry about that. You know how to fight, Rojon, but your mind and heart are your true strengths. I don't want you to have Graysword, because you're better than it. Better than me, and better than all those before me who wielded its magic. If you pick it up"—her voice trembled with the need to be heard—"you will be changed forever. And that doesn't have to be your destiny, Rojon." She looked deeply into his eyes, and he felt he saw her for the first time as more than just a warrior and mother. But as a person, as scared as he was, of losing those she loved.

"Its power will call to you, Rojon." Her eyes flashed with fire. "You know it. You've felt it, and you're already losing your temper because of it."

"I can't blame the sword for poor choices."

"Rojon." She took a deep breath. "Even if you're annoyed with me, which you have every right to be, you've been acting a bit out of character for you."

"I don't think…" He took a step back. "It's just been so much. I mean, I'm known in Elihor, and here I'm no one, and I stand out for all the wrong reasons. I thought being heir to Elihor made me stand out. This is much worse."

His eyes lingered on the sword. The red jewel in its pommel.

"Don't trust the magic, Rojon. It is not safe." *It's not for you*, he heard her say, though she didn't speak the words. He felt himself grow angry again, at being denied his chance to do more. His mom shifted, blocking his view of the sword. Placed a soothing hand back on his shoulder, and he looked into her familiar eyes riddled with unfamiliar fear.

"Do you understand me, Rojon?"

"I think I do," he said, then fortified himself. "But I

want to help, too. I won't carry a sword, but I don't need to be shoved aside, either. You taught me to be observant and to think, and Shirina taught me some basics of magic and details of Graydon and Elihor... I can be useful in other ways. Don't shut me out, Mom. Not here, not now."

His voice trembled now. "I've already lost Grandfather, Mom. I don't want to lose you, too."

At that, she gathered him in her arms, and he still felt like the little boy, except this time, he could hold her in return, too.

"I won't promise you won't ever lose me, Rojon," she whispered in his ear, "I'm not a fortune teller and I live by the sword. But I do promise you that, no matter what happens, I will always be looking out for you and proud of you. I maybe have never expected to be a mother, but that's because in all of my imaginings, I couldn't imagine a wonderful son like you."

She broke free, still held his arms. "Now make smarter choices than me, Rojon. This world is at peace, even if rebuilding. Nothing makes me prouder than to see you doing something more than dedicating your life to the blade."

"Something different," Rojon quickly corrected her.

"Different?"

"Than the blade. Not more," he spoke softly, like they spoke as adults for the first time, despite all their chats. "I'm proud of you, too, Mom. You picked up the sword when you had to, to protect your people, and you keep getting up, again and again, to make things right. That part I got from you, too. I want to help make things right, even if it's not with a blade."

Avarielle looked at him as though seeing him for the first time. Then she gently kissed his cheek.

"My brave, smart boy," she said. "Thank you."

A quick grin, and his stomach plummeted. He knew that look. That mix of guilt and excitement she always got before leaving him behind, to protect Cassara or travel to Graydon, to go somewhere away from him.

"Well, you might not think so much of me after this." She grew serious. "I have to go and get some information from someone."

To leave him behind.

"I'm coming, too," he said, not wanting to let her go. He'd built a life for himself and he was proud of it. Were they in Elihor, it would be different. But here, her leaving him would mean he'd truly be alone, without purpose. And that terrified him.

He tried to glimpse Graysword again, to find comfort in the jewel, but his mother seemed intent on keeping it from his sight.

"I wish you could"—she winced—"but I'm reliant on Circle magic to travel, and they can only take one. But you'll be safe here, and I'll come back as quickly as I can."

"You won't be in danger, will you?"

"I won't," she sighed. "To be honest, I think Shirina is sending me there to get me out of harm's way, which is all kinds of annoying."

Rojon felt better for hearing that, and something wound tight within him released.

"She cares about you," Rojon said with a smile.

"She's irritating, is what she is." Her voice held no bite. "And she'll make sure you're safe, Rojon. If anything happens while I'm gone, listen to her and move quickly. Trust your instincts. You're a Grayloft, and you've got them in spades, understood?"

He nodded, then hesitated.

"Will you tell me where you're going?" He wanted to see if she would bring him into her confidence, like she always did Cassara and Shirina. Or if she would leave him out in the cold, waiting for her to come back, imagining all the darkness that could have befallen her.

She pondered for a few moments and then, to what seemed to be both their surprise, answered. "In Kosel, the forest country east of here, to chat with some old friends. The worst I'll face there is indigestion from their cooking."

"And they can help you figure out what's happening in Massir?"

"That's the plan," she said, then looked annoyed. "That, and get me out of here until things cool down a bit. But I'm not thrilled about leaving you behind, Rojon. I'd much prefer to have you with me."

He believed her. A gulf he'd always felt dividing him from his mother seemed to narrow.

"Be safe," he said.

"You too." Then she added, "And be smart around

Altessa. That girl's as much trouble as her mother was when she was young, and believe me, that was a lot of trouble."

She kissed him again and walked out of the room without another word, his eyes lingering on the red jewel of Graysword until it vanished around the corner.

34

The outpost at the back of the gardens lay nestled between cherry blossoms and apple trees from Edoline, surrounded by lilacs. Each outpost had some form of magically fortified and everblooming flower with a strong, recognizable scent, to help guide witches from outpost to outpost. Edoline's outpost was surrounded by cherry blossoms.

"Pol." She turned to one of her first Circle adepts, a member of the old Circle. A longtime friend of Shala, she trusted him with this mission. "We'll heighten the magic to get you quickly to Kosel. With as few stops as possible, and then only to continue onto the next outpost, no one should be able to interfere with this mission."

He nodded, focused on the pad. He seemed a bit nervous, which wasn't unnatural for him. His power was great but his confidence not as sturdy.

"We'll watch for your return," Shirina said. "You will be tired, so rest up, and we'll await you in the morning."

"Thank you, Crimson Circle Elite," Pol said, nodding nervously.

Shala stepped up, grabbed him in a giant hug, their crimson cloaks mingling. "Be safe," she told him.

Her farewells to her son made, Avarielle walked back toward Shirina. The only other person there not of the Circle was Altessa. Not many knew of Avarielle's departure, and even the guards had been placed in other locations to keep this mission a secret.

The fewer knew, the better their chances of success.

"I will look after your son," Shirina said, keeping her voice low as the warrior reached her.

"Thank you," she said. She glanced back, made sure the two weren't being heard. "Listen, I have one more favor to ask of you."

"You're very demanding, Avarielle."

"Think how I feel, needing to keep asking favors of you." She ran her hand in her hair, a sure sign of both hesitation and resolve. She didn't want to have to ask Shirina whatever she was about to, but would regardless because she needed the sorceress.

"Look, if anything happens to me, I need you to promise me that you'll destroy Graysword or at least hide it away. Far away."

Shirina locked eyes with the warrior, seeing only determination blazing within them.

"I don't know if I'll be able to destroy it," Shirina said, "but I can make sure it's kept away from Rojon."

"Not just him," Avarielle said, surprising Shirina by taking hold of her arm, as though intent on being heard. Desperate to be heard. "His descendants, too. No one in my bloodline should ever take up the oath to Siabala, Shirina. I need you to promise me that you'll do whatever you can to make sure I'm the last."

Realizing her hand clutched the sorceress, Avarielle broke free, but her eyes held Shirina's, waiting for an answer. Shirina wasn't sure how she could destroy Graysword, should that feat even be possible. She guessed Siabala would not have created a weak sword, and not once in all the enemies that Avarielle had encountered did the blade ever weaken of fail. It might be unbreakable, at least by her magic.

Could she keep it at bay? Maybe. If buried far and deep enough, she thought she could at least buy her descendants generations of freedom, until the Circle could prove powerful enough to destroy it or Siabala could be destroyed.

Ideally the latter.

"You have my word," Shirina whispered. "But, with any luck, we'll actually destroy Siabala next time and never have to worry about it."

A grin slowly spread on the warrior's face. "Once for practice, twice for the kill."

Shirina nodded. Avarielle turned to leave.

"Spare us both the trouble of owing each other

anything and just come back," Shirina said. Avarielle shot a grin her way, then walked toward Pol.

They were headed to Kosel and would be safe there. Safer than in Massir. Still, both she and the warrior were on edge, probably because of yesterday's attack. The sooner they had more information, the better.

"Prepare your spell, Pol," Shirina said, as she, Shala, and two Orange Circles closed around them. Pol began chanting, Avarielle standing closer to him, hand on her sword. She wouldn't activate her magic before the spell was complete, even if needed.

Two other teleportation Circles would help propel them all the way to Kosel, to get answers on the green flames. Avarielle nodded to Shirina, and the sorceress returned the gesture, beginning to chant, the three others joining her.

Pitch and cadence matched, thanks to years of practice, magic leaping around them, closing over Pol and Avarielle. Shirina used the Sight to ensure the magic still acted properly as it held them, growing so bright that it proved hard to look at Avarielle.

Just before they vanished, she saw the warrior look to the side, toward her son, shooting a smile his way before her eyes grew harder and she focused on Shirina.

She expected battle.

And so did Shirina.

With a nod, the warrior and Pol were gone. Shirina used the Sight to watch the magic arc away, toward the next Circle outpost at the border of Rashim, unchallenged.

Perhaps they were all on edge for no reason.

Tingling spread from her elbow to her fingers, beneath her silver bracer, indicating a warding spell had been broken. The rebel was finally on the move. She indicated for Shala to join her.

"Shala, remain here and keep the others safe," she commanded.

"You can't go after her by yourself!"

"If an Elder is at the end of this, I've the best chance of escaping with my life," Shirina responded. "And don't worry, I hardly intend to engage. I'll follow and withdraw as soon as I know where they are."

Shala had protest written all over her face, but she bit it back as the others approached. Their circle of confidence had been small here, too, for all their safety. Secrets upon layers of secrets, and Shirina fought back against the worry that this Circle was becoming eerily similar to the old one.

These secrets were necessary to keep others safe, not simply to keep the Circle safe.

Shala would know to keep an eye on Rojon. And Cassara. She had to trust that the Crimson Circle would make the best decisions in her absence.

"I'll be back," she whispered to Shala as she left. Shala nodded, eyes a bit wider than usual. Shirina turned and walked back into the palace, to follow the trail of magic before it grew too thin.

It chewed her up, no matter how she turned the question in her mind. The rebel had escaped just as Avarielle vanished from Massir, and Shirina found it hard to dismiss that as mere coincidence. With a flick of her wrist and a quickly worded spell, she hid herself in shadows, vanishing from plain sight.

With any luck, Elder Tally would be caught unawares and would be dead before the day was over.

35

The scent of evergreens mixed with old earth, of pine-soaked humidity, enveloped Avarielle, insects buzzing the heat of the day in mournful crescendos. The spell completely vanished, and Pol stumbled and would have fallen had she not caught him.

"Steady," she said, not being too familiar with the adept. Three other Circle witches stepped forward, one Orange and two Blue. These weren't high on the pecking order.

"Thanks," he mumbled, managing to right himself. He looked about ready to keel over. According to Cassara, the old guards would be about an hour to the north of there.

"We heard from Crimson Circle Elite Shirina that we were to provide you with whatever aid you needed," the Orange Circle said, an older woman who looked like she belonged in Kosel, with an honest and open face, unlike most adepts. Avarielle found herself taking to her right away. The old Circle only stole children for new recruits, but Shirina had welcomed anyone, from any walk of life or age.

"I'm Tisha," the adept said. A grandmother, Avarielle guessed.

"Avarielle." They shook hands in a strangely common gesture for the Circle. "How long have you lived in Kosel?"

"Pretty much my whole life, save for some time learning in various Circle outposts." Pol was taken away by the two younger adepts. "I know what you're thinking," she said, looking sharply at Avarielle. "That I'm old for an adept. Well, I am, and it's been a challenge!" She laughed, the sound unapologetic, coaxing a smile to Avarielle's lips. "But I've always wanted to learn magic, and I met you all when you were doing your song-and-dance routine twenty years ago."

"Ah," Avarielle said. The three of them had been traveling through Kosel and needed a way to make money, and, well, Cassara played the flute, Shirina sang, and she could dance. It had been more fun than washing dishes.

"So, when the singer came back to ask if anyone would willingly join, I figured why not." A wide grin split her lips, eyes lined by the stamp of time. "I've raised a family, fought off Eloms, survived famine... figured I'd do something for myself, and this is what I chose."

"I admire your guts," Avarielle said, meaning it. "This wouldn't be everyone's cup of tea."

"Or pint of dark ale, as my preference." She winked. "But I have no regrets. Now, how can I be of help?"

Avarielle looked to nearby bark, to see where moss grew, and up, to see how the shadows struck the top of trees. Once she'd found north, she took a deep breath of nature, ripe and old. She loved it, but the humidity proved stifling. She missed the West, where the heat didn't drown you. Sweat already ran down the back of her shirt, cotton sticking to skin, making the leather armor uncomfortable.

"If you can make sure Pol rests up so we're ready to go when I'm back," she offered, "that would be great. I'll come back by nightfall, hopefully. But in the morning at the latest."

The Orange Circle nodded, then handed her a pack filled with cheese, apples, and another waterskin. Avarielle had come prepared, but she didn't refuse.

"Old habits die hard," Tisha said. "Now, be safe. Kosel is much safer than it used to be, and even the old thieves and bandits have moved on. It's a quiet place, but"—she glanced down at Graysword—"I have a feeling trouble tends to follow you wherever you go."

"Well, like you said," Avarielle smiled, "old habits die hard."

The old woman laughed, the grainy sound belonging to this harsh but beautiful landscape. With a quick farewell, Avarielle made her way up north, through the trees and thick mosses, looking for small tracks that would point to the village.

After about an hour, she found what she was looking for. A slope leading down, wooden walls and doors poking out between tree trunks and from underneath vast evergreens, a settlement partly hidden from view. The sound of children laughing and running perked her ears, and she smiled and relaxed. The last time she was in Kosel, Eloms were running rampant and the people had mostly hidden.

She knew she'd been spotted and walked ahead like she belonged, feeling two people trailing her. They were good but not so good as not to be spotted. She couldn't fault them the extra security and ignored them as she kept walking forward. She was the stranger there, after all.

She found a building a bit more noticeable than the others, a doorway through an old lightning-struck thick trunk where had spawned an inn. Avarielle stepped in, the atmosphere thick with booze and spices. A few people smoked pine needles, the air ruined with the foul scent. She glanced around. Tables were strewn around the edges, cut from old bark, as were benches.

A kitchen filled the back, a bar blocking it. Stew bubbled over the hearth, and warm bread cooled, the smell captivating once the pine needles died down. Cheeses had been cut, and not just basic hard cheese, either. There were different types, some covered in truffles. Bottles hung from above the bar, showing a fine and wide variety of wines and ales, and Avarielle's stomach grumbled like an angry desert cat.

Whoever ran this place loved food and drink, and had good taste, too.

She selected a seat at the bar, keeping her back to the side wall and her eyes to the few other patrons. She didn't know this place well enough to trust a knife wouldn't find its way into her ribs.

After everything she'd lived through, this would be a ridiculous place to die.

A young woman, dark hair tied back in a ponytail, dark skin contrasting with her beige shirt, eventually popped up from the kitchen, carrying a sack of flour. She crouched and placed it down near one of the working stations, then wiped her hands on her previously brown pants, now rather marked with flour prints. Eyes narrowed as she spotted Avarielle, probably unused to strangers.

"What can I do for you?" She came forward, movements fluid and slow, her training reflected in every movement.

"I wouldn't mind some of that delicious bread and cheese," Avarielle asked, "and I'm looking for a couple of friends who live in this area."

"I can do the first, but I don't offer information to outsiders."

"Fair enough," Avarielle said, "but if I tell you their names, will you be willing to let them know I'm here and I'd like to chat with them?"

She pondered the offer, a quick glance down to the counter.

Of course. Avarielle slid over two Massir crowns, which would buy ten meals there, if they were recognized as currency.

"Got anything unmarked?" she asked, taking the crowns regardless.

"Not anything I'd trade away," Avarielle said, hand on Graysword, which thankfully she'd covered before teleporting. Red jewel at its hilt, the blade looked too expensive and precious to leave exposed for a common thief to try to take. Seeing the woman's eyes stay on the hilt, Avarielle added, "Or that I wouldn't fight to keep, and I put up a good fight."

"I bet you do," the woman said. "Fine, I'll take your marked money, then. Give me your friends' names and yours. Then I'll decide."

"Their names are Kaden and Carsyn, and they moved here about twenty years ago." Retired after the Days of Blood. "And my name is Avarielle Grayloft."

Avarielle wasn't sure she detected recognition in her eyes at the old guards' names, but she definitely did at her own name. She looked at the woman, waiting to see if she said anything.

"Wait here," she said, "and be kind enough not to leave."

A quick movement of the hand, and swords emerged from beneath tables, everyone turning from patron to mercenary. Avarielle's blood pumped in her veins, the familiar adrenaline kicking her senses to life.

There were five of them, and she glanced across the room casually. One's blade was so rusty, it hadn't seen combat in years. Another favored his left hand, his right shoulder sporting an old injury from the way he held himself, she wagered. The other three might give her a challenge all together, but she could easily get them to funnel their way to her by knocking over the nearby table. And, from the strength flowing to her muscles, she knew she could easily finish them.

She sighed. For a second, she thought this day might have turned interesting. She turned to the woman.

"I'll stay for the food, and please add some ale with that. One of your better bottles." She leaned against the bar, looking as bored as she felt. "Tell them to put their weapons away and not embarrass themselves. It's painful to watch and might ruin my appetite."

The woman waffled from amusement to annoyance, but she brought Avarielle her food and drink. Siabala's magic gave her some advantages. She couldn't be affected by most Circle magic, for example. And poisons of this land had no effect on her. So, she bit heartily into the bread, pleasantly surprised by the crust opposite the perfectly chewy center.

"This is delicious; thank you," she said. Then she looked the woman in the eye. "Now, can you get my friends, or should I start stacking up some of your friends to work up more of an appetite?"

She didn't hurry out of the place, but at least she went, hopefully to get Carsyn and Kaden.

If not, at least Avarielle would get to fight on a full stomach. Slowly, purposefully, she cut a piece of cheese, placed it on the crusty fresh bread, and took a bite. She closed her eyes, enjoyed the flavor. Then, even more slowly, opened her eyes again and took a long drink of what turned out to be a delightful bitter cider, with strawberry and rhubarb notes. Kosel had certainly come a long way since last she'd been there.

She turned to the five men staring at her, weapons on tables.

"You should probably just enjoy your food," she offered, "because you certainly wouldn't enjoy fighting me, though I'm sure I'd get a kick out of it. For the few seconds it lasted, anyway."

One of the men growled at her, flexing his muscles. She ignored him and enjoyed another bite of her cheesy bread. Did she detect garlic?

"So, you've heard of me," she asked around a mouthful of deliciousness. Definitely garlic. "What did you hear, exactly, that's got you all on edge?"

"We just don't like strangers in Kosel," the closest man, a wiry bearded man, answered.

"You liked me fine when you thought I could be a target."

He shifted in his seat. She took another bite.

"So, you've heard I like a good fight and I generally win?" she practically cooed, and finished her cider. "Let me assure you that whatever you've heard, it's worse." She paused, looked at each man in turn, made sure to catch their eye. "And I'm way, and I mean *way*, less patient."

She stood up as seats toppled backward, and metal scraped wooden tables as they reached for their weapons.

"Well, that was an excellent meal," she said, stretching. "I wouldn't mind working some of it off."

Eyes darted from one to the other. Just as Avarielle though they'd never work up the nerve to attack her, the doors flung open. The woman from behind the bar stepped in, followed by an old man. He gazed from her to the men standing, weapons drawn.

"Put down your weapons, you fools." He shook his head. "I've seen her fight packs of Eloms and not break a sweat. You'll all just embarrass yourselves."

"But, Kaden—"

"Get out of here, and if I ever catch you doing anything this stupid again, I'll ban you from this place. Got it?" Kaden said, voice like steel. The men studied him, the old man staring them down with deep gray eyes. Even without weapons or uniform, the old Royal Protector of Edoline did his rank proud.

"Now put away your weapons, son," he said more softly, "and go on home. Come back once you've cooled off. All of you."

They mumbled a few words, obviously respecting Kaden, and slipped out.

Kaden then focused on Avarielle. The man was in his eighties, but he seemed stronger than the last time she'd seen him, twenty years ago. Of course, back then, things were a bit more dire and few people were at their best.

"Avarielle Grayloft," he said, walking up to her, the woman keeping a close eye on her, obviously protective of Kaden.

"Kaden Trawel," Avarielle said as they clasped arms.

"Still making friends, I see."

"It's my charm. It knows no bounds. And you? You own this place?"

"A little side business Carsyn and I started after the Days of Blood." He indicated a table where they could talk. Avarielle joined him, and the woman brought over another cider for her and a caramel ale for Kaden.

"Pakana, you can close off for the afternoon," he said gently to the woman. "My friend and I will catch up on old times, and it's bound to be boring."

"I doubt that," the young woman said, glancing at Avarielle. "But I'll get out of your hair if you want privacy," she said, kissing his cheek. "I'll be in the back, chopping wood and tending to the animals. Let me know if you need anything."

"I will," he promised, and she headed out, the door closing gently behind her.

"There were lots of orphans after the Eloms were finally all killed," he offered as an explanation. Avarielle knew exactly what he meant. Even after Siabala had been destroyed, Eloms still ran in Graydon for months, years in some places. She'd been busy healing and in Elihor with Rojon, and always felt guilty she hadn't been able to help get rid of them. Graysword could cut them down easily.

Of course, that was because they were the people of Elihor, transformed into monsters by Siabala.

"Is Cassara well?" he asked, worry slipping into his

voice. He hadn't been her protector for more than half of the queen's life, but old habits apparently died hard.

"For now," Avarielle answered honestly. "But there's been an attack in the palace, by a faction of discontents. Rebels, they call themselves."

Kaden's eyes turned to steel as he waited for her to continue, grip on his drink tightening.

"She and Dayshon are fine, as are the kids," she added for good measure, then leaned in. He followed suit. "But they had access to a certain kind of magic that was… unexpected, and of concern, to say the least."

Gray eyes widened slightly, hands began to tremble. Avarielle reached and clasped his hand in hers.

"Cassara told me because she had to," Avarielle said, "and what's done is done, Kaden. I know you for the man you are now. A man I've grown to respect."

Hand still on his, she held his eyes, forced him to see the truth of her statement. Eventually, very slowly, he nodded.

"We suspect an Elder survived, one allied with Siabala." She couldn't bring herself to speak loudly, like the walls might hear. "Shirina doesn't know how the green flames were given to the original users, and hoped you might be able to shed some light."

"I'll do what I can," he said as softly. "But know that I don't remember much from those days."

"Any detail might help Shirina figure it out." Avarielle withdrew her hand. Sharp eyes looked at her.

"Shirina stayed with Cassara to protect her?"

"It made more sense, since the attacks are magical," Avarielle said, though part of her hated admitting she wouldn't currently be effective protecting her friend.

He nodded as though satisfied.

And then he started to speak.

orty years earlier, the Circle had needed a special force to ensure the Western Wars continued while they sought to decipher a message sent to them through Stormhold, the messengers themselves turned into monsters.

Kaden was almost forty-five, a veteran of several skirmishes in the south as the countries fought for dominance over each other. He'd dedicated his life to the sword and, when the Southern Coalition was finally formed, he found himself without purpose.

While he was drinking away his anger at being useless one night in a dirty bar, a witch from the Circle approached him and promised purpose.

Purpose. That was all he'd ever wanted. All he'd ever craved. A reason to get up in the morning, to put his skills to the test, to carry out orders or give them. She didn't need to ask twice before he followed her, as did other veterans, just as the war in the West exploded with stories of hidden gold and Westland greed.

It was easy to hate the West, its people living in harsh conditions and so independent that they'd never opened trade with the East. It was so easy to hate and fear the unknown, and so the armies of the East decided the riches should be theirs. The West fought back, arguing riches didn't exist. Eloms began attacking the Eastern troops, an act blamed on the West, even as the Westlanders struggled to survive, their villages torn to shreds by the monsters.

The Westlanders tried to move out of the shadows of the Bloody Mountains from where monsters erupted, as the Eastlanders moved in toward the West, seeking reputed treasure. Caught in the middle with nowhere to go, the Westlanders fought tooth and nail, using the land to their advantage. Meanwhile, the Circle stoked stories of the Westlanders moving east to take over eastern lands and kill their families. That for years they'd kept riches and power, and were finally ready to deploy them.

The Eloms being a part of it.

Stupid, Kaden thought now. But back then, his blood lusted for purpose. And for the chance to make his blade sing.

The leader of the West went by the name Grayloft, reputed to hold a sword that slew the demons in one stroke. To break the West's spirits, they had to break him. Kill him and hang up his bloodied sword as a sign that everything they fought for was destroyed.

It had made sense then. For Kaden, Carsyn, Klar, and

many others who'd sought a cause. Supporting the recently war-torn East had been their cause, though now Kaden couldn't understand his past self.

He'd agreed to become part of an elite unit, to stop the West before they destroyed the East.

And now he looked into the eyes of the daughter of Grayloft, who held his sword, had wielded it to save his ward, Princess Cassara. He respected the warrior, seeing in her the same need for battle he had once known. Except, unlike himself, she had purpose. He wondered if she ever questioned it or wished her life had been different. He wondered but didn't ask. It wasn't his place to do so, and it never would be.

Because he was part of the reason that purpose had become hers, and the magical sword of her ancestors now belonged to her.

"They told us we would make a difference," he said, like an apology.

"You did," she answered, her words cutting. Yes, he'd certainly made a difference for her.

He swallowed, pushed forward. This wasn't about receiving atonement for his sins. He didn't deserve it and would never ask it. She'd come there, willing to face him, requiring his help, all for Cassara. Her willingness to hear him out would be his forgiveness. It was all he would ever get, and he would learn to make peace with that.

"They brought us to the West first," he said, focusing on the details as much as he could. "Just on the border of your lands."

"My lands have no borders," she responded. The West didn't divide their land into ownership as the East did. The East considered the edge of the desert to be the West. But the Westlanders had never ratified anything, and their own maps were in their minds, not on papers scarred with imaginary borders.

He nodded his understanding and pushed on. "It was to the north of the West, and south of the Salir Hills. Underground, accessible through a large bolder at the base of the hill. A door appeared on it when the witches cast a spell." He winced. "Sorry, that's not very helpful."

"Every detail helps."

"We went down three sets of stairs, all stone, to a chamber below. The place was quite large, with Elders and a few Crimson Circle Elites. There was a large room in the basement, with stone slabs forming a large circle, at least thirty of them all lined up. Before we knew it, we were all tied to one, hands and feet, large bands across our bodies to hold us still, our heads held down." He swallowed, his mouth getting dry.

"The Elders walked to each of us and forced a liquid down our throats. It tasted bitter, thick and brown. Before we'd finished choking it down, sweat just started pouring from me. It wasn't nerves but something the potion did."

Avarielle nodded encouragingly.

"And then... I'm not sure. My vision doubled and I had to fight to stay conscious. I remember movement. Like all our slabs moved in a circle, making me dizzy. I think I threw up some of the potion, because next thing I knew, more was being shoved into me. I could hear chanting. Several voices, all together, clear and confident."

He finished his ale, coughed. Avarielle handed him the rest of her cider, which he gratefully took. His hand shook, but he ignored it. He hadn't gone back there in all these years. But if Cassara had betrayed his confidence, it meant she needed him to share what he knew. Even if he no longer watched over her daily, he took his oath to protect her at heart.

And he would do so, no matter the cost to himself.

"There was light. So bright it hurt my eyes and kept waking me up. I heard screaming, and the light was broken by dark cloaks once in a while. It didn't burn, the light. Not until it turned green"—his voice turned to a whisper—"and then it burned. Moved around our bones, like they turned to snakes, like swarms of insects ate my organs from within... I can't describe the pain. I've never felt anything like it, not since."

He sincerely hoped never to again.

"It was all green light and pain. I don't know for how long, but a while. When I finally came to, I was still bound to the slab. The light was gone, only that strange glow from the witch light. Several Crimson Circle Elites tended to us. One of them smirked when she saw I'd survived. Like they hadn't expected any of us to."

He paused, drank again. "And most of us hadn't."

"How many do you think lived?" Avarielle asked, snapping him back to the now. A thin coat of sweat covered his brow, and he wiped it from his forehead with the palm of his hand.

"We were about thirty, like I said. Three of us lived."

Avarielle's eyebrows shot up. "That's not a great success rate."

"Rather not." He managed a chuckle, then grew sober again. "Which isn't a bad thing, really. Between us and a few other batches, if you will, we did enough damage."

Avarielle grew silent, as though she wanted to ask him about that night.

"I wasn't there," Kaden whispered. "But I know someone who was."

She knew who he meant, of course. Carsyn, his brother-in-arms, best friend, and life partner, who lay slowly wasting away at home, age and battle wounds finally claiming him. Even a year past, Kaden and he would have been tending to this place with Pakana. Not now, as Kaden tended to Carsyn, and Pakana tended to them both.

Avarielle seemed to struggle with herself.

"If you'd like to ask him anything," he said, "the time is now, Avarielle. He doesn't have long left."

"Will he actually speak to me?"

"I think he wanted to, years ago," Kaden said, "but his health was never the same after the Days of Blood. And he didn't want to implicate me."

Carsyn needed redemption, which Kaden knew Avarielle was in her rights to withhold from him. But as his mind slipped from him and death pecked at his body,

Carsyn had mentioned the night more than ever before. It ate at him.

If there was a chance that Avarielle would grant him forgiveness or at least listen, then it was a chance Kaden would offer his friend. But only if she agreed.

He'd vowed to never again hurt a child of the West, or of anywhere. And he intended to stick with that promise.

Still, when the warrior nodded gently, Kaden found himself able to breathe again, even as his stomach churned with worry.

*A*varielle had smelled death before. On the battlefield, and on healing beds. A certain sour sweetness, a turn of the usual scent of humanity, that proclaimed its desire and willingness to release its earthly coils. When she entered Carsyn's room, she could smell death on him.

One of the first memories she held was of the smell of death. Burning flesh, her mother consumed by green fires. No screams or cries. It had either been too quick or her mother had held them in. Avarielle didn't know. All she remembered was that light. And that smell.

Her father had suspected the Circle, though green flames weren't part of their arsenal. She'd grown up hating the Circle, for good reasons. It turned out he was right, though he'd not lived long enough to find out.

How did you take your blood oath with Siabala, Father? She wished she could ask him. Or ask her brother. She didn't

OATH BREAKER

know the details, but she knew without a doubt one detail would be true to all of them.

The stench of death.

The dying man before her had taken an oath too and claimed it with lives. Her mother's.

Kaden waited outside, leaving them be, maybe not wanting to hear the details of what his friend had done. It was easier to look someone in the eye when you weren't fully aware of the details of the worst moment of their lives.

Avarielle waited, standing in the entrance, looking at the bed. Then the form shifted, a blanket moved by a wiry arm bearing a scar received by an Elom years before, and familiar eyes looked at her.

"I always knew you'd be the one to take me to the Afterfate, one way or the other." He coughed, and Avarielle closed the gap and handed him water. He drank with shaking hands, and then she placed the glass back on the log that served as a bedside table.

"I'm not here to kill you, old fool," she said softly, kneeling by his bed so he could easily face her. She wanted to look him in the eye. "But I am here to hear what you have to say."

"You know," he said simply.

Avarielle nodded, focused on her breathing. Calm, steady, riddled with the stench of death, both past and present.

"I've gone over this in my mind thousands of times, since meeting you in these woods decades ago," he

271

whispered. "No, that's not true. Since seeing your face, eyes lit up by green flames."

He'd seen her. He'd known he'd killed her mother, and he'd seen her.

"I lost control of my powers, Avarielle." His eyes filled with tears. "I was terrified, having heard of your father's might and sword, and the second your mother turned the corner, you trailing behind her, I thought it was him. And my flames... they just... I just lost control." His voice wavered.

She said nothing, focusing on her breaths, on the creases around his eyes, the tremor of his voice.

"I looked into your eyes, and I saw what the war truly did. For the first time, like a daft old man. It left children without mothers, and scarred... I couldn't hurt you. They told me to leave no witnesses, but I'd already gone too far. I'd already lost the war by taking your mother's life." Energy deserted him. "And part of me always wondered what happened to that little girl, the shock turning to grief on her face. Until I met you, and you protected Cassara. I'd never felt like life had come more full circle, or had mocked me more."

Another coughing fit, arms shaking too much to take the glass of water. Avarielle pushed herself up to the bed, gently held his head, and brought the glass to his lips. He drank slowly, barely anything, body wracked by coughs and rattling. That rattling that filled the lungs before choking life. She'd heard it often enough, her life always in the shadows of death.

And there she comforted the man who'd killed her mother, finding herself unable to hate him. Twenty years earlier, she would have run him through. Now? Life just didn't seem as clear. And he'd made different choices then, to become someone she'd counted as a friend.

"Thank you for telling me." She helped him lie back down. It wouldn't be long, and she intended to make sure he was surrounded by family, not by her. "There's a saying in the West," she said, his slitted eyes focused on her. "*The shadows are richest before the sun sets.* And yours are rich and long-reaching, Carsyn, and I will remember my friendship with you, and honor what you've told me this day. You leave for the Afterfate with a friend in me."

He opened his mouth to say something, but no sound came out. He held out his hand and they grasped wrists with what little strength he had left.

She stood and walked out of the room.

"You should go in," she told Kaden and Pakana, both seated at the cozy kitchen table. "It won't be long." They stood, Pakana's eyes wide, terrified of losing him. Kaden walked more slowly, used to the cadence of death, knowing speed would change nothing and that everything had already been said.

Avarielle stepped out of the house, away from the stench of death, gulping in fresh air.

It had been forty years, and never once had she wept for her mother, part of her trapped in that moment, coils of shock and pain around her heart. As she heard Pakana's sobs from within, Avarielle found those coils loosening, and she finally found the tears for her mother. And then, she even found some of her old friend, Carsyn, whom she would remember as brave, grouchy, and loyal to Cassara.

And strong enough to tell his truth, in the end, knowing it would change nothing for him but it might change everything for Avarielle. Kaden joined her, sitting beside her silently, the two looking up at the constellations slowly moving overhead, marking the unstoppable passage of time.

38

*B*rick walls cast large shadows on the dirt street. Shirina followed the trail, invisible to regular eyes but not necessarily to those with the Sight. Green magic winked in and out of existence, an effective —and almost successful—means of hiding their tracks.

She didn't really have a plan, taking a page from Avarielle's book. She needed answers and didn't want to risk any of her adepts in a simple scouting mission. She hoped it would be a simple scouting mission, anyway. She'd already lost Feylam and wasn't ready to sacrifice anyone else. Whether that was strength or weakness right now, she simply didn't care.

A breeze ruffled her cloak, which danced silently behind her, sound also muffled by her spell. She'd been following the rebel for two hours now, walking down the streets of Massir, beautifully set stonework and cobblestone streets left behind long before for muddy bricks and dirt as she headed down the hill that held Massir. The sun would soon reach high noon, but she doubted this place ever lacked shadows.

Shirina slowed her pace, spotting her prey. The rebel stopped, looked around with cunning eyes. Shirina had stayed far enough back so as not to be spotted. Maintaining her spell for so long had sapped some of the strength she'd hoped to keep for the upcoming battle, but she couldn't risk being spotted, either.

She hoped to catch Elder Tally by surprise, though the chances of that were not necessarily high. It was still a risk she was willing to take. She wished Avarielle were there with her, or Cassara with her magic. But she had made her choice, and now she had to live with it.

Hopefully live with it.

Shaking her head, she cleared her mind, focused on her breath and the movement before her, and followed the rebel down a cramped, dark alleyway that reeked of urine, the rebel pausing to pet a few felines. One of them looked toward Shirina and hissed at her. The sorceress paused, as did the rebel. The cat scampered away, and the rebel looked long and hard toward Shirina.

For a moment, Shirina wondered if the rebel could see her, with her green flames. That was a possibility, after all, though from the little Shirina knew, the green flames were wild, untamed magic, mostly created to destroy instead of manipulating the strands of power.

Apparently deciding no danger lurked there, she knelt, touched the ground before her. With closed eyes she chanted an incantation. A simple opening spell, teachable to even new Green Circles. So, she had some training, though the Sight only came to Crimson Circles, so Shirina wasn't worried.

Pebbles hovered up and the ground before the rebel vanished, stairs leading down below. Shirina waited a few moments after the rebel headed down the stairs and then quickly followed, slipping in before the spell reset.

Careful not to slip down the uneven stone steps, Shirina used her Sight, intent on avoiding potential warning spells. A soft glow greeted her at the bottom of the stairs, the lights following the rebel as she walked down a narrow corridor. Shirina paused, looked at the lights, recognizing them. They were the same lights that had graced Ravenhold, which would follow individuals around until dismissed.

With a softly spoken spell, Shirina ensured the lights would not follow her.

She paused a moment longer, not for fear of being caught but rather to try to work through what she'd just witnessed. The lights of Ravenhold were old, so much so that people often assigned intention and personality to their movements. In Ravenhold's final moments before crashing down into the sea, Shirina had witnessed the franticness of the lights as they urged her to move faster lest she be caught in the Keep's destructive wake.

No one knew who had cast the original spell or how to replicate it. They had been with Ravenhold since its inception, before Graydon's time, even.

Yet there it they were, unmistakable. Intent on not letting her prey escape, Shirina picked up her pace. The passageway took her to more stairs, some leading up, some down. Corridors led to darkness in both directions, and although she really wanted to see how far this network of underground channels reached, she kept following the rebel. Whoever had constructed this place had done so with some planning, some chaos, and a lot of power.

Walls were chiseled clean without any signs of tools, rendered smooth by magic or some other force she wasn't familiar with.

"Welcome home, child." Shirina recognized the grating voice.

Slowly, she peeked around the corner, to where Elder Tally greeted the young woman. The Elder looked right at her, and Shirina did not fool herself into thinking she hadn't been seen. Still, she waited, meeting her gaze, staying cloaked in her spell.

"Now go change," she told the young woman.

"But I have much to tell you." Eagerness dripped from her voice.

Shirina raised an eyebrow. Tally narrowed her eyes, focused on Shirina.

"Soon, I promise. There's something I must tend to first."

The young woman didn't seem to understand, but she took off, looking annoyed.

"I see you're just as good now as you were then with

students," Shirina said, not bothering to remove her spell. Should another rebel be around, there was no need to make this easier for them to harm her.

"And you're just as foolish as ever," the Elder replied. She shook her head. "I gave you the chance to serve the greatest master of them all, and what did you do? You killed an Elder with brute force. Some Crimson Circle Elite."

"I will never bow to Siabala. Why do you continue serving an imprisoned master? He's not even corporeal anymore. His head was lopped off his body, in case you missed it."

This had the desired effect, Elder Tally hissing at her, her skin blotchy red.

Good, Shirina thought. *Let her get so angry she forgets herself and tells me more than intended.* Shirina's mentor never thought much of Tally, and that belief had been justified and Tally's weakness exploited by Siabala.

"That Grayloft could have been the general to his armies, marching on to Graydon and victory," she spat. "Instead, she turned on him, like a dog biting his master."

"I doubt Avarielle would enjoy that description," Shirina said, "but I see. You're angry she was favored by Siabala, and not you."

At that, Tally grew still. Shirina observed, waiting. If she knew why she hunted Avarielle, she might be able to figure out the rest of her plan. Any detail could build the tower of logic upon which her plan rested.

"How do you do it, Shirina?" Tally asked, her voice distressingly soft and, even more disturbingly, present.

"How do I do what?" Shirina asked, not liking the calm presence in the Elder's eyes.

"How do you go on, knowing there's nowhere left for you to go? Knowing that you'll never make Elder, never walk in Ravenhold again, and that your so-called Circle is overshadowed by every single magical force in existence?"

She struck close to home, and Shirina took a deep breath, forced her emotions to stay contained. Then a plan took hold, and she glanced down, for just a split second, to show uncertainty. Tally bit.

"You could have a place here," Tally said. "You and your adepts could finally know true power, instead of using the dribs and drabs left behind by Graydon."

Shirina narrowed her eyes. If she looked too eager, even Tally would clue in. "I can't just abandon everything I hold dear and know to be true." And then she looked at Tally expectantly. And the Elder looked back at her.

"I bet the Grayloft would come to me if I had you in my grip," she cooed. Shirina's eyebrow shot up, but she grew worried for the first time. In all the scenarios she'd imagined, she'd never once considered being used as bait for Avarielle.

The stupid warrior was noble enough that she'd feel the need to rescue her, too.

Shirina fed her frustration and worry for Avarielle into her next words. "Why will you never let me into your plans, Tally? You keep asking me to give up everything to serve your master, but I still don't understand what you want from me or how your Circle works."

"I will teach you everything if you stay here."

"You know I won't do that," Shirina said, then her eyes flickered to the dark cloak behind Tally's red robe. Red for Siabala. Black for the Elder.

"You still want the power," Tally cackled. "I knew it! Tanja always said you were driven, not ambitious. I could never figure out how these two things could be different from one another. And now I know they can't be. Tanja always tried to fool me with her haughty airs. I'm glad she's dead."

Shirina's jaw hurt, locked hard. Her mentor had died trying to protect Graydon. She'd been killed at the hands of Siabala, but by the Circle.

"I know you'll leave," Elder Tally said, "but there will come a time where you will need me. Where you'll have no one else to turn to except me. And when that time comes, come to me, and I shall answer your questions."

"Why should I trust you?"

"Because no one else can answer the questions you have, Crimson Circle Elite, and when I'm gone, no one will ever be able to."

The truth of her words pierced Shirina. But, deep down, Shirina knew that was why she'd chosen to come, and by herself. She'd come there to face the Elder and ask questions of her. To know more about the power of the Circle and how she could use it.

"How do I become Elder?" Shirina asked softy, hating

that she had to. But some magical secrets and powers were simply out of her grasp. She didn't care about the cloak color or the title. She just wanted answers and the power to help Graydon and the Circle.

"You must be mentored by another Elder from your coven, Shirina," she cooed. "You know that. And as I'm the only Elder left…"

Shirina pointed to her robes. "We are no longer from the same coven."

"We are," Tally said. "My robes may be red and my magic from Siabala, but my learning is from Ravenhold. You need me, Shirina, much more than I need you." Her eyes shone, and she managed to look down at Shirina, despite a shorter stature. "You will be swept away in tides of blood, Shirina, you and all of your adepts. Don't they deserve the chance to choose survival?"

"Siabala is survival?" Shirina scoffed. "That's not how I remember it."

"That's because you allied yourself with the wrong magic, Shirina. How could you understand what you lack when you've never gleaned what it's like to be complete?"

Tally moved her hand, a simple gesture. Shirina braced herself as magical strands danced toward her, dark and red, blood and death. She recognized the magic as Siabala's, and her stomach plummeted.

"How…"

"Because I'm an Elder, Shirina, and I know things about magic that you'll never understand." The hairs on

Shirina's arms stood on end, and she took a step back. "And you'll not live long enough to learn them, either."

She unleashed her magic, the spell held in her bracers surprising Tally. *Good.* The Elder wasn't the only one with surprises. Her teleportation spell shimmered around her as the black and red strands mixed in, trying to wound her.

Shirina had anticipated the green flames, not Siabala's magic, but still her magical filters worked just as well as she pulled them through both bracers, using them to strengthen her spell. Tally's shout echoed as she tried to rip Shirina's spell to shreds.

She would have succeeded, had another strand of magic not been waiting for her.

Shala. The familiar magic called to her, like a rope pulling her from thick mud. Their magics mixed, and Shirina let Shala, and then other witches from her coven, pull her free of Tally's grasp. The Elder had not anticipated this move. The Circle had not shared magic like this before, expecting the individual to survive on will and strength alone.

Shirina had said she would build a different Circle, and she had, appearing back in Massir's royal garden, to the chant of four adepts.

"Thank you," Shirina gulped.

"What was that?" Shala asked, looking at the whisps of magic.

"Our call to battle," Shirina said. "I must speak with

Queen Cassara. Assemble all Circle adepts in Massir to the castle. I will speak with them after."

Shala nodded, but Shirina could see even her pupil was nervous. Shirina placed a hand on her shoulder, steadying her, and looked at each assembled adept in turn.

"It's nothing we won't be able to face together," she reassured them. "We have prepared for this."

They nodded, taking her at her word.

Just as she hoped that she hadn't lied to them, the ground shook, and a large *crack* echoed across the air. For a moment, everyone held their breath. Then the Unity Tower began to topple sideways, to screams below.

Without pausing to think or plan, Shirina ran toward the noise, hoping against hope that Cassara hadn't been in the middle of it, knowing full well that she probably was.

39

The air smelled off to Cassara. A strange tang, nothing she could quite put her finger on. She once again wished she had the Sight, then pushed down her frustration and focused on what power she did have.

"We have delegates from various sections of the city coming to meet with us over the next few days," Cassara told Altessa and Rojon, both following her in the barely risen day, getting prepared for a long day. Her daughter trailed her eagerly, while Rojon proved a bit more restrained. "We'll have them in small meetings instead of a big assembly, to reduce risks of attacks. We also must attend the funerals of those who passed in the original attack."

"Are they not yet buried?" Rojon asked, surprised.

"No," Cassara said. "Well, they've been cremated, and their ashes will be released by their families."

"Oh," Rojon said. Cassara glanced curiously at him. "In

Elihor"—he flushed at the look—"we bury the dead so that trees may be nourished from them for generations to come."

"That's beautiful," Cassara said. "In Edoline, my home kingdom, we bury people in crypts, a home for the afterlife."

"So, what do you want Rojon and me to do?" Altessa asked, cutting in, impatient.

Cassara stopped, sighed, and turned to face them.

"I know it's been a lot." She focused on both, then turned to her daughter. "And you want to do something, so I'm involving you, though many would prefer I didn't. But you must remember your patience, Altessa. Hot heads will only make things worse."

"They're the ones who attacked *us*." Altara crossed her arms.

"The rebels attacked us, yes," Cassara said. "And we won't find answers unless we connect closer to our people and get to the root of it. Our heads must remain calm so that we don't enflame an already-deadly situation."

"So, you want us to basically smile in the background?"

She loved her eldest but sometimes wanted to smack her.

"No, I want you to listen and pay attention. You might see things that I do not, and it's good for us to look united. And to *listen*."

"Won't my presence hurt the talks? I'm not at all from Graydon," Rojon said.

"I considered that," Cassara admitted. The youth's

completely black eyes and red hair were different in both lands, and according to Avarielle, he stood out no matter where he went. "But I'd like you there, too. You hold no preconceptions here and so might see things that Altessa and I might miss. I would value your opinion, Rojon."

"Thank you." He flushed at the compliment.

"Wouldn't it be more effective if we took the army and rooted out the rebels?" Altessa asked. Cassara felt her patience slip, patience that she would need for a long day of talking with angry and frightened people.

"First, we don't know where they are. Second, we'd get citizens injured, basically sending the army to kill our own people. Some of which are veterans of our own armies, Altessa. Rash, unmeasured actions like that lead to civil wars, which would undo us all."

"I still think we should do more than talking," Altessa mumbled.

"We are," Cassara reminded her in a whisper.

"Not *us*." Altessa pointed to herself and Rojon. Cassara sighed. *Back to this.*

"Helping isn't aways about running into battle. Sometimes, it's about listening, Altessa. Now, come on, or we'll be late." First on the agenda were merchants from the lower city, who'd requested an earlier hour so they could tend to their shops during their regular hours. She'd been happy to oblige, though now she wished she could still be curled up in bed near Dayshon.

"They can wait for us," Altessa muttered, angry. "They attacked *us*."

"Stop it." The steel in Cassara's voice surprised Altessa and Rojon. "*They* did nothing except suffer their own losses. And yes, some of them might be rebels. But let them see us for how we are, Altessa. Unafraid, willing to listen, and *punctual.*"

She turned around, done with the conversation, taking deep breaths and grounding herself back into her surroundings. The base of the Unity Tower was beautiful, with elongated windows, purple carpets, silver trimmings.

The odd scent from earlier struck her. Her stomach turned, her head ached, her heart raced. The tang grew metallic, reminiscent of blood.

"Something's wrong," she said, uncertain why or where but knowing beyond a measure of a doubt that something terrible was about to happen.

"Wha—" Altessa barely got the word out before Cassara turned and grabbed their arms to drag them away.

Too late. The air stilled, her heart stopped racing, and she knew she was too late.

Air exploded outward from the nearby wall, something collapsing against the side of the tower, bricks and arches tumbling down, dust choking them, and Cassara pushed Altessa and Rojon away from the falling stone wall.

Her magic pulsed deep in her gut, but she fought it down, bit her cheek, and ran.

Too late.

*A*varielle jumped up, her skin burning as if on fire, her instincts screaming that something was wrong. Terribly wrong.

"What is it?" Kaden stood up slower, the old man having fallen asleep near her on the porch. Pakana joined them, the first time she'd exited the home since Carsyn's passing.

"I have to go," Avarielle hissed, with no knowledge of *why* she had to move, just knowledge that she had to. "Back to Massir."

Kaden squelched the thousands of questions that had been dancing in his eyes when she mentioned Massir. He suddenly understood as well as she did.

Cassara.

She'd never felt this way, in all their time being friends. Without another word, she started to stride toward the forest, in the direction of the Circle outpost.

"Wait," Kaden said, and Avarielle bit back the anger that bubbled within her. This wasn't her. The magic propelled her forward, forced her to move.

"Pakana will get you there faster," Kaden said, nodding to his daughter. Her face twisted in protest, stilled when Kaden placed a hand on hers. "Please," he said. "There is no greater way to repay Carsyn than to help those he loved. And that includes Cassara."

"How does this involve Cassara?" Pakana asked, suddenly intrigued. Kaden and Avarielle both kept silent, and she sighed.

"Give me a second," she said. "I just have to get him out." She grabbed a bucket and vanished in the forest.

"Kaden, I don't have the time..."

"This will be faster," he said. "Trust me. I wouldn't put Cassara's life in unnecessary danger, would I?"

"No," Avarielle admitted, though every fiber of her wanted her to run toward Massir, energy vibrating up and down her core. Standing still proved painful. The sun had barely risen, tall shadows creeping across Kosel.

"Has this ever happened before?" Avarielle barely heard him over the buzzing in her mind.

"No," she answered, then forced herself to grow still as he took hold of her arm, making sure she paid attention.

"It did to Carsyn and me once," he said. At that, she snapped at attention, focused on the clarity in his eyes. "When Prince Jayden returned to Graydon from Elihor. Our magic had never worked that way before, but suddenly he needed us, and we heard the call."

"The green flames helped you save Jayden," she whispered, the buzzing growing less intense.

"I don't think magic is good or bad," Kaden said. "It simply does what the wielder demands of it. And I know from experience that sometimes, that magic changes. In times of great need."

"Like the Days of Blood," Avarielle said.

"Like now, too, apparently," Kaden said, a hint of regret in his voice. He looked back toward the door to his home. "Carsyn would have hated more fuss."

Avarielle placed a comforting hand on his shoulder but glanced back to where Pakana had vanished.

"She'll be back shortly," Kaden said, "and it will be worth the wait. Avarielle." The hesitant way he said her name forced her to focus back on him. "You owe me nothing and I'm in no position to ask anything of you."

She wouldn't argue the point, but she did like the old guard, despite her better judgment.

"Pakana is gifted, and funny, and wise… and she's lived most of her life with two old men, taking care of a pub."

"She seems happy with her life."

"Soon, she'll be alone." Seeing her about to protest, he shook his head. "I'm not saying I'm imminently dying, but I'm two years older than Carsyn and closer to ninety than I'd care to admit. It's a numbers game; that's all."

"I'm not going to take care of your daughter," Avarielle said. "She seems plenty capable of doing so herself."

"She is," he acknowledged with a smile. "But if ever you're passing through these woods again, and you stop here… maybe tell her of the world outside. Maybe, and this is a big ask, but maybe encourage her to visit some of it. I don't want her to live her entire life in shadows, Avarielle."

"I make no promises," she said, "but I'll keep it in mind."

"That will do," he said, and before she could reply, a sound made her turn. A large lizard descended on them, brown and green skin disguised in the forest floor, shadows only making him even more impossible to spot. By instinct, she took a step before Kaden and pulled out Graysword.

"It's all right," Pakana said, her head popping above the reptile's face, grin wide. "This is Rolly. He can get us to the outpost in a third of the time you'd spend walking."

"I was planning on running," Avarielle said, not sure she trusted the sight of the beast. A forked tongue slipped out and licked a bug from its large, round green eye.

"Time's wasting," Pakana said, turning the lizard so Avarielle could climb behind her. Only a blanket covered the lizard. She'd ridden bareback on horses before, but she'd never ridden a lizard.

"Go make sure Cassara is all right," Kaden said. "I'd go if I could…"

"See that Carsyn's soul finds the Afterfate," Avarielle kindly said. Then she turned to the lizard, impressed with its height. She placed her hands on it and leapt up, eager to get going, swinging her legs open and staying on the blanket behind Pakana.

"You might want to hold on to me," she said, voice teasing.

Avarielle's hands slipped around her waist just as she somehow urged the lizard forward, sending a flying kiss to Kaden.

"I'll be back shortly. Get some sleep!" she said, and he waved her off, shaking his head.

The beast was fast, Avarielle had to admit, body hugging the forest floor, six muscled legs climbing stones and trees with ease. His entire body contracted around obstacles, and she barely felt a bump. The fresh forest air revitalized her, and the movement toward the outpost calmed her.

"What is this thing?" Avarielle asked. Looking up at the trees made her dizzy, they moved so quickly. She preferred horses, but was grateful for the speed of this creature.

"A colisso," she replied. "There aren't many left, and they live only in deep Kosel, where no one in their right mind lives. But this one was wounded and Kaden and I helped it. It took some doing, but the work was worth it."

"No kidding," Avarielle said. Despite its speed, she still willed the creature to go faster, to head toward Cassara as quickly as possible, hoping against hope that Shirina had everything under control.

And that Rojon was nowhere near them.

41

*A*ltessa tried to blink away the tears from her eyes, dust crowding out her senses, ears whistling. Her hand lay before her, covered in ash and blood.

Why is my hand there? she thought as she managed to move it, a jerky twitch that made her cry with relief. She couldn't feel it, but she could move it.

Slowly, she lifted her head, coughing on dust. The whole world tasted like dust.

Shouting. There was so much shouting, somewhere far away. Maybe not. Maybe it was close and her ears betrayed her. She pushed up, forced herself to sit up. To see what happened.

Arms wrapped around her, helping her up.

"Rojon?" she asked, voice laced with confusion.

"We have to go," he said. "They're coming!"

"Who?" she muttered, looked around, then she saw it.

A silver crown on the ground.

"Mom!" Snapped back to her senses, Altessa pushed herself up, Rojon urging her to move, but she followed the blood—*blood!*—leading from the crown to a section of collapsed wall. How had this happened? They'd just been walking. She'd been so mad. So intent on being heard. On being seen.

And now...

"Mom!" she screamed. A slender hand covered in dust. She knew those hands. They'd held her, kept her safe.

Where were the guards?

"Help me." Rojon didn't hesitate, throwing himself on the larger rocks to push them off Cassara. Her face was drawn, blood dribbling from her lips, skin gray from pain or blood loss. Her hair, usually so perfect, tumbled around her. The blue of her dress, now gray, grew dark with blood.

"Mom?" Altessa leaned down to make sure Cassara heard her. Her ears no longer rang, and she could hear a battle raging. She glanced up, unable to quite grasp everything happening around her. The guards fought in the nearby entrance, where they'd been headed. Green flames licked the edge of the stones, guards screaming as they were burned alive. Where was the Circle? They were supposed to protect her mother, weren't they?

"Altessa—"

"I won't leave her!"

"Okay." Rojon nodded, face grim with determination.

He bent down, put his arms under Cassara as gently as he could. Gingerly, he started to lift her, but her entire body convulsed, blood erupting from her lips. He put her down gently, dark eyes wide.

"We have to get her out of here," Altessa said, tears in her eyes. "Mom!" she screamed again.

Green flames grew closer. Rojon's own clothing was covered in Cassara's blood, and her mom rattled, chest heaving... and nothing. A guard fell nearby, arrow in his throat. Rojon jumped up, grabbed the man's sword, and moved gingerly to meet an attacker.

They were so close, and her mother... Altessa looked down, willing her mother's chest to move up and down.

"Mom?" Her voice was soft as she reached down with a finger to touch her pale and drawn face, and gently wake her up. Her skin touched Cassara's still-warm skin, and she felt the slow breath trapped in her.

"Altessa!" Rojon screamed as he was flung back, green flames burning his arm even as he fought off rebels, striking them with the now-shattered sword.

Her mother was dying. Rojon would die too. All because of what? What in the two worlds would this accomplish? She looked toward the rebels, eyes filling with tears, shaking with anger, thoughts growing clearer.

She wanted them gone. She wanted them dead. And she wanted Rojon and her mother to live.

For the first time in her life, it wasn't the castle walls holding her in, as she'd always thought. It was some other wall inside of her. And it crumbled under the weight of her need to do something, anything, to stop the attack.

She touched the magic of Graydon, anxious to be courted by another of Graydon's descendants.

Her world exploded in light.

42

The magic of Graydon buckled, strands of white magic twisting into shadows, writhing like dying snakes. Something was wrong. Very wrong. And Shirina knew exactly what was happening.

Cassara. She was calling on the magic of Graydon. The Wall of Loss would fall if she did so.

"Protect Cassara at all costs," she told the witches running after her, her crimson cloak in a flurry as she turned the corner into the northern tower, and immediately had to shield her eyes. Magic exploded in light, as though the entirety of Graydon's powers had slammed this room. She'd seen this before, when Cassara had called it all to her.

Grunts. Screams cut short. The scent of burning flesh. And she saw one of the rebels burn in white magic, his skin turning to ashes before he'd even collapsed.

Breath catching in her throat, Shirina spotted

Cassara's broken body on the ground, blood pooling beneath her. Her life force ebbed away, and with it, the magic of Graydon danced wildly. But it wasn't Cassara who held the magic. It was Altessa, kneeling in her mother's blood, head snapped back, arms straight at her sides, magic wild and uncontrolled.

"Stay back," Shirina ordered her witches, and headed into the light.

43

A sea of light engulfed Altessa, drowning her in fire, power, hopes, and dreams. Washed over her with the stench of ashes and blood as her knees grew cold in her mother's blood.

"My mother is dead," Altessa said to the sky, looking up where a ceiling had been but moments before, the top half of the tower crumbled around her. Without looking back down, tears warm on her face, she let those fires wash out from her, into the rebels who had killed her mother. The white mists around her fed her, and she let herself drift on them, watching the life of the rebels leave their bodies, destroying their souls.

She'd done that. Killed. And she didn't regret it. She wanted more blood, to find whoever led them and destroy them.

"My mother is dead," she repeated to the sky, unable to fully understand a world without Cassara's steady presence by her side. The arguments, the laughter, the frustrations, all wrapped in the love of the woman who'd brought her into this world.

"She's not dead yet," a crisp voice said, "but she will be if you don't release the magic."

Slowly, she lowered her head. Shirina knelt on the other side of her mother, red blood on white robes, hands on her mother, as though she intended to hold her together herself if necessary.

"Shirina." The name grounded her. The familiar features. "It's keeping us safe, Shirina. Why would I let the magic go?"

"The magic is too powerful, Altessa, and if you keep using so much of it, I won't be able to use it to heal your mother."

She blinked, examined at Shirina, sought the truth in her eyes. She looked tired. Exhausted. And something she'd never seen in the leader of Ravenhold's Circle: she looked afraid.

"Please, Altessa."

"You can heal her?"

"I can," Shirina said, "but first you must trust me. You know how to use magic, Altessa. I've trained you for this. You need to close the dams of power."

Her whole life, she'd studied something she couldn't touch. Her whole life, her mother had insisted she learn. For this moment. She closed her eyes, imagined those dams shutting, the magic fighting against her, lashing out at her. She cried out, clutched her arms, and folded on herself.

"There's too much magic. I can't. I don't know how."

"You do." Shirina's tones weren't gentle. "You do, and you must. Your mother could do it, and so can you."

Her mother could do it. Her mother *had* done it. All the times she thought her mother was choosing to simply talk instead of act... if she could do it, then so could Altessa.

She opened her eyes, unfolded herself, and met Shirina's eyes.

"You can do this," Shirina repeated. "You must."

Altessa nodded, nausea creeping up her throat. Magic lanced through her arms and legs, her gut, her head, until she thought she would throw up. Cold sweat trickled down her face and back, and when she felt at her weakest, her vision doubling, she managed to lock the magic away. Her hands shook, her mouth was dry, and she fought not to slump forward. She'd never wanted more for her mother to hold her in her arms.

Shirina touched her face and chanted a few words, and Altessa sensed walls erecting around her, guarding her from the magic.

"This will keep you safe from the overflow of magic," she said, and Altessa wanted to know why she needed to be kept safe from something she needed so desperately. Something she craved above all else.

"I can heal my mother," Altessa said. "I have the power." Her voice was distant. Faint. Coming from somewhere not entirely her own.

"Let me do it," Shirina said, hands already glowing on Cassara. "Healing spells are tricky and require time. Let the guards escort you to safety, Altessa." The sorceress looked toward her, and in her eyes Altessa saw something else she'd never once seen in the twenty years she'd known her.

Uncertainty.

Altessa nodded, swallowed hard. She glanced to the side, trying to see Rojon. He stood nearby, though his left arm was badly wounded. In his right he held a sword. He spoke with a few guards while they checked on the fallen rebels. He caught her looking at him, and they locked eyes. He read something in hers and came to join them, standing near. As though keeping watch. A role his mother would have assumed, had she been there.

"I'll stay with my mother, please," she said. "I promise I won't do anything."

Shirina studied her and then nodded. The sorceress's features were already drained. Shala joined her, mixing healing spells, her mother's skin turning less ashen.

"You can hold her hand, Altessa," Shirina said. "Comfort her."

Altessa bit back the tears that threatened to overwhelm her. A moment before, she'd been in control of the world, could see and touch everything around her. Now she was scared, felt so small, and just wanted her mother to hold her. But her mother couldn't, and all Altessa could do to help was hold her limp hand.

She didn't know how long she stayed kneeling in the

blood, but by the time Shirina and Shala stopped casting their spell, Shala could barely stand.

"Rojon," Shirina said, holding out a hand to him, who still stood by Altessa, keeping her safe.

"I'll heal you next," she said, her words long and languid.

He shook his head. "You're exhausted. Save your strength in case another attack comes."

Shirina opened her mouth and closed it again, as though too tired to argue. She did find the energy to give him a slight smile.

"You remind me of your mother," she simply said. "Bring Queen Cassara to her chambers, carefully. I'll take a short rest and then heal her some more."

Captain Tralin brought four guards with a stretcher. Altessa noticed they were surrounded by guards, and that the sun shone through cracks in the tower. The sky had been so bright when filled with magic. With a tired sweep of the head, she looked around, at the burnt remains being carried away.

I did that. The numbness evaporated, and she feared she'd be sick.

"Come on," Rojon said kindly, as though sensing her distress. She let him help her up, even though he was the one sporting a bandaged arm. The guards gently placed her mother on a stretcher and carried her to their home, the way lined with guards and Circle witches.

Shirina followed slowly, standing tall and proud, though she looked like she was about to collapse.

Altessa focused on her mother, on the hand gently resting on her chest, and how it rose with each breath. In that sight Altessa found she could breathe again and allowed herself to lean in to Rojon's strength more. The world had felt so big and now felt so small.

She wanted to conquer it, to run away from it, and she couldn't even talk to her mother about it, the one person who might understand what she was going through.

44

They reached the outpost within minutes, saving Avarielle an impressive amount of time. The sun had broken the horizon as they traveled, and the lizard's skin turned brighter green in the morning light.

Avarielle's urgency had turned hollow, like something had been cut from her, only to return as a slight buzzing. Between that and the lizard's movement, she'd started to feel sick, and focused on taking deep gulps of forest air.

"Do you think Cassara is in danger?" Pakana asked as they slid off the beast. He squeaked once and she gave him some kind of treat before he vanished into the forest again.

"I don't know," she said, "but maybe."

"I've never met her," she said, "though Carsyn and Kaden spoke of her so much that I feel like I know her. Like she's the sister I never met."

"Well, someday you might," Avarielle said absentmindedly as an Orange Circle witch approached.

"I need to get back to Massir." Her voice left no room for disagreement. "Now."

The witch looked like she might protest, but one more look into Avarielle's eyes and she decided against it.

Smart.

"Be careful," Pakana said.

"Thanks for the ride." Out of respect for Kaden, Avarielle added, "If ever you're in my neck of the woods, let me know."

"I will," she whispered, and Avarielle followed the Orange Circle back into the camp.

"What's happened?" the Orange Circle, hair red like drying blood, asked in quiet tones.

"I need to get back to Massir," Avarielle said, blood flaming.

"I can take you," she said.

"What about Pol?" Avarielle asked, not keen on trusting another witch with her safety. Shirina had trusted Pol, and so Avarielle was inclined to trust him.

"He's still exhausted," she said. "It would be dangerous for him to attempt the jump so quickly."

Avarielle's instincts warred within her, part of her screaming caution, but a louder, more important part of her screaming to go to Massir, like a knife planted in her gut and turning slowly.

"Step close to me," the witch said, "and don't activate your magic until we've reappeared."

"I know the drill," Avarielle hissed, "now get me there."

The witch nodded, began chanting, magic enrobing them both, the sight of the tall pines of Kosel vanishing into the light. Avarielle took deep breaths, preparing herself for whatever battle awaited her.

Blood pumped in her limbs, her thoughts were focused, her breathing relaxed, her body ready to move as needed, for as long as needed. Another deep breath, and the scent of junipers, acrid and unexpected, struck her nostrils, as they hit another outpost and kept teleporting.

They hadn't encountered juniper on their journey there and so should not on their way back.

They were not going to Massir. Wherever the witch was taking her, it wasn't Massir.

"Where are you taking us?" she hissed at the witch right beside her. She didn't answer, maintaining her spell, but a slight smile crept onto her lips.

Avarielle had been captured before, an experience she didn't care to replicate.

"Which do you think will be worse," the warrior asked casually, voice diffused by the surrounding magic, "me using my magic, or me stabbing you through?"

The witch's smile vanished and her eyes grew wide. Without waiting for her answer, the warrior took hold of Graysword and called its magic forth, the power creeping down the blade and surging into her hand, up her arm.

"No!" the witch screamed as her spell collapsed. Air sucked out of their immediate surroundings, sound crushing Avarielle's skull for a second before they were catapulted out of the spell, Avarielle hitting something hard before managing to land on her feet.

What in the two lands did I just hit? Blood poured in her mouth and crumbled stones lay at her feet. She'd hit a wall, hard, taking half of it out. And breaking her bones as well. The magic of Graysword started to heal her quickly, keeping her in one piece while she fought to get her bearings. In the distance, to the south, she could see Massir, the towering palace of silver and white surrounded by dark walls, a vain attempt to withstand another attack.

Avarielle looked to see the witch but couldn't find her. She spat blood, wished her ears would stop ringing, and crouched low as she headed into the fields, using tall wheat to hopefully hide her tracks as she made her way back to Cassara, the call of her need outweighing the ringing in Avarielle's ears.

Shafts of wheat danced in the breeze, the morning light treacherous. Keeping low as she ran, Graysword burning her palm, she didn't dare to leave the sword in its sheath, in case a split second might save her life.

The Circle witch might have lived, and she'd spent a lifetime studying their abilities. A Crimson Circle could use the Sight and easily detect magic. Avarielle's magic would remain hidden from the Sight of a witch of Ravenhold, but she wasn't certain this witch was from Shirina's coven.

Shirina. She needed to warn her of the treachery. She hoped the witch kept her wits about her and protected

Cassara. Moving in zigzags to throw off anyone trying to pursue her, Avarielle tried to balance speed to her target with difficulty of tracking.

A rustling to her left and Avarielle dove. Fires erupted above her head, missing her by a hair, the wheat bursting into flames. Her side exploded in pain, one or two of her ribs definitely fractured. Gritting her teeth, she flung a dagger where the flames had erupted, not bothering to make sure she'd hit her mark. For all she knew, there was more than one witch hunting her, and hunting them all down would use up too much of her time.

Clutching Graysword and calling its magic to give her muscles speed and to heal her, she raced past the quickly spreading fire, the dry fields going up like kindling. This was the last thing Massir needed, but there was little Avarielle could do except keep moving, stay ahead of the flames, and hope the fire would be contained.

Surely, someone would soon notice the orange-and-red glow and the rising smoke? Her feet slid on the edge of a ditch, and she pushed herself off the edge onto the other edge in a bid not to fall, the brown water at the bottom thick and muddy. A break in the wheat might help contain the fire but not for long.

Avarielle heard splashing and looked down the ditch. Something big headed her way, powerful legs pounding soft earth, slipping but not slowing down, mud flying up. She'd never seen anything like it. Skin sickly pale and without fur, nose more like a pig but jaw like a wolf, the yellow eyes close enough for Avarielle to see the red veins throbbing in them.

Eli's tits. She knelt, planted Graysword in the ground before her, and pulled out her bow, firing two shots. Arrows stuck out of its large chest, above two of its powerful legs, but it didn't slow.

She dropped the bow and grabbed Graysword in one smooth motion, using her momentum to bring the blade across the creature's legs. The magic ignited and the creature screamed, a shrill not unlike a pig in slaughter, and it collapsed.

But only for a split second. It scrambled back up, spit flying from its teeth as it snarled at Avarielle. The clean cuts on its legs were already healing, its mouth frothing.

Great. At its speed, it could run her down easily enough. She hoped it wasn't that smart as she dove back into the wheat. The creature leapt after her. Avarielle moved back several paces to let it pass, blinded by the wheat, and this time, she sliced its side, pushing the blade deep into its flesh, Graysword's flames plunging into it, stinking of overcooked pork by the time it collapsed on the ground. It didn't move. Avarielle wanted to look at it more closely, but the fire had crossed the ditch and ignited the wheat around her.

Without a glance back, she crouched and kept running, keeping an eye out for witches or monsters, the burning wheat crackling behind her and annoyingly loud.

In the distance she could see Massir's great towers. She blinked, looked up. Had one of them collapsed?

Before she could figure it out, something large hurtled into her out of nowhere, knocking the wind out of her and throwing Graysword from her grasp. A large and surprisingly silent boar, with six eyes on each side of its head and three sets of large tusks, snarled over her.

"Your choice," the Circle witch said, stepping out from behind the boar. She sounded hurt, but apparently not hurt enough. "You stay down or you die fighting."

She started chanting. If she'd known anything about Avarielle, she'd have known that was hardly a choice. Hand held out, she called on Graysword, the weapon returning to her grasp. She twisted the blade up and jammed it into the beast's mouth and through its brain. She'd been quick but not quick enough, its smaller tusks ripping out part of her shoulder. Avarielle gritted her teeth and ignored the pain, pulling her sword free and rolling away from the witch as the beast fell.

She pushed herself up, Graysword before her to run the witch through. With a look of victory on her face, the witch finished her spell. Avarielle felt the magic materialize around her, a strange tingling but nothing more.

Without bothering to inform her that Graydon's magic didn't work on her, Avarielle thrust her sword toward the witch, intent on ending her before she had another idea, but a wall of force shoved into her from her left and sent her to her knees.

"Graydon's magic doesn't work on her," a coarse voice said. "But there are other ways to skin an oath breaker."

A warlock walked out of the woods, black cloak billowing, white robes turning dark red. Siabala's Circle. She didn't know this warlock, or this Elder, and her stomach dropped. They'd vastly underestimated the size and strength of this second Circle.

"Queen Cassara is dead." He cocked his head, waiting for her to react. She fought against her rage but knew he lied. Were that true, the Wall of Loss would have crumbled. Siabala would have made himself known already. She glanced toward Massir, now clearly seeing the missing tower, smoke lazily wafting up.

Rojon.

Four other witches and warlocks surrounded her, and more creatures stalked the wheat, rustles and shadows. Fire raged all around them, avoiding them in whatever magical circle kept them safe.

Avarielle really wished Shirina were there but was also relieved that she was with Cassara. She would keep her safe.

"No witty words?" the Elder said. "I heard you liked being witty. I expected more repartee."

"I save it for better company," Avarielle said, not liking her odds. Siabala's magic was like hers and could hurt her. She couldn't cut down all the adepts before they killed her. And the creatures obviously obeyed their orders. Not to mention the wall of fire surrounding them.

No, Avarielle didn't like these odds at all.

"We could try to make a deal with you," he said, almost regretfully. "We've heard so many fine things about you."

"Oh?"

"We heard you were… impressive."

Avarielle's mouth grew dry. *Impressive.* That was what Siabala had called her after weeks of torture, his voice still rumbling sometimes in her nightmares, the pain of old wounds haunting her on rainy or cold days.

Impressive.

She focused on the Elder. "Then you must have also heard how hard I am to kill." She kept her voice low, relaxing her hold on Graysword. "And how I don't like to play games."

"I have," he said, looking disappointed, like a child not allowed to keep his favorite toy. Avarielle shifted her foot and lunged at him, intent on at least taking out the Elder. He held out his hand, without chanting, and a force snatched her, held her above the ground, crushing her bones. She gasped and gritted her teeth, looking down at him with hatred. She'd felt this before, too. This power of Siabala, somehow freed from the Wall.

How had they gotten his power? The Circles were supposed to be watching it! She didn't trust them, but she trusted Shirina. She glanced toward the tower, willing her friends and her son to stay safe. Her family.

The Elder followed her gaze.

"Of course, you know she's not actually dead," he said casually. "Not yet, anyway. We know Queen Cassara's magic is what's keeping up the Wall of Loss. We're just biding our time until Lord Siabala is ready."

Avarielle slowly turned her head toward him, hatred

pumping in her limbs but still unable to break free, wanting to tear the look of victory from his eyes. They knew. They knew Cassara was the key. And she was powerless to warn them.

She tasted blood in her mouth. "Siabala won't need you anymore once the Wall is down, and he'll crush your puny lives. I hope he makes it painful."

For a second, his eyes narrowed, like he considered her words. Then his mouth broke into a dark smile.

"And that's a glory I'll unflinchingly witness, unlike you, oath breaker."

The pressure increased. Avarielle tried to break free, to push back, but couldn't. Air escaped her lungs and couldn't be refilled, and something snapped and popped. Avarielle gasped, looked once more toward Massir.

Be safe.

Grayword tumbled to the ground, its blade dark and silent.

45

*S*hirina sat in a dark corner of Cassara's room, needing rest but unable to tear herself away from her sleeping friend. She'd almost lost her. After years of preparing for the inevitable, it had almost come to pass, and she hadn't been there to help.

Her tired mind spun and grasped at the details of the day, trying to make sense of the chain of events that had brought them there, to Cassara's near-death.

Near-death. She took a deep breath, tried to focus her thoughts, like the Elders had taught her to do years ago.

May your steps be steady and your thoughts heavy.

She didn't believe in the mantra anymore, having seen Ravenhold crash down into the sea, and it was taught more as a piece of history than necessity to new adepts. But she'd learned to tap into magic with these words, and they helped still her mind.

Cassara's chest rose steadily, three adepts having

pumped all their healing magic into her. Altessa was in her own room, having locked herself in there. She'd used magic. Graydon's magic. Shirina would have to speak with her once they'd both rested.

Another deep breath. Shirina's hands rested on her lap, forming fists. She willed her fingers to untangle and loosen, stopped looking at Cassara's sleeping form, and closed her eyes.

Slowly, as though meandering in a garden, Shirina retraced the steps that had led them all there.

First, Avarielle's home had been attacked, as had she. Shirina had brought her to Cassara, imagining the attacks might come for her, too. Intent on protecting her.

She forced her growing frown to release, took more deep breaths, let go of the thought that she'd doomed them all.

Cassara was attacked right after they arrived.

No. She'd been attacked *as* they arrived. Had that been coincidence? They could have killed Cassara and Dayshon but hadn't. That had bothered her, but she hadn't had time to coddle her worries.

They'd followed the green flames, sending Avarielle to Kosel. Then the rebel had escaped.

Right after Avarielle left.

Was that coincidence? This time, Shirina didn't even notice her frown. Shirina had then followed the rebel, as had been the plan all along.

And, when she'd returned, the next attack had started. And the Elder could have probably made more of an effort to stop her. Unless... unless Tally was testing her. Or something about her.

A hollow formed in her chest, filled with iron as she forced deep breaths in and out. She needed to objectively look at the facts.

Attacks occurred after they made a move of some sort, as though someone waited for the proper pieces to be in place before unleashing the next attack. Like someone orchestrated all of this.

Slowly, her eyes drifted back to Cassara. Her mind spun with possibilities, each worse than the last. She felt like she had to act quickly, but also desperately needed to wait and think things through. She closed her eyes, dizzy from fatigue. She needed to ponder this with a fresh mind, but could she afford the time?

There were three linchpins, as far as Shirina could see: Cassara, Avarielle, and herself.

The three who had stood against Siabala.

But why let them live at all? Why let Cassara live when her life could have so easily been claimed? What had they been testing of her Circle? And why attack Avarielle?

She opened her eyes, turned to the window. A field burned far from town. Her witches would have to try to help put it out. She should tell them.

Despite wanting to move to help stop this calamity from impacting the still recovering food supplies, Shirina stayed rooted, staring at those flames, a deep sense of dread crushing her ability to move.

She needed to make sure Avarielle was all right. And

she needed to make sure now. She finally found the strength to move, though it took her a few moments of unsteadiness before she could take her first steps.

"I won't be far," she told the unconscious Cassara, and then swept out of the room, her thoughts still crashing into each other but her worry bubbling over into the need for action, trying to ignore the fear that she continued walking to their enemy's beat.

46

A timid knock at the door of Altessa's room. She shifted her head slightly but didn't answer, remaining seated by the window, legs pressed against her chest, her knees a convenient place to hide her face.

She'd used magic. And she'd killed people, turned them into burning carcasses of who they'd once been. It had been self-defense, but she couldn't help but think it had been murder, too. Her mother had rarely spoken of the magic she'd once used, but she'd described it as warm and comforting. She'd helped protect all of Graydon with it, keeping her people safe.

Altessa's magic had been anything but comforting. It had burned, and unleashed darkness within her that she hadn't even known existed. And she hadn't been scared of it. In fact, she'd relished it and had wanted more of it. She would happily drown in it.

Seeing her mother there, dying... she'd wanted to burn them all down. She would have, too, if not for Shirina.

The knock sounded again, this time a bit more forceful.

"Go away," Altessa mumbled, mouth against her knees.

"I'm coming in," Rojon said. "I just want to make sure you're all right." His voice was a comforting whisper. He hesitated at the door, then closed it and pulled a chair beside her bed and sat down.

"You're not supposed to simply walk into a princess' room like that," she said, peeking over her knees at him. A cut lined his cheek, and his arm was in bandages. He wore clothing from Graydon, not Elihor, and the loose slacks, freshly pressed light shirt, and brown overcoat looked good on him.

"You're not supposed to let friends mull themselves into depression," he replied, leaned back against his chair.

"I don't have friends," she said. That was true. She intimidated most people and had acquaintances at best.

"Me, neither," he said. "Not really."

He said it so simply that she looked at him, forgetting her own worries.

"Well, if neither one of us has friends, how do we know we're even friends, then?"

"Because I'm here, and you're not screaming at the guards to drag me out."

"I guess that's as good a sign as any." Her chin settled back on her knees. The day was beautiful, the sun shining in where her window faced east. In the distance to the north she could see Kosel if she craned her neck.

"Shirina said your mom would be all right," he said, then hesitated. "You kept her safe while more guards rallied."

Altessa would have snapped at anyone else but found that she couldn't snap at Rojon.

"I didn't even know I could use magic before today," she whispered. "And I killed people."

"It's not your fault. You'll get control of it."

Altessa turned to look into his strange dark eyes, trying to gauge what kind of a person he was. *The kind who stays by you when the world is burning.*

"Friends can tell each other anything, right?"

He nodded, looking unsure as to where this was going, shuffling in his seat.

"And they keep each other's secrets?"

He pondered it, then nodded. "I feel like our moms have been doing it since before we were born," he said.

"I agree." Altessa hesitated, gathering her words. She needed to tell someone, for her own sanity, but feared anyone else's reaction. She trusted Rojon. Partly because of how Avarielle spoke of him, and partly because of who he'd already shown he was. And his alliances in the palace were nonexistent, which she admitted helped. She didn't need to worry about his telling others, except perhaps his mother, but even then, he seemed to share the same issues with his mother that Altessa shared with hers.

If she was honest, he was the only other person in the

world she'd ever felt actually understood what she was going through. She decided to confide in him. To take a chance and not be crushed by worries.

"I felt them die, Rojon," she whispered, then looked away from him, unable to face the sight of his judgment, should there be any. And there should be. "I felt them die… and I didn't care. I *wanted* them to. If I could have, I would have hurt them more."

Speaking the words didn't come with the catharsis she'd hoped it would. She'd thought maybe she'd cry or feel relief. She didn't. But she didn't feel as alone, trapped in the cocoon of her own mind, and that helped.

The city came to life down below. Altessa focused on the small movements she could see—a cart going down the street, shutters opening, guards walking along the ever-present walls of Massir. She imagined the gossip flying through the streets. An entire tower had fallen. And the queen… she didn't know how her father would handle that. Aside from quickly making sure she was fine, she hadn't really seen him since the attack.

The bed shifted as Rojon sat on it and placed a hand on her shoulder.

"I don't think it's a bad thing to love so much, we're willing to kill to protect those we love. I think it's about loving too deeply, not about hating."

Loving too deeply. The thought of losing her mother had terrified her. Ripped parts of her to pieces, and that was where her magic had escaped, formed from despair and fear.

And love.

At that thought, at his words, a tear finally did break free. She ignored it, reached up, and took his hand, holding it on her shoulder as they both stared out the window in silence.

47

*S*tanding up had been easier when Siabala's powers flowed through her veins, a feeling she desperately missed. Tally managed to get up without grunting, a small feat in itself. Things were unraveling quickly, and little time remained trapped in this crumbling mortal shell.

They'd retreated to their secondary location, avoiding the guards and adepts Shirina had sent to capture them, knowing they had more than likely moved on. And they would move again and again, as often as necessary, to avoid being stopped.

Not while so close to their goal.

She sifted flour and mixed it with water and yeast. A pinch of salt and a bit of fragrant honey, a treat for her tastebuds. Kneading bread always calmed her, something the Circle never let her do while she was an adept there.

She had to give Shirina credit—her new Circle seemed entirely more balanced than Ravenhold's vanished coven, with a focus on nature, history, magic, and life. Weaker but more balanced.

How Ravenhold ever believed trying to separate magic from life and emotions would work was beyond her.

Fools.

She'd had friends there once, or so she'd thought. But one by one, they'd fallen when approached by Siabala to fulfill a purpose greater than Ravenhold's. Her right wrist flared, the joint crippled by arthritis, but still she kneaded, using her palm to absorb some of the shock. Lightning jolted from the joint up her elbow and shoulder, down to the tips of her fingers.

Pain mimicking magic.

"Elder," Ramelia asked, the young woman standing in her doorway, ancient dust clinging to its edges. Her features looked sharply cut, but Tally knew that was but a trick of the witchlight. Beside the surrounding granite, she still looked quite soft.

"Yes, child," Tally said, leaving her bread to rise, wishing she could put it in the sun but having to satisfy herself with placing it near the hearth's heat. She'd have preferred a woodfire to get that delectable crust on the bread, but this ancient home's magical fire would have to suffice.

"What's our next move?" Ramelia asked, hands in fists. Her parents had been veterans of the Days of Blood, and they'd taught her to fight, whether they'd intended to or not. It had made her easy pickings—little power and eager to champion a cause, like her parents had once done.

"Now we wait," Tally said. Seeing the look of annoyance on the young woman's face, she laughed. "Things are moving beyond your knowledge, child. Once the magic of Graydon is silenced, only yours will function. Then we take Massir."

Ramelia studied her, as though not trusting the Elder's words. That was unexpected. She'd never questioned her before.

"What is it?" Tally asked softly. "Is something bothering you?"

"It's just... We could have taken the king and queen back there, and we almost killed the queen. Instead, we killed regular folk... and that's... It's not..." She spread her arms and huffed, "I don't understand why we don't just kill them and start a new government."

Tally poured herself another cup of tea, wrapped her hands around the warm cup, soothing her aching hands.

"Because that would make them martyrs," Tally said. "And there are still many sympathizers to the king and queen. It would be better to get them to step down and throw them in jail while Massir rebuilds." She paused. "Of course, that would be a perfect-case scenario. But there are other powers in play, child, and you must trust that all will be well."

Ramelia seemed unconvinced. The child might prove a

nuisance more than a boon, and Tally made note of it. She could deal with her later. The quality of the light changed, dimmed for an instant, and grew strong again.

It was time.

"I must finish the ritual," Tally said, regretfully putting down the warm cup and throwing on her black cloak. "You prepare yourself for the next attack." She looked the young woman in the eye. "The world is about to change, Ramelia, and you are on the right side."

"Elder… why did my magic not work?"

Tally paused. "You escaped, didn't you?"

"Yes, but before that… I simply couldn't access it. Not even when the Grayloft chased me down. If emotions are to power my magic, then surely that would have done it."

Little fool, Tally thought. *Your magic will work when I need it to and not before.*

"I truly must go," she said, sounding regretful. "But let us resume magic training tomorrow. We can figure it out together."

She nodded and Tally walked past her, eager to find the other Elders. So far, everything had fallen into place. Only Shirina remained standing, and barely, from all reports. They just needed her to make her next move, and they'd be ready with theirs.

She would fall soon enough, and all of Graydon would be theirs for the taking.

∾

Ramelia stalked out of the Elder's home, then turned to watch her walk slowly down the old stone path, up toward the center of the cave. Shaking her head, she shoved her hands into her pockets and waited for that black cloak to vanish. The odd shadows of this place held on to her impression for a few moments after she'd turned the corner.

This whole place gave her the creeps. She'd grown up at the edge of Massir, right in the path where the Eloms had destroyed people and buildings. It hadn't been perfect, sure, but there had always been the sky. Here, beneath the city, in ruins she had no idea existed and doubted many did, Ramelia missed that sky. The unnatural lights of the cave didn't warm her, or make her pause at the vast beauty. The stone and magic of this place just made her feel empty.

Just like the green flames, even though she'd welcomed the magic at first. A chance to make a difference and help Massir into a new era. Stop building walls and build farms and homes instead.

She stalked down the road to the small home assigned to her. This place was huge, and everyone in the ever-growing group had their own dwelling. If they opened this place up, it could be a fresh start to so many families. Except there was no sky.

And the place was crawling with witches, wearing different-colored robes. The usual white, which she was used to. Then there was black, and even gray. The most disturbing of all was the red, especially after listening in to Tally's conversation with the Crimson Circle Elite Shirina.

Siabala. Her hands turned to fists in her pockets, and she forced a deep breath in. The very monster that her parents had fought, bearing the scars of that battle still, especially on their souls. And the Elder served him instead of the greater good.

Ramelia hadn't told anyone what she'd heard and didn't know where to turn. She wasn't sure who would help her instead of Tally, or believe her, for that matter. She'd been pumped full of Circle magic, the green flames at times writhing across her bones, twisting her dreams into nightmares until she started awake, drenched in sweat. She heard others whimper, and scream, as magic unleashed their nightmares, too.

She'd made a deal she regretted, and Ramelia had no idea how to get out of it.

I should have asked the queen for help. She squashed the thought down, way down. The queen had already betrayed so many during the Days of Blood, so why would she help Ramelia now? No, Ramelia needed to help herself, just like her parents had learned to do.

She stopped short of her room, hesitated. Then she turned and walked back toward where the Elder had headed.

~

Tally glanced at the ceiling above the ruins, then down to the surrounding broken chairs around her, where they sat in a circle atop the large altar, almost like a stage. The forgotten shrine had been broken, but its beauty could not be denied. Its power. Lights danced above, the roof a perfect curve without chisel mark. It was high enough and her eyes poor enough that it might be full of makers' marks, but she doubted it. This place had been constructed with magic. She could sense it in her bones.

"She's not moved yet," Elder Rale hissed. "We need her to move faster."

"We've waited twenty years," Elder Morik answered before Tally could. "We can wait another few hours."

Rale turned to Tally, apparently dissatisfied with Morik's answer. Tally waited patiently for him to speak, his raven-black hair a trick of magic and certainly not nature, getting lost in his black cloak and robe, not to mention his fully black eyes.

"Are you sure she'll head to the fields?"

Tally leaned back, letting the curved shape of the chair support her back. "As soon as news reaches Massir, Shirina will move."

"She's too exhausted to use her magic." Rale snorted. What a tiresome man. "She'll have to wait until tomorrow."

Morik looked to her, his gray robes covered by his black cloak, green eyes focused on her, also curious about her answer. She couldn't read him as well as Rale, who spouted emotions like weapons. But she knew she could trust Morik, because her master had deemed him worthy.

"I believe she can," Tally said. "I think she's learned to use not just her magic but the magic around her as well. We tested her earlier, and it definitely wasn't all magic drawn from her."

"Ravenhold's Circle is tag-teaming magic," Morik said with a sneer.

She ignored his tone. "Clever, I know. Except"—a tint of a threat dripped into her voice, and Morik sensed the shift in her mood, standing straighter—"that is not Ravenhold's Circle. That is Shirina's pet project, and nothing to compare to the powers of Ravenhold." She held his eyes. "Is that clear?"

He nodded without a word. Tally looked to the ground between them, where the sacred item had been set on the altar. Nobody had noticed it going missing in the attack, nor had they spotted the switch since. And they probably wouldn't. She allowed herself a slight grin as she looked on the amulet of Queen Cassara glinting in the magical light.

Yes. It had been a long road, but soon, everything would fall into place.

A ripple of magic danced up above, heading to Massir. A familiar teleportation spell, supported by the adepts at Massir's teleportation circle. It had been clever on Shirina's part, really. A way to extend the distance a witch could travel, while sparing magic. A shared burden made lighter through many hands.

And how it would break Shirina when it all came crashing down.

4 8

*S*he sensed it, the teleportation flowing back to Massir. Most of her adepts were asleep now, regaining their strength, including Shala. But Shirina still stood, near the teleportation circle, as four of her younger adepts joined in helping the spell reach its destination.

The scent of pine wafted from the spell, dragged from Kosel to Massir. Shirina found that she didn't know what to do with her free hands, exhaustion and worry rendering them useless. She wanted to step in and help the spell re-form more quickly, but she was too tired and too likely to make a mistake.

She had trained her adepts and had to trust them to use their magic for the strength of her people.

Please.

The one thing she had never really figured out how to replace from Ravenhold was the focus for her magic. The old Circle was full of mantras and solid stone walls. Hers was made of outposts and shared hopes.

But when her mind grew dull with fear, she found that she missed the old mantras most of all.

Please.

A single figure appeared in the circle. A bad gash ran across his left cheek, and his robes were burned, with blood that might or might not belong to him.

The adepts took a step back, and he took one forward, focused on her and her alone, holding her eyes with his tired ones.

"We... we were ambushed." He took another a step forward, and Shirina continued to focus on his eyes and words, unwilling to look down at what he grasped so firmly in his hands. "There were so many of them. Green flames everywhere, and the Grayloft... they... they tore into her. I couldn't save her... She... So much blood... and I just managed..."

His voice cracked, and his arms shook at the mere effort of lifting the sword. She ignored the blade.

"We may be able to save her," Shirina hissed, adrenaline spurring her into action. "Help me teleport." She walked to the middle of the circle. Her adepts were all exhausted. They'd used too much magic keeping the rebels at bay and then saving Cassara.

"I saw her head ripped from her body," Pol whispered. Shirina's hands grew numb.

"Are you sure?" she whispered, feeling stupid but

unable to stop herself. Pol simply looked at her, eyes downcast. Her adepts shuffled uncomfortably around her. One of them looked like she was about to collapse. Too much magic. Not enough magic.

It always seemed to come down to this.

Shirina finally lowered her eyes to the familiar, red-jeweled hilt, the blade covered in blood. She'd seen this blade covered in fire, killing formidable foes, wielded without pause or fear. Part of her never believed this day would come, though she knew chances were high it would.

Slowly, with numb hands, Shirina reached out, finger gently touching the symbol of the Graylofts. The blade was silent. Avarielle was freed from her oath.

Her hand dropped to her side, and she took a deep, shaking breath, speaking in a whisper lest her voice crack.

"Did she speak to Kaden and Carsyn?"

He shook his head. "She didn't find them in time and wanted to come back quickly. Said something was happening to Queen Cassara and she was needed."

Shirina wasn't looking at him anymore, eyes focused on the red jewel on Graysword's hilt, dull in the gray day. The scent of burning wheat could be smelled all the way there, even though the fires were thankfully under control, thanks in part to her witches.

Too much was happening. Too much all at once. She needed time to think and regroup, but her witches were falling quickly, and now, without Avarielle...

"I'll go find them," she said, her mind made up. She

would not send another witch to die there, and could teleport closer to where Cassara had indicated they lived. She would then walk back to the outpost, to properly bury Avarielle's remains.

Or perhaps not. The West's customs were to leave the bodies uncovered.

No. In Elihor, Avarielle could be buried, and a tree would grow, holding some of her memories. Someday, Rojon could learn of everything she'd sacrificed and lost. Someday, he could get to know the side of his mother she never let him glean. Shirina would do this, a final gesture of friendship, or whatever it was they shared that connected them so deeply.

She looked up from the jewel, feeling drained in a way she hadn't before. All the adepts looked to her, waiting for her to gather herself.

"I'll go speak with Rojon," she told Pol, the Crimson Circle looking about ready to fall over. "I need you to take Graysword to King Dayshon and ask him to place it in the kingdom's safest vault. I'll deal with it later."

Pol nodded. Shirina would make the time to speak to Rojon, then she would go to Kosel. She could sleep there and return in the morning. She'd have to wake Shala, though she hated doing so. But she needed her to know what was happening.

"Speak of this to no one except Shala, Pol. Do you understand?" He nodded. She glanced to the other adepts, who all nodded in turn.

"Good," she murmured. "Now go quickly, and hide

Graysword with your cloak. The fewer people know, the better."

"Of course, Crimson Circle Elite," Pol said, his voice sounding a bit stronger, and he headed off, his stride quick despite his fatigue.

Shirina took a deep breath of fresh garden air and headed back into the palace, the walls smothering, her feet uncertain, wishing someone else, anyone else, would speak to Rojon in her stead, wishing even more so that Avarielle would reappear and scoff at the idea of being dead.

~

The sandwich before him looked about as delicious as anything he'd ever made, and he pushed it across the table to Altessa, whom he'd finally coaxed out of her room after her stomach rumbled like an angry brush beast.

After a few seconds, she took a tentative bite, followed closely by another.

He smiled and started making himself one, cutting more bread slices and roasted meats.

The door to the residence opened and closed, and Altessa and Rojon shared a look.

Altessa stood, her face pale but resolute as the Crimson Circle Elite filled the doorway, red cloak like blood against her white dress. White peppered her raven hair, too. Rojon had never noticed before, but with the sorceress's exhausted look, it highlighted the slow stamping of age on her features.

Rojon took a protective step toward Altessa, figuring the sorceress had come to punish Altessa for her use of magic. He was surprised when she took another step in and turned to face him. He was taller than her by quite a lot but always felt like she towered over him. Now, at the look in her eyes, covered by a thin veil of tears, Rojon had never felt smaller in her presence.

He wanted to ask her what happened, but his mouth wouldn't work. His heart skipped a beat, and gently, slowly, the sorceress lifted her hand and touched his cheek. She'd never once done that in his life. She'd been affectionate in her own way, giving him learning he was interested in, but never physically affectionate like his mom.

His mom.

He tried to speak, but his voice failed him.

"She fell in Kosel, Rojon." Shirina's voice cracked, making the moment even more devastatingly real. "I'm so sorry. I'm so very sorry."

Altessa made a choking noise, but Rojon just stood there, trying to understand what he'd just been told. His mother had always been there. She'd fought monsters and won. She'd gone up against Siabala and lived. She couldn't…

"She can't be," he whispered, and at the tear running down Shirina's high cheek, Rojon's denial came crashing down, and he folded in on himself. Without hesitation, the sorceress gathered him in her arms as he grieved.

49

*S*hala had only ever seen Shirina this drained once before. Right after Ravenhold and the Wall of Loss had collapsed, and she'd teleported herself and the remaining surviving adepts out of Ravenhold. The Crimson Circle Elite had looked ready to fall over and never stand again, but she'd of course done it.

This time, however, anger boiled deep within the witch. Shala had spent years studying with Shirina, intent on being the best she could be. She'd seen Shirina get spat on by angry people, only to just walk away. She'd been insulted by politicians and Elders, chased out of some towns, and had always borne the people's ire with no complaint.

Their anger is justified, she'd simply said once. *It's our job to show them that we have changed. And that will take time.*

And not once had she shown them anger, knowing full

well that one slip would set them back years. She'd imprinted that very concept into every adept.

Now, however, anger seethed at Shirina's core, energizing her when she should have been down. She'd been gone for over an hour, to speak to the young Grayloft. Pol sat at the table near her, looking exhausted.

"You should get some sleep," Shala told him for the hundredth time. "Shirina will understand."

She wasn't sure if he'd heard her. His features were taut, face grim, robes dirty. Pol wasn't the type to ever get dirty. Shala was known for throwing a punch, but Pol was more the bookish type. They'd joined the Circle during the same Harvest and had decided to remain under Shirina's guidance.

He was, for all intents and purposes, her oldest friend.

"Pol," she said more forcefully, reaching across the small ebony side table to take hold of his hand. His head jerked up and he looked her with wide eyes. "You're okay," she immediately said. "And you're safe. But you need sleep."

"I couldn't save her." His voice was just a whisper. "She told me to go, and, and…"

"Avarielle would not want you to dwell on that." Shirina's voice was crisp as ever as she entered the guest lounge, on the second floor of the royal quarters. "She was a warrior and knew someday she would fall in battle." The sorceress looked more drained, but her back was ramrod-straight. "Shala is right, Pol." A gentleness crept into her voice. "You need sleep to be of use come nightfall. Because we don't know what to expect."

"I want to help with the next steps," he said, looking up at her hopefully. "I want to help make sure that Avarielle's sacrifice wasn't in vain. That I… that I was worth saving."

"If she saved you," Shirina said softly, "then you were worth saving. Now get some sleep. Be prepared to fight. If you want to honor her legacy, do so by being prepared for battle."

He looked like he might argue, but one look from Shirina silenced him. With weary feet he stumbled out of the room.

Shirina looked to Shala as though debating something important. Shala stood up, looked her in the eye. Despite now being a good friend, she still always wanted to impress her mentor. Shirina muttered something, moved her hand quickly, casting a warding spell.

Shala looked at her in surprise as Shirina slowly sat down, her dark eyes holding Shala's. They were alone, as far as she could tell. Whatever secret she would confide in her had to be of utmost importance, and despite her worry and fatigue, Shala felt a thrill.

"Shala." A pause. A slight hesitation. And then she seemed to make up her mind. "What I'm about to tell you cannot be spoken to anyone else, no matter who they are or what they say. Do you understand?"

Shala nodded, her throat growing dry, knowing her eyes grew wider and unable to stop them. Shirina was taking her into her confidence, sharing forbidden knowledge. Would it be something from the Elite rank? No, she would have done so officially, not like this.

She shifted her legs, suddenly uncomfortable.

Shirina hesitated again.

"This will change how you view the world forever," Shirina said. "And put you in the middle of dark battles. Are you sure you want me to tell you? I will think no less of you if you say no, Shala."

Shirina had always done that, given them the option. She'd let them walk away from the Circle, even. If a witch chose to wield magic, she could choose a different path, too.

But Shala had always known this would be her path, from the moment she returned to Shirina's side after the Days of Blood. And if Shirina needed to ask for help now, it meant that her mentor was in dire straits. Shala didn't believe in abandoning what, and who, she believed in when things got rough.

"I'm not going anywhere," she said. "Let me help."

Shirina looked both proud and sad, the anger tempered for a few moments. And then she started to speak. And Shala knew she could never look at her in the same light.

And she wasn't sure if it was good or bad.

~

Shirina walked slowly toward Queen Cassara's room, where she would sleep near the slumbering queen in case she was needed. Sun streaked down the corridor where she walked, dust from the earlier destruction dancing in the shafts of light.

She'd told Shala everything. That Cassara's magic was the only thing holding back Siabala, and when she died, the magic would become corrupted again. And nothing Shirina had tried succeeded. She told her about the green flames and the second Circle. About Elder Tally's treachery.

Shala had absorbed it all, but slowly she'd physically backed away from Shirina, unaware of her own movements, as though needing more distance. Because of all the secrets she'd kept. She'd vowed not to become like the old Circle, but what choice did she have?

No. She stopped herself. She had made a choice, for better or worse. She simply had to accept the consequences now and hope that history would judge kindly. If anyone was left to judge.

With Avarielle gone and Cassara badly hurt, she'd had little choice but to break her word and bring someone else in. They'd kept knowledge of the Wall's magic to themselves to protect Cassara, after all. All she was doing was protecting her as best she could.

Shirina walked past the guards and into Cassara's cozy living room, and toward the chambers. This looked more like Edoline's simple royal manor than it did the royal palace of Massir.

"Shirina." Dayshon wheeled out of the kitchen. He looked exhausted too. "I'm making tea. Would you like some?"

She just wanted to get to bed but sensed the king needed to speak with her. He had never once before simply invited her to join him for tea. She nodded and joined him at the table where she'd held Rojon barely an hour before.

"Rojon will stay with us for now," he said. "Will the magic of Graydon hurt him?"

"It does not seem to have so far," she said honestly, "but even if it begins to, I doubt he'll notice. At least not for a while. And it will be uncomfortable, but it won't kill him."

He handed her a gold-rimmed teacup and sat down. His posture always looked kingly, his back straight, his eyes keen. And those eyes settled on her.

"Is she really dead?"

"I intend to go check for myself in the morning."

"You'll go to Kosel?" He seemed surprised.

"I don't intend to send one of my adepts into a trap."

"Of course not." He took a slow sip of tea. Shirina had never chatted much with Dayshon. He was Cassara's husband and king of Rashim, but there had been no reason for the two to ever discuss much beyond formalities.

Cassara had married him to get an army. But she loved him now, deeply and fully. And, more importantly, she trusted him completely. Shirina took a deep breath, focused on the tea, the acrid scent reviving her brain. A lot had happened, and she still worked to puzzle it all out. She suddenly remembered something odd.

"Is the field fire out?" Dayshon didn't seem as surprised by the question as she'd expected him to be.

"It is," he said. "Barely any damage. We were lucky."

"Indeed," she said. He looked at her, and she knew that look. Was painfully familiar with it, in fact. He was deciding if he should trust her. With his wife almost killed today and her protector dead, Shirina couldn't blame him, though she hated to admit that it hurt her.

"There have been a lot of strange coincidences lately," she chanced.

"I agree." His voice was soft, calculated. He'd allowed her access into his home. And no guards were around to stop her. He trusted her with his life, but something had happened today that bothered him.

"What did you find in the field?" she asked, landing on the only logical conclusion she could. "You suspect magic."

He looked her deep in the eye and nodded, barely perceptible.

"Tell me what you saw," she asked.

"First, tell me why so much magic is suddenly being wielded against my kingdom. Against my family. Is the Circle our friend or not?"

She held his gaze steadily.

"*My* Circle will always be Massir's friend."

He shifted, tea forgotten.

"*Your* Circle."

"An Elder survived and created a rogue faction."

"But you're not an Elder," he said. Dayshon had earned his reputation as a quick thinker. She hoped his reputation for kindness was also earned.

"I am not," she said, "and cannot become one without an Elder's knowledge passed down to me."

The air in the kitchen suddenly seemed thicker.

"Would you betray us to get that knowledge?"

Shirina met his gaze, unflinching. "No."

Seemingly satisfied, he refilled her cup. The warmth felt good in her hands.

"The origin of the fire seemed oddly positioned, at the top of shafts of wheat, not the base. And, oddest of all, a perfect circle of trampled wheat was left unscathed, even though everything around it was singed. What do you make of that?"

She pondered, enjoyed the dark brew, her mind firing again, fatigue pushed aside by the mystery.

"A magically set fire and then teleportation of several witches, for it to be a circle like that."

"Why would they do that?"

"Of that, I have no idea," she said sincerely. Why would they bother burning down crops? "If they were trying to seed more discontentment in your people by making them fear for food, they would have ensured the crops were completely destroyed."

Dayshon seemed both reassured and disturbed all at once.

"Cassara's magic is holding the Wall of Loss, isn't it?" he said more than asked. Shirina schooled her features and simply stared at him. "You don't have to answer. I know you won't. But I remember hearing her flute as the wall reset. And now she doesn't have her magic, and you and Avarielle are crazy secretive about this... All I'm saying is if I figured it out, I'm not the only one who heard her music that day. And I'm certainly not the only one who knows she had magic once and now doesn't."

Shirina's hands felt numb as she clutched the teacup too tightly. "You heard her music?"

"The Traveler's Song. Everyone did." His voice sounded far away, like he spoke from a different room.

"Why have we never heard this before?"

"No one wanted to talk about it, especially not to you three. And others attributed the song to the magic and nothing more." Shirina had heard some stories of the music of the Wall but attributed them to magical waves, not the Traveller's Song, which Cassara had used to unleash her magic. Had she truly been that gullible? No, she'd been distracted. Hopeful. And preparing for the next attack.

"I've heard Cassara play that song since, Shirina. I know it was her."

Her anger collided with her dread, mind spinning with possibilities. One thing was certain. Cassara wasn't safe anywhere.

"Why haven't they killed her?" Shirina said, ignoring Dayshon. "Why let her live?"

"Altessa's magic might have been a surprise?" Worry and pride lined his words.

"Her magic draws from the same source as her mother," Shirina said, "and it would be best if she didn't use it until we're certain it won't impact the Wall."

Dayshon slowly nodded, and suddenly he looked very tired.

"So, what do we do now?"

"I may have to take Cassara somewhere safe," she ventured.

"You haven't been able to stay ahead of them," Dayshon said, "so Cassara will stay here, where we can protect her. With your help." The last part was added with weight. Shirina fought back the urge to argue.

"Of course," she said.

"So, how do you get ahead of them?" She'd never noticed before the piercing gray of his eyes. But he'd never focused so much on her before this moment. "They've been one step ahead of you the entire time. How do you get ahead of them now?"

"A difficult thing to know when I'm not sure how they know what our next move will be."

"You're intellectualizing it too much." Dayshon leaned forward. "We're led by emotions more than logic."

Shirina bristled at the thought. As a Crimson Circle Elite, she'd been brought up to use her judgment and logic, not follow her gut instinct.

"Think about it," Dayshon said. "When I'm trying to

think ahead in negotiations or warfare, I count on people reacting emotionally." His voice lowered. "I'd expect you to run to Kosel and let no one else do it."

"I need to make sure she's—that Avarielle is…"

"I know," Dayshon said, "and you can couch it whichever way you'd like, but in the end, you want to pay final respects to your friend. Maybe even claim vengeance. Avarielle was one of your closest friends, Shirina, which both of you would have realized had you any ability to express your emotions."

She gave him a thin smile. "You've just insulted me multiple times."

"Think on it," he repeated, and stretched, pushing his wheelchair from the table. She went to stand, but he waved her off. "No need to stand on ceremony in my home. Finish your tea and make your move, Shirina. But Cassara stays here, where I can keep an eye on her."

"Of course," she said softly as he vanished.

He'd been right. Which annoyed her deeply. Perhaps even more so than the fact that the Elder seemed to always be one step ahead of her. And he'd been right about Avarielle, too. She needed to see her. To lay her to rest. She'd been a constant in Shirina's life for so many years that her absence proved piercing.

It didn't matter that they didn't see each other that much. What mattered was that she always could. Now there was a void where Avarielle Grayloft once breathed, and Shirina didn't care for it.

She imagined Avarielle making fun of her.

The witch discovered she had emotions and it broke her ability to think. Avarielle would want Cassara safe more than she'd want Shirina to have closure.

What if Dayshon was right? What if the enemy counted on them to react emotionally? They'd done so, so far, if she was honest. They'd come to Cassara to make sure she was safe. Kale's death had made it all too clear that something dangerous was afoot. She'd chased the green flame down because of what it represented, and wanting to confront the Elder.

Shirina slowly sipped her tea as she relived every event, looking at them from an emotional point of view. And what she could glean from them. Tally might not have expected her to be able to escape, nor that Altessa could draw on the powers of Graydon. That would have changed the course of the attack, and Cassara might have died.

But why kill Avarielle? It suddenly struck her, the one obvious thought she'd been too tired to ponder. What if Avarielle wasn't even dead? What if Tally had captured her?

No. She squashed down the trembling hope. Pol had seen her get torn to pieces. Even Avarielle couldn't survive that. With a quivering breath, she stood up, her mind made up.

She'd told Shala she'd head to Kosel in the morning and that she'd be in charge of keeping Cassara safe. But now, mind clearer despite her fatigue, Shirina had no intention of deserting her.

She'd already lost one friend. She didn't intend to lose another. She just had to start reacting with her mind instead of her heart.

May your thoughts be heavy.

50

*R*ojon had always felt his roots deep in the land. A descendant of Elihor, beloved by family and his people, supported in his learning and ambitions, he'd become a builder focusing on plants to design buildings that would survive the test of time. So that, no matter what may come, the next generations could count on roots his generation simply couldn't. Not in architecture, most of it burnt or melted.

He'd wanted to build structures that would help redefine what Elihor looked like. Strong, with deep roots, from the plants that held their memories and hopes, the pride of a people who had survived no matter what.

Now, in a foreign land, alone, his only remaining relative dead... Rojon had never felt so rootless. He walked quietly down the palace, where guards stayed out of his way, though they kept a close eye on him. He ignored them, trying to focus on the stone detailing instead. He'd have to ask Shirina to make sure, but he thought the detailing had been carved by magic, not chisels. It was too fine and too perfect, showing off symmetry in a way that seemed impossible.

Then again, perhaps he was being unfair to a hardworking artist.

A few magical lamps lit the palace, round orbs filled with glowing mist that provided a cold but comforting light. He followed the walls, ignoring the fine furnishings, looking at the strength of the stone instead. Trying to find roots in a place he didn't belong. He could feel it, churning within him, the magic of Graydon. It sapped him of strength, though it didn't hurt him.

Would he stay there? Would they ask that of him, at least until he was safe? And was he even in danger, or had his mother been the target all along?

He longed to be back in Keshmeer, with his mentors, working on window placements to capture the most light, on irrigation systems built from roots to keep the cities thriving, and on the movement of air within a building so that fresh sea air filled every breath. Or in Raklar, helping the villagers come to grips with the recent attacks, helping Torbolem's parents navigate their new reality.

Torbolem. He'd been Rojon's friend. With some guilt, Rojon realized he hadn't thought about him since arriving in Graydon, his death overshadowed by fear, wonder, and grief for Kale.

A sound caught his attention, and he followed it into a quaint study, an imposing oak desk at the back, large windows letting the fading daylight in. A familiar figure pored over books. He almost left without saying a word, not wanting to disrupt her nor necessarily seeking company, but his hesitation cost him the chance to escape as she sensed his presence and looked up.

"Rojon," Altessa said, stood up, then hesitated.

"What are you up to?" he asked, trying to sound casual, like his mom hadn't just died.

"I'm just studying a bit," she said, flushing slightly.

"Your family's magic?" he asked, and she nodded, sighed, and collapsed back into her chair. "I'm trying to, anyway, but there's very little written down as far as I can tell. I'll have to ask Shirina and my mother." At the mention of her mother, she looked up to Rojon, like she'd said something wrong.

"It's okay," he said, approaching the desk, looking at books, not sure why he lingered. Maybe he did want company after all.

"I'm really sorry about Avarielle," she said, voice trembling. "She was amazing."

"She really was," he whispered. Altessa had lost her too, and it felt nice to share that burden. "You know what I can't stop thinking about?" he said, not sure why he felt the need to tell her anything, or why she'd really care. She looked up, waited patiently.

"In the West, they let their dead be eaten by wildlife, like a back-to-nature thing." He shuddered. He'd hated the idea of that, but her mother had always spoken of it in the way people who'd never really known anything else spoke. "In Elihor, we bury the dead and let fruit trees grow their roots through them. They feed the tree, and their memories are trapped in the pulp of the fruits, so we can still revisit them."

She looked at him with wide eyes. He gave a shy smile. "I guess it kind of sounds like we eat the dead."

"No," she was quick to deny, "not at all. It sounds like a lovely way to reconnect with loved ones."

"It is," he said, "and what really bugs me is that I don't know if Mom wanted that or if she wanted to be left in the West somewhere... I just... We never talked about it because she seemed, I don't know, eternal, I guess."

"And now," he continued, "I just... I feel like there are all these questions I'll never get to ask her, and I'll never even be able to get to know her more through the sweet taste of apples, and it feels... Death feels so *final* here." He cleared his throat.

"So many of your people died here," she said softly, "during the Days of Blood. You've lost so many memories, where orchards should have bloomed instead."

He looked at her slowly, the tears welling in her eyes unmistakable. She got what he meant, so easily and simply, that he was stunned.

"There are vast orchards in my mom's home kingdom, Edoline. She always said they brought her peace. I wonder if that's part of it, and some of your magic is in Graydon too?"

"Maybe," he said, then focused down on her book. "So, what did you learn?"

"Not much at all," she said. "I think most of what I know is from what my mother told me."

She looked chagrined again. The volume before her was about magic, with lore he didn't think he could understand.

"You studied magic?" he asked, and she nodded.

"My mom and Shirina insisted, just in case the magic of Graydon ever found me. I didn't want to become part of the Circle, though my parents said I could if I truly wanted it. But I loved learning about magic, even if I'd never actually experienced it until today."

She stopped and flushed. "I'm sorry. You've got other things on your mind."

"No, I always like hearing what you're thinking about," he quickly said, but felt hollow. "I think I'll walk around a bit, if that's okay?"

"Guards won't be far, I imagine," Altessa said, "but please take the space you need."

"Thank you." He turned to go.

"Rojon." When he looked at her, she seemed uncertain what to say. "I… I'm glad you're here. That's all. If you need anything…"

"I'll make sure to ask."

She nodded, and seemed to want to say more but respected his need for time alone. He wanted to comment how funny it was, really. That she thought she'd lost her mom but he'd been the one to lose his, in the end. But it didn't feel funny to him at the moment, and so he kept silent as he walked away. To replenish his heart and mind, to think things through.

To try to find footing in this new world without his mother.

51

*C*assara's head had been stuffed with silk, until room for thought no longer existed. It wasn't uncomfortable, lulling her back to sleep, a gentle comfort promising beautiful dreams.

Her mouth, however, felt abrasive, sucked dry like the deserts of the West. The two sensations warred with each other, but her mouth was winning out, her throat closing uncomfortably. She wanted to get some water but found that she couldn't figure how to move her arms or legs. That was strange, and slowly teased her out of her silk-filled mind.

She followed her breath, coldness rattling all the way to her lungs, where they rose and fell. She found she couldn't open her eyes, either, like a heavy weight held them down. Was she dreaming? Memories skirted the edges of her mind, dancing just out of her reach.

She wanted to shift to feel the cushions and bed beneath her, but her body proved too heavy.

A cough escaped and she wanted to cry from relief. The sound gently knocked her back to her body, out of her mind, the silk unraveling to reveal pain. Not as terrible as it could be, as though warm water had been poured on her wound. She knew this sensation well. She'd been badly hurt and had needed healing spells.

"Here." Dayshon's voice seemed distant, but she felt her head being held up gently and water dribbled down her throat. It felt good, and cold, and she wanted more, but he gave it to her slowly. Her lips managed to finally move, and she took a few small gulps.

He lowered her back down, gentle fingers pushing hair out of her face. She was home. She was in bed with her husband, and she'd just woken him up. They'd cuddle and go back to sleep, until the duties of the court summoned them anew.

Not for a while yet. A curtain slid, and through her closed eyelids, the soft glow of the sun came pouring in. Had they overslept? No, the light was wrong. It wasn't dawn. It was sunset. She tried to push herself up, but her body refused to budge.

"Don't move too fast, Cassara," Dayshon said softly. "You were hurt pretty badly."

And then she remembered. The attack, the collapsing stone, pushing Rojon and Altessa out of the way, and feeling Graydon's magic dancing all around her... *Altessa.*

She tried to say her name, but it came out a garbled whisper. Dayshon understood her nonetheless.

"She's fine," he said, "and so is Rojon."

He stopped when it seemed like his tongue wanted him to continue. Cassara forced her eyes to open, Dayshon appearing out of focus in front of her. She took a few deep breaths, feeling the threads of sleep completely leaving her, along with whatever drugs still worked through her system, keeping the worst of the pain at bay. Now that she knew to expect the pain, it wasn't as bad.

"What is it?" she asked Dayshon, bracing herself.

"You need to concentrate on getting better." He tried to brush her off.

"Dayshon," she pushed. "Tell me."

He looked at her, his pain obvious, either at the loss or that he'd failed to keep it from her. He sighed, lay down and wrapped his arms around her. He kissed her cheek gently.

And then, he spoke.

"It's Avarielle. She's gone."

Cassara stiffened, ignored the pain in her body, and sat up. He followed with her, arms still wrapped around her, holding her. Holding her together.

"You shouldn't overdo—"

"What do you mean, *she's gone?*" Her voice trembled.

"She was killed in Kosel, Cassara."

Instead of the expected grief, a deep calm fell on Cassara instead.

"Where is Shirina?" she whispered.

A flicker of annoyance crossed Dayshon's features. A rare sight on her husband's usually calm demeanor, or at least rarely projected her way.

"She's exhausted and needs sleep." He looked at her pointedly. "As do you."

"I need to speak with her first," she said, but kept her eyes riveted on his. She wouldn't back down from this.

"All right." He slid into his wheelchair and called back, "But once I'm back with Shirina, I'm not leaving the room. Not this time, Cassara. This time, I'm staying."

Before she could answer, he was gone, shutting the door gently behind him. Cassara hoped Altessa slept soundly. She sometimes looked at her daughter, surprised to find a full-grown adult instead of her baby. She'd always laughed, Altessa, even as an adult. And always gotten into trouble. She was eighteen, well travelled and beloved, and just the gem of her heart. Her, and her two siblings, Traina and Alexavier. She hoped they were having fun. They'd kept her brother advised of events, and she'd asked that they not be told what exactly was happening. They needed peace too.

Edoline was well protected, despite its small size.

Her thoughts wandered to Avarielle. *Gone.* That's what Dayshon had said. Cassara couldn't wrap her head around it. Avarielle had always been present. A force to be reckoned with. Unstoppable, and too stubborn to die. What could have possibly killed her in Kosel?

The door opened again, and Shirina stepped in, followed closely by Dayshon, who closed the door behind him. Shirina looked exhausted, white robe and crimson cloak dusty, eyes small from fatigue. Cassara felt guilty at demanding the sorceress's presence when obviously she needed sleep.

"I'm sorry," Cassara whispered. "You should get your sleep."

"As should you," Shirina said, walking to her bedside and sitting on its edge. In someone else, this would be a friendly, comforting gesture, but Cassara knew that Shirina did so because she was too exhausted to stand.

"Are you sure about Avarielle?" she asked without preamble. The pain in her side had begun to spread to her back, like a vise, and she didn't want to injure herself more. That would simply mean that Shirina would have to cast another healing spell on her, sapping her strength even further.

Shirina didn't hold back. "Pol saw her get torn to shreds. I have no reason to doubt him."

"And Graysword?"

"He brought it back."

"Did he?" Cassara raised an eyebrow. "How would he have gotten it through the monsters?"

"He used his remaining magic to get it. It would be unwise to let our enemies get hold of such a powerful weapon."

"If Avarielle could have," Cassara said, her voice losing fire as realization crushed her hopes, "she would have destroyed Graysword, or ensured it could never harm Rojon."

"Agreed," Shirina said even more softly. "It must have happened fast. Let us take what comfort we can in that."

"Why would Graysword harm Rojon?" Dayshon asked from where he listened by the door. Cassara started. She'd forgotten he was there. She held out her hand, and he wheeled to the other side of the bed and reached to hold it.

"The sword is cursed," Shirina said. "She did not want to pass it on to her son."

"Graysword is cursed? How?"

"That is not for us to say," Shirina answered. "But you must trust that Avarielle would never have let the blade go in the middle of battle, and certainly would not have sent it back to her son."

"Where is it now?"

Shirina's eyes widened, then narrowed as she reached a conclusion. "I instructed Pol to bring you the blade," she said, rising, uncertain on her feet for a few seconds, "so that you could put it somewhere safe."

Dayshon squeezed Cassara's hand and sat back in his chair, back straight. She began to struggle up as well.

"You need to rest, Cassara," Shirina and Dayshon both said at once.

"Not while Rojon is in danger," she said, wincing as she pushed herself up.

"I'll tell the guards to find him," Dayshon exited the room.

"Cassara." Shirina helped her up but mostly looked

annoyed. "You're hurt and almost died today. If not for Altessa..."

"What of Altessa?" Cassara asked, a faint memory tugging at her mind. The warmth of Graydon, dancing all around her.

Shirina's voice softened, though she still obviously struggled to contain her annoyance. "She used the magic of Graydon, Cassara, and saved you."

Cassara closed her eyes, took deep breaths. Her daughter had called on the magic, without the amulet. She'd trained for this. Cassara had made sure her daughter would not be caught unawares as she had been.

"I need to go talk with her." Cassara took an uncertain step, pain wrapping around her middle.

"If you hurt yourself," Shirina said, "I'll have to heal you again. I don't have that kind of energy right now, and neither do the rest of my adepts."

Cassara paused, gritted her teeth. "I'll heal fine with time, Shirina. Right now, I need to talk to my daughter. Besides"—her voice softened—"you're the one who looks like she's about to fall over. Get some rest. I promise I won't be long, and I do feel better."

Shirina sighed. "You're a terrible liar. But very well. Altessa is trained somewhat in magic, but this could easily overwhelm her. Please ask her not to use her magic until I can ascertain whether or not it's pulling from the Wall of Loss."

She held Shirina's gaze but knew the sorceress knew exactly what she'd asked.

"Avarielle is gone," Shirina said, dark eyes small. "And things are progressing quickly. We kept this secret so your children wouldn't have to bear an unjust burden, and to keep you safe. But now that burden is falling on them, and your life is already targeted, regardless of our intentions. The more informed they are, the better decisions they'll be empowered to make."

"Agreed." Cassara ignored the churning in her belly. "But we finish this ourselves. We don't put this burden on them."

"We will certainly try, Cassara," Shirina said, "but we may not get a choice."

Cassara's hands turned to fists at her side. "There's always a choice."

"Avarielle would still be here if there was always a choice." Cassara reeled at the sorceress's words.

"She didn't want her cursed magic to be passed down," Cassara said, after gathering herself again. "So, we make sure it doesn't."

"You don't have that choice," Shirina said more kindly this time. "The magic courts Altessa as it did you. The power is hers, and the choice must be hers too." She held up her palm in a bid to stop Cassara's protest. "You never let anyone tell you how to use your magic, myself included. And it turned out to be a good thing, might I add. But at least warn her against using it until we know more. Just to be safe."

"I will," Cassara said. "Now go to sleep. I promise I

won't be gone long. And you look like you're about to fall over."

"I have been trying to get to sleep for over an hour now," she said. "Please wake me if you need anything."

"Of course," Cassara said.

"Shirina." The sorceress stopped at the door, turning her head just enough to look at Cassara. "Thank you. For always being there."

Shirina nodded and vanished. Cassara took a deep breath and put on a respectable housecoat before stepping toward her daughter's room, the walls and corridors of her home seeming foreign to her, unable to shake the feeling that a hidden layer of the world that once courted her had just betrayed her.

52

*R*ojon walked slowly through the main palace, watching the last of the day's light vanish through the windows. He suspected that the throne room had been angled to welcome the first light of day, though sadly no one made use of it at that time. But the entire palace faced the east with large mosaic windows. In the mornings, it must reflect stars toward the silent thrones. Perhaps he'd come there for first light, to witness it.

He couldn't sleep and so distracted himself with architectural details. Arches that drew the eyes to look up. Mosaics that would split the light into explosions of color. Stone nestled in herringbone patterns to create interest on the floor.

His eyes feasted on the sights around him, but his ears were crushed by the silence, filled only with the whispers of ghosts.

You don't have to follow in your parents' footsteps. Find your own path, Rojon. I'll always be proud of you.

It wasn't just that his mother had been supportive of him. She'd steered him away from the path of the sword.

I have to go keep an eye on Cassara. It's part of the Grayloft oath, one that you'll never have to take, Rojon. Not every legacy needs to survive.

Every six months, she'd leave for Graydon, and come back six months later. Trevon and his grandfather looked after him as a kid. He'd learned the sword with the Westland warrior, and stories of the West, though he suspected Trevon had a penchant for exaggeration. *Trevon.* He missed him. Maybe he could go visit him in the West.

He shared no blood with Trevon, but he was family.

His grandfather would teach him about magic, and Elihor's legacy, and history. About nature and the Wall of Loss. And he'd tell him stories about Rojon's father. He'd heard his mother and Kale arguing about it once, late at night, when he was barely ten.

You need to tell him of your heritage, Avarielle.

No. He has Elihor's, and that's enough for one child to deal with. Kale, this stays between us, understood?

He'd asked his grandfather, knowing his mother would shut him down. He'd just shaken his head, with a smile. Told him that some legacies were not worth exploring and to respect his mother's wishes. That she loved him deeply and wanted him to have different choices than she'd had.

But he'd never know what those choices might have

been, though he knew all of his mother's roads had led to Graysword and Graydon's descendants. Two days later, Rojon always suspected because of Kale and Trevon, Shirina had shown up, books in hand.

Your grandfather tells me you're eager to learn more about Graydon. I've brought you some history books that might prove of interest.

She'd come back a month later and answered all of his many, many questions. Shirina had understood that he loved architecture and plants before he did, and she'd made sure to always bring him books on the subject, and his grandfather had secured him apprenticeships.

Then his mother had returned, a fierce warrior with shining eyes, and he'd wanted to learn more about the sword.

Your grandfather tells me you've been learning about history and architecture. Why don't you teach me about those?

She'd forged his love for buildings and gardens, bringing him around Elihor to see what was being rebuilt, visit ruins, talk to people about how things used to be. He absorbed it all, and she knew it. It was always like being on an adventure when she was around, and it felt like they'd explored every nook of Elihor.

And then she'd leave again when the seasons changed, and Trevon would return to watch over him and Kale.

I took an oath I regret, Rojon. Cassara is a good friend, but I hate leaving you. Keep studying. Take care of your grandfather. And forge your own path. It's what your father would have wanted, too.

She'd leave him with books under Trevon's watchful gaze, Kale's health deteriorating slowly. Shirina came more and more once he became sicker, conferring with him in whispers about magic, then answering Rojon's questions with patience and good humor.

His life revolved around his mother's comings and goings, until he'd turned sixteen and asked to be apprenticed to one of Elihor's top architects in the capital, and had been accepted. He'd made his own way, fusing his love for plants and buildings into architecture that literally grew and paid homage to his people. Well, to the people of Elihor, for he didn't really know his people in Graydon, though he kept reading about their history.

His mother had been so proud of him, returning every six months to see his progress, listen to his stories, visit every site he'd worked on.

But still, every time she walked away from him to return to Graydon, his gaze didn't linger on her red hair nor her powerful walk. His gaze lingered on Graysword, its hilt calling to him, the red jewel peering into his soul, which he tried hard to hide so that his mother would be proud of him.

Your hands are meant to build, not destroy, Rojon. And they're a much more powerful tool than Graysword.

Sensing a presence behind him, Rojon turned to come face-to-face with a Crimson Circle warlock.

"My name is Pol," he said, eyes deep wells of sorrow. "I saw your mother... I was there..."

Rojon stood rooted in place as the warlock brought up

a covered sword, shifting aside the blanket to reveal Graysword's pommel. Dirt filled every crevice and detail. No, not dirt. Dried blood.

His mother's blood.

"She wanted you to have this." The hilt came closer to Rojon, who stood rooted in place. He realized he wasn't breathing and let the breath escape, slowly, seeing his life split in two paths before him.

In one, he followed in his parents' footsteps. His father had been only five years older than he was when he was killed. His mother had made it to forty. A short life, and one bathed in blood. *Drying on her own sword.*

On another path, he would continue his studies, learn from Graydon's architecture, and help Elihor rebuild. Forge a family. Find his own way.

His hands trembled with the desire to hold the sword and uncover its secrets. But his mother had never raised him to be weak, and he knew that the greatest way he could honor her life was by honoring his own.

"Give it to Shirina," he said with a tremor. "She'll know what to do with it."

He wanted to hold the sword and see if its magic would now work for him, since his mother was gone. His hands formed fists at his sides. He would stand firm. He might not have received his mother's love of fighting, but he definitely had her stubborn streak.

Tearing his gaze away from the sword's red jewel, he looked up into the adept's eyes. And saw fury shining in them.

"Rojon Kolder," a guard shouted, "you're needed immediately."

Rojon wanted to take a step back from the adept, but the man's hand gripped his arm. Surprised, Rojon stopped.

"Hands off the Grayloft," the guard said, shouting back and joined by another guard.

"What is…" Rojon said as the adept's grip tightened.

"Time to go," the adept hissed, and light filled Rojon's world.

53

Water dripping. The stench of wet dirt. A slight tremor from deep below. A rumble.

No, that last one was her stomach. Well, she'd been crawling in this infested area for hours, with no sign of finding an exit.

"Where in Siabala's shadow did she end up?" someone mumbled near. She leaned more closely against the wall, counted her breaths. The adepts were distressingly quiet, using their magic to block signs of their passage. Their growing impatience would be to her advantage.

Dagger in hand, she jumped down a broken section of wall, kept to the shadows, a strange yellow light flickering above. She was underground; that much she knew. Or guessed, having been in a similar place before, a city stretching beneath the West. Perhaps beneath all of Graydon, if she was still under Massir.

Which Avarielle did not know, because the bloody

Elder had teleported her. But to do so, he'd had to drop his binding spell, thinking she was too hurt to fight.

That had been a mistake he wouldn't make again.

And now she was trapped in this cursed place, row upon row of stone houses filled with adepts and, as far as she could tell, rebels.

Great. She longed for Graysword, left behind in the field, probably taken by an adept. She'd tried to call it, but something interfered with her magic. She still had her bow and arrows, several daggers, and her fists. That would have to do.

The adepts seemed unable to track her with their Sight, so must have been using Graydon's magic. Was the now-dead Elder the only one who could use Siabala's magic? She hoped so. She'd lost a dagger in his eye, stabbed too deep in his thick skull to pull out before she'd had to retreat.

Keeping low, she skirted three more houses, witch lights flickering within. The houses started and ended without any noticeable pattern, some with doors, others without. Windows seemed to be an option, and not a popular one. The ground wasn't smooth, but at least it was of dust and so didn't leave a trail. That would complicate her escape. Not that this was much of an escape. No, she had a better plan than to escape.

If the Elder had been foolish enough to bring her to their hideaway, then she'd take full advantage of it. If that witch Tally was behind this, she intended to end her this time.

The roads skirted the tightly built houses and bigger buildings, zigzagging upward, the ceiling so far away that Avarielle wondered how far beneath Graydon they were. She dared hope, for a moment, that perhaps she'd been brought under the West and she'd soon find a path to emerge there.

But she'd been in to those ruins and knew she would see shafts of skylight, were she still there.

She also knew that up usually meant a way to the surface or to one of their large round shrines.

"There!" the adept shouted seconds before fires slammed near her, Avarielle throwing herself to the ground. Without pause, she pushed herself back up, pulled out her bow, and sent an arrow flying toward the fire. She had no clue if it hit, running down the back of a row of round stone houses, hearing adepts in pursuit.

With a quick glance around the building, she saw a witch casting a spell. Avarielle let loose another arrow, striking her in the neck. She crumpled, gurgling.

Even she knew that had been a lucky shot, and she couldn't count on taking out all of the adepts so easily. She needed to find a place to lie low, and she needed it fast. But where in these bloody buildings could she find such a place?

She took off again, crouching and heading up still, leather boots silent and swift on the stones. Another few arrows, and the witches at least considered not approaching her too quickly.

"She's heading toward the shrine!" someone, a smarter someone, shouted.

Avarielle swore and veered left, no longer following the upward curve of the city, choosing to head into deeper shadows as the stone houses grew thicker, nearer to one another. She opted to climb one of the taller buildings and get a view of the area, and hopefully not be too easily spotted.

Gripping the rocks with her fingers, she flexed her muscles and pulled herself up, finding the next perch for her feet, then again for her hands, until she was atop a flat-roofed house or some kind of official building. A stone buttress would give her enough cover, she hoped. She crawled toward the edge, risking a peek.

The whole place crawled with witches and rebels, calling out to each other, looking for her. They'd find her, she had no doubt. She just had to be ready for them, and she'd survive this. At least long enough to kill another few Elders.

"What do you want from me?" Avarielle's heart dropped at the familiar voice, then her anger pulsed in her limbs. "Let me go!"

Rojon. They had her son. Her hands trembled with rage, but she forced herself to stay calm. To form a plan that would see him to safety. She didn't mind being reckless when only her life mattered, but never with his. She shuffled to the other side of the roof, fairly certain she could tell where he'd called from, though the echoes in this cave might prove treacherous.

Without hesitation, she slipped down from the building onto an adept and slit her throat, making sure not to get a gush of blood on her. That would leave a trail.

Then, slowly, carefully, she started making her way up, intent on getting her son back and killing anyone who might get in her way.

54

"Shirina, we have to find him." Cassara's voice shook with exhaustion, refusing to return to bed despite her injuries. She'd thrown on simple, practical clothing, a pair of pants and cotton shirt, with a shawl wrapped around her shoulders to keep her warm.

They stood in the courtyard, where Shirina had a better chance of using the Sight to hopefully find a trail. But no matter how hard she looked from the royal quarters to the sky, or the ground, she couldn't see anything to indicate someone had teleported out.

The air was refreshing, an insult on such a terrible night. Avarielle was gone, and Rojon had been taken. By one of *her* adepts. Shala stood by, features drawn, anger pulsing in her limbs. The rest of her witches stood in a circle around them, green, blue, yellow, orange and crimson cloaks billowing in the breeze. Beyond them, layers of guards stood watch.

Dayshon had spared no protection for his wife. But none of it would help. Her witches were exhausted and terrified. They'd been betrayed by one of their own. The guards' weapons were useless against this Circle.

"I don't understand what the end game is," Shirina whispered to Cassara. "Cassara, what are we missing? What do they know that we don't?"

"Let me pass." Altessa's commanding voice sliced through the air. Shirina motioned for her adepts to let her join them in the center.

"Rojon was taken," she said, joining them. "By one of your adepts?" She turned to Shirina.

"So it would seem," Shirina said, bracing for the usual anger.

Instead, Altessa turned to her mother. "I want to help find him. I can, and you know I can." She now turned from her mother to the sorceress, back and forth, meeting their eyes. She reminded Shirina so much of Cassara. The drive to help, to take on an unfair burden.

Cassara turned to Shirina.

"No," the sorceress said. Cassara hadn't seen how much Altessa had lost control, how much power she wielded. It was entirely too dangerous.

"We'll need to risk it or lose Rojon," Cassara said.

"One man, Cassara." Shirina hated herself for her words. Avarielle would hate her. But Avarielle was dead, and Cassara was soft, and all that remained between them and the fall of the Wall of Loss seemed to be her dedication to keeping Graydon safe. "One man versus all of Graydon. And Elihor."

"This is Avarielle's son, Shirina!" Cassara spat. "We can't let him die. He's our responsibility!"

"Graydon is our responsibility, too." She hated herself, hated her words, but pushed forward. "As is the Wall of Loss."

Shala made a quick motion, a warding spell to keep the others from hearing. The Crimson Circle had gotten a few hours of sleep, but Shirina doubted she could cast many more spells today. Nor hold this one for long.

"What does saving Rojon have to do with the Wall of Loss?"

"Everything," Shirina said, not shying away from the angry look Cassara shot her. Her Circle had failed Graydon once, and the Wall had fallen. She'd vowed it wouldn't do so again under her watch.

And she intended to keep that vow.

55

The adept named Pol, along with what felt like endless numbers of other adepts, escorted him toward some kind of shrine. Rojon tried to tame his fear by focusing on the details around him. The architecture was unlike anything he'd ever seen, but he'd read about the ancient ruins beneath the West, and heard Shirina and Avarielle's stories of ancient gods living there.

Siabala's brothers, now dead. By his mother's hand.

A moan wanted to escape his throat as fear ripped through him. He'd refused Graysword. He'd tried to get as far from his mother's legacy as possible. For what? To die because of her actions? As revenge?

"Well met, son of Kryde Kolder and Avarielle Grayloft," an old woman said as he entered what seemed to a round shrine. It had been large once, but its dome had cracked and fallen, crushing chairs that formed an amphitheater.

He was marched up a few stairs, to what he could only guess was the stage.

Or the altar.

"I have to admit," the old woman continued, walking slowly around a chair to face him, "that we didn't expect you to refuse to take Graysword."

Cold dread and realization washed over him.

"You killed my mother." The words slipped from his mouth, anger pulsing against his temples, as hard and unforgiving as the stone of this place.

"Yes," she simply said. "And you're too weak to avenge her, aren't you?"

She held Graysword before her, the red stone pulsing with light, calling him to look into it.

Thinking of his mother and how the blade danced in her hand, Rojon felt himself drawn in, wanting nothing more than to take up the blade and destroy the ones responsible for her death.

56

Cassara turned to Altessa, focusing on her daughter. Her beautiful, adventurous, powerful daughter.

"Look toward the West," she indicated. The palace stood on the top of the hill that formed Massir, but the city's height was dwarfed beside the Bloody Mountains, even if they were three days' ride in the distance.

"Cassara—" Shirina started, but Cassara cut her off with a look. She would not lose Rojon. She would not betray her friend's confidence by letting her son perish. No one else would die on her watch.

Except it wasn't her watch anymore, Cassara realized, pain flaring in her side. She was powerless, having spent all of her strength in her youth.

The pain turned a hollowness, and she filled it instead with love. For her daughter, for Rojon, for the legacy they left behind. But still, she couldn't fill the hollowness, hating feeling like she needed to stand on the sidelines.

"Relax your eyes," she instructed, "and summon the Sight."

"I'm not good at Circle magic," Altessa said. It was true. Altessa knew the theory of magic, but she'd had little innate talent. But that was before she'd tapped into the powers of Graydon.

"I had no talent for magic before I stumbled into the same magic you found this morning," she said. Altessa turned to her, brown eyes large, as though seeing her mom for the first time. "So, forget everything you think you can't do, and focus on what you actually did. Now try again; relax your eyes."

Altessa turned and frowned, but before those lines could turn to annoyance and impatience, her eyes grew wide again. Cassara imagined what she saw, which she no longer could. The magic dancing in the Wall of Loss, bright and pure. Not just the shimmer that people saw during sunsets and sunrises. She would see the magic of the Wall for what it truly was.

"It's… it's beautiful," Altessa whispered, and swallowed hard, overtaken by the beauty.

"It's your mother's magic," Shirina said. "She spent all of it bringing back the Wall of Loss. And you more than likely draw your magic from the same well. Draw too much of it, and the Wall falls. Siabala runs free."

Altessa's eyes snapped to the sorceress, then turned to Cassara.

"Is this true?"

"It is," Cassara admitted, "but we don't know if your power draws from the same well. It may be safe for you to cast at least smaller spells, like the one needed to find Rojon."

"And what about when we need to fight adepts and probably Elders to get him?" Shirina held her ground. "Will you draw on more power then? And doom all of Graydon?"

"I would never do that." Altessa stood defiantly before Shirina. The sorceress studied her for a moment.

"Not willingly, no."

"Do you want to let Rojon die?" Altessa spat. "I thought Avarielle was your friend! This is her son!"

"We vowed to protect Graydon," Shirina said, tired eyes focusing on Cassara. "We vowed to keep everyone safe, Cassara. We won't if you pursue this."

"We don't know that she draws from my magic," Cassara said, the tightness in her chest growing. "She could save Rojon."

"We know that drawing on magic has consequences, Cassara. Especially untested magic."

"I won't abandon my friend," Altessa said, arms trembling by her side. "I won't let you stop me!" Altessa moved her hand in a swift motion, and although Altessa did not physically touch her, Shirina flinched like she'd been hit, blood streaking from her hairline.

"Altessa!" Cassara said, looking from daughter to friend. Her daughter stood rigid, in shock at what she'd done. Shirina ignored the blood, simply looked at Altessa.

"I will not abandon him," Altessa said, though her fire was gone.

"What if she could use a conduit to control it more?" Cassara asked suddenly, reaching for her amulet.

"She'll still be drawing from the same well... Cassara?"

Shirina stopped as Cassara held her amulet. It had been around her neck most of her life, since her mother had given it to her as a child. She knew its curves, how it felt, the way the gold disk nested in the silver crescent, representing the two lands. Even when it had been filled with Elihor's and Graydon's magic, she still knew it for what it was. It had been the key to access her magic, before she'd grown so powerful that she no longer needed it.

She knew this amulet. And now, holding it in her hand, she could feel the weight of it was off. The metal not quite right. Slowly, she looked up to Shirina.

"This isn't my amulet."

The heir of Elihor looked toward the sword, the red stone glowing brightly, Siabala entangling the boy's mind with his. Avarielle Grayloft had refused to lead his armies and would be too dangerous to break. But this boy... he would do, for when her master returned. He would do, to house the glorious soul of Siabala, his bloodline so blessed with Siabala's own as to be a natural extension of him.

Slowly, Tally turned toward the amulet. She knew they would come if they could. Cassara's daughter had strong magic, unexpectedly, and would bring down the Wall of Loss. It was not time yet. Not until they were ready to ensure Lord Siabala's soul would find a body and reclaim his full power right away.

The amulet of Elihor, gifted by Graydon, kept by his bloodline. It had once housed the powers of both ancient mages, and their magic lingered yet. It had been used to lower the Wall of Loss once. For now, it would ensure the Wall remained standing and that their magic remained strong.

"I will give you what you crave," she told Rojon, hands opening and closing at his sides, wanting to grasp the pommel of the sword. "All you must do in turn is use it."

He looked up, the worried eyes from earlier replaced by anger and hatred.

"On you?" he asked.

"Of course," she offered, holding the amulet.

In a slow, calculated motion, she handed him Graysword and waited for the blow.

~

Rojon's hand closed around Graysword, and his head felt like it would split in two even as his limbs grew more powerful. His heart hammered in his chest, his throat dry, his skin raw.

Take an oath with me—a thunderous voice split his mind in two—*and I will gift you with my power.*

Rojon fell to his knees, found he couldn't drop the sword, and screamed, his own echoes answering him.

~

Avarielle heard her son scream and abandoned all caution. Two crimson cloaks were dead before they knew she was there, and she ran into the shrine, toward her son, fallen to the ground before that wretched witch Tally, a smile on her face.

"I thought you'd never come," she said. Avarielle threw a dagger at her face, but Tally casually flicked it off. Before she could open her irritating mouth again, the warrior leapt at her, tired of her words and her smug attitude. She'd hurt her, she'd hurt Rojon, and that would be the last thing she ever did.

She flicked her dagger around, twisted, and, in one smooth motion, slit the Elder's throat, not taking a chance on a spell. The Elder collapsed, unnaturally black blood pooling, a smile on her face. Then she saw it, Cassara's amulet, a second before it vanished into that dark blood, dissolving in it.

"What in Graydon's sewers..."

"Mom?" Rojon asked, and she turned to him, to find him standing before her, Graysword in his hand, looking at her.

She knew that look. She'd had it herself, years before. The look of someone who was about to take a blood oath with Siabala.

"Rojon—" Before she could finish, the entire cave shook. She managed to stay standing and so did Rojon, the other adepts and Elders staying back. Of course they did. Because of course that witch Tally had orchestrated all of this.

Well, at least she was dead for it.

She looked down at the Elder only to find the witch pushing herself back up despite her head lolling at a strange angle, thick black blood covering her robes, eyes filled with red flames.

Avarielle hissed. Rojon's knuckles turned white where he gripped the blade too strongly. He turned to her and, before she could say anything, he screamed and lunged at her, blade first, intent on a kill.

"Rojon!" She shifted, let his thrust carry him past her, and kicked his legs hard to send him flying. But she knew his limbs were powered by Graysword, and he could easily overpower her.

He pushed himself back up, snarling, thirsty for blood, for *her* blood. She barely recognized him. Before he could strike, the cave trembled, and a section of the ceiling shattered. Chunks of rocks the size of Massir's palace crumbled down, screams from above and below as houses were crushed. The ground shook, air rushing down, the entire cave filled with thunder. Buildings stood atop the fallen debris, dust swirling into them as the bang echoed in their skulls. Avarielle realized she'd been thrown to her knees, and recognized buildings from the outskirts of Massir above the crumbled underground city.

They would take down all of Massir. She pushed herself up, Tally gurgling laughter from her neck. Avarielle threw a dagger at her, but the disturbingly standing Elder only grinned as it plunged into her cheek.

Eli, she hated Circle tricks.

Rojon stood up, dust falling from him, Graysword tight in his grasp, its red magic reflected in his black eyes.

58

Standing near the palace, shielded by Circle magic, Ramelia knew she had to help or perish fighting for Siabala. *Siabala.* Her skin crawled at the very thought. He was the one her parents had fought against. The one who'd tried to kill them all.

Now they all stood, more than a hundred strong, waiting to unleash green fires upon the palace. To take down Massir once and for all, and bring Queen Cassara alive to Elder Tally, as an offering to Siabala.

Tally had of course not said that, saying instead she would be made to see their point of view. But Ramelia knew what she would do. And, despite hating the queen and what she stood for, she would sacrifice no one to Siabala.

She glanced around, having stayed at the edge, physically ill at the thought of integrating with all of them. There were so many, mostly young, mostly from her part of Massir. Children of veterans, of farmers who'd lost fields, of parents killed by Eloms in the Days of Blood.

Quietly, she slipped away, using her wards to get her past the guards. She'd escaped this place once. Now she would use her magic to sneak back in and warn the queen.

She was willing to pay the price for insurrection. She wasn't willing to pay the price of her soul for cowardice. She'd just entered the palace when the ground shook. She looked north, where clouds of dust drifted up at the edge of the city.

My parents!

Her breath trembled, but she knew she was too far to help, and so focused back on the mission at hand, running full speed toward the throne room, and the orchard near them. She would be there, Tally had said.

And Tally seemed to have more spies than Ramelia had breaths.

~

"What's happening?" Altessa asked, eyes wide and terrified. To the north of the city, smoke drifted up, the entire city shaking. A few buildings collapsed nearby, and a piece of wall cracked, though it held.

"We have to get you to safety." Shirina stepped toward Cassara, her circle of witches closing in, though most looked afraid. How many more would she bury after today? She shoved the thought deep, dissipated it with focus on the present. Anything else would get them all killed.

A scream. From the corridor. Orders barked as guards moved to intercept their attacker. Shirina had a pretty good idea who it was, and guessed few guards would survive this day.

"Shala, do you have enough energy to teleport Cassara to safety?" They had safehouses nearby, just in case. Close enough to teleport and slip away.

Shala closed her eyes, looking deep into her wells. Then her eyes snapped open.

"I have no magic, Shirina."

"We'll find another way," she said, but Shala took a step forward and grabbed her arm.

"I mean I can't find the strands of magic!" At her words, a ripple flew through her adepts. Shirina tried to draw on the magic around her, finding no strands. Like someone had just blown out its candle.

"Shirina?" Cassara asked.

Green flames licked the courtyard's hedge, where guards screamed and fell. They were running out of time.

"Altessa, can you use your magic?" The sorceress asked.

"I... I don't know how!" She sounded terrified. To the north, smoke billowed.

Cassara stepped up to her daughter. "Just reach deep within, to your deepest desires," she said, voice calm and commanding. "There you will find your magic."

Altessa swallowed hard, closed her eyes, and then

shook her head. "There's nothing." Tears lined her eyes. "Mom, there's no magic!"

"It's okay," Cassara told her daughter, then calmly turned to Shirina as rebels began to break through the line of guards.

"Adepts, take cover," Shirina hissed. They were not trained to fight by hand. Most of them didn't even know how to use battle magic. Their only hope was to run. "Shala, take them to safety. Get them out of here!"

"What about you?"

"Quickly," she ordered, and Shala hesitated for just a split second before ordering witches and warlocks to follow her, multicolored cloaks streaming away from the battle as even more guards poured in, swords drawn, the silver-and-purple armor of the royal guards flashing in the moonlight.

"This way," Cassara said, indicating the back of the gardens, where tall hedges formed a dead end. Shirina didn't argue, following Cassara, who grabbed her daughter's arm and practically dragged her along.

"They're getting slaughtered," Altessa said, not with fury but shock.

"We have to move, Altessa," Cassara said evenly. "We have to get out of here."

Shirina reached deep into her bracers, where she stored magic from Graydon and Elihor. It still existed there, trapped, but too weak to teleport, especially to teleport two people. Cassara would never go without Altessa.

The battle intensified, the scent of burning leaves and bitter bark swarming them. Cassara pushed aside the hedge, revealing a secret exit. Just like in Edoline.

"Quickly, now," Cassara told her daughter, who slipped in. She went next, and then Shirina. They'd been spotted, of course, but hopefully they could reach a safe room quickly. If the magic in her bracers still existed, then it stood to reason the wards on the rooms would also hold.

There was no reason to think differently, and no other choice.

They turned the corridor, moving quickly, when the rebel from the dungeons stepped before them. Shirina stood protectively before Cassara.

"I'm not here to hurt you." She held up her hands. "But you must get to safety, Queen Cassara. They want to sacrifice you to Siabala."

"Siabala," Altessa moaned, voice trembling.

"Behind you!" the rebel screamed, holding out her hand, green flames unfurling. Shirina threw herself on Cassara, dragging her down as she pushed Altessa to the ground. The green flames erupted above them, swallowed a red-cloaked adept. Not one of hers, his screams engulfed by magic.

Shirina pushed herself up. Magic slammed into the rebel, sending her flying back. Large hands pulled Cassara up, the queen kicking back and connecting. Before she could get away, they grabbed her again, holding her tight, making her cry out in pain.

Then she felt it, the familiar buzz of a teleportation

spell, activated by the adept who now held her. Shirina threw herself at Cassara, wrapped her arms around her, refused to let go.

"Mom!" Altessa screamed from somewhere in the distance.

"Get to safety!" Cassara screamed back as she tried to kick the assailant off, pain squeezing breath from her body.

Then the magic sucked them all up, green flames whirling chaos around them as they teleported away in a magic that was never meant to exist in Graydon.

59

*A*varielle fought against the magic that tried to hold her still, binding her legs and arms apart, readying her for the sacrifice at the hands of her own son.

Her own son, who would take the oath to Siabala, through a will not his own. She had done the same. Killed her beloved dance mentor and some of her people, seeking magic to protect them.

"Coward," she scoffed, looking not at Rojon but at Graysword. Then she turned to Tally. "You want to replace me? You think you'll find more power in my son?" she spat. "He can't kill me unless you hold me with your wretched magic, you coward!"

Rojon's steps stopped, Graysword so close to her stomach. Her leather armor would prove useless against its magic. She'd cut through enough monsters to know.

Oath breaker, the voice resonated in her mind. *Do you*

really think I cannot break you? You have a son now. A weakness I can so easily exploit, fool.

"Siabala," she gasped as Tally's laughter erupted in the cave. Large creeping monsters like the ones she'd encountered in the field crawled up the walls and remained on the ceiling of the cavern, eyes glowing red.

"How did you get out?" she hissed through gritted teeth, the magic pulling her apart.

Don't you know, Grayloft? I've always been with you.

The laughter resonated in her mind, echoing deep into memories she'd hoped to forget.

~

Rojon held the sword, its power feeding him. He craved it, and feared it. He could no longer move of his own accord, fueled by Siabala's will to take the oath and activate Graysword.

To spill blood, and gain power.

His mother had done the same. He could see her, in his mind's eye, younger than he was, angry and screaming, covered in the blood of her people. Felt her power, the strength of her strike.

Then he stood in a stone room, recognized it. He'd been there recently, wondering if a stain on the floor had been his father's blood. She stood there, younger, angry tears staining her face. Before her stood the man who could only be his father. Without a word, she ran him through with Graysword.

He gasped, shuddered, felt sick. Almost dropped Graysword, but the blade refused to relinquish its hold on him.

His mother had killed his father. His mother had killed his father, and he'd crumpled from the blow, gone before he'd hit the ground.

His grip on Graysword tightened as green flames erupted beside him.

~

Shirina and Cassara appeared as the green flames dissipated, the adept who'd cast the spell so spent that they consumed him. Avarielle felt hope for a second as Shirina stood protectively before Cassara. Her heart dropped as Tally flicked the sorceress aside, trapping her against a stone.

Green coils wrapped around Cassara, holding her in place.

Tally gurgled, unable to speak through her slit throat.

"Why don't you just die, you hag?" Avarielle hissed, then focused on Cassara. Determined blue eyes met hers. If the queen was frightened, which Avarielle had to imagine she was because the warrior herself had skipped *scared* straight into *terrified*, she hid it well.

"Queen Cassara." The Elder from the fields strolled in, red robes an insult. Avarielle fought against her bonds, but they held tight.

"Release me," she ordered.

"I'm afraid I can't do that. We need the Wall to fall, and we needed all the pieces in place."

Shirina struggled but couldn't get up. The sorceress looked from Rojon to Cassara, then locked eyes with Avarielle. There was no plan there, no hope. The sorceress looked spent and out of ideas.

"Rojon," the Elder said, and Avarielle snapped her gaze back toward him. "Time to take your oath. Kill the queen."

Rojon turned, slowly, as though he struggled against the power of Graysword.

"Rojon," Avarielle said. "You don't have to do this. You're stronger than I ever was. You have the protection of Elihor. You can stand up to Siabala. Don't give in to him!"

The Elder turned to her as Rojon slowly walked toward Cassara, who looked at her son not with fear but sadness.

"Renew your oath to Siabala, and we'll spare your son." He smiled. "Kill the queen in his stead."

"It's okay," Cassara said, voice entirely too calm considering the circumstances. "Save Rojon. That's all that matters."

Avarielle saw it then, the trembling in Rojon's hand, the sweat trickling down the side of his face, the grim determination of his locked limbs. He was fighting it with everything that he was.

Everything.

Rojon had his father's magic, and his grandfather's. He wasn't like any Grayloft who had come before him. But

Elihor's magic wouldn't protect him. It would protect those he loved.

He didn't know Cassara enough to have that amount of selfless sacrifice toward her, but... Avarielle pulled hard on the bonds, felt them weaken as the creatures crawling on the walls and ceiling began to chitter nervously.

"Enough of this," the Elder commanded, holding out a raised palm toward Rojon, pouring red energy into him. Siabala's magic.

Rojon took another heavy step toward Cassara. The bonds holding Avarielle weakened as the magic was redirected to her son. She pulled again, straining muscles, old injuries sparking to life and ripping, groaning as she didn't relent.

Rojon screamed, a deep cry of fear and anguish, hatred and loss. So much of him remained. Avarielle could hear it. Hatred didn't feed his scream as hers had. It was fear.

With a scream of her own, she managed to pull herself free of her bonds, crashing down to her knees as Graysword came up. Cassara looked straight at Rojon, ready for the final blow. Avarielle threw herself up, without hesitation, and landed straight before Cassara as the blade came to claim her blood.

And pierced the warrior through. Warm blood filled her throat, but she used her remaining strength to hold Rojon's hands to stop him from slamming the sword through and piercing Cassara. She heard her name screamed but focused on Rojon's eyes.

MARIE BILODEAU

On the eyes of his father. On the power of Elihor to save those they loved, even if it could not save themselves.

Blood dribbled down her chin, and Rojon screamed, anguish in his face, the red flames flickering in his eyes. She'd wagered everything on his love and his goodness. On his ability to fight off Siabala even when she couldn't.

And as Elihor's magic exploded around them, Avarielle knew her faith had not been misplaced.

EPILOGUE

Altessa hid near the edge of the garden, uncertain where to go. Rebels swarmed every path she tried to take, guard bodies strewn around, parts of her beloved home still burning. Her mom and Shirina were gone, teleported away. She couldn't find her magic, didn't know where to turn for help. And she hoped her father lived and had escaped.

Smoke drifted up from the palace, but no one came from the city.

They hate us, she thought, pushing deeper into the nook against the wall, closed in by stone, knowing she'd have to move soon. But to where? There were escape paths, of course, but none near her.

Get it together, she chided herself. Slowly, she emerged from her hiding spot, looked around at the clear corridor. She stifled a scream when a hand landed on her shoulder.

"Shhh," she heard, and turned to see the rebel from

earlier, the one who'd helped them. "I can get you out of here, but we have to move quickly, and you'll have to trust me and stay near," she whispered, holding out her hand.

Altessa hesitated, looking at the callused hand. Those hands had wielded magic. And they'd killed others.

So have I.

Terrified and never having felt so alone, Altessa took the offered hand.

To be continued in Keepers of a Broken Land 2:
Magic Breaker

Milton Keynes UK
Ingram Content Group UK Ltd.
UKHW010654091123
432260UK00006B/277

9 781738 061419